Empathy

Siri Pielski

© 2024 Siri Pielski

All rights reserved

The characters and events portrayed in this book are fictitious. Any similarity to real persons, living or dead, is coincidental and not intended by the author.

No part of this book may be reproduced, or stored in a retrieval system, or transmitted in any form or by any means, electronic, mechanical, photocopying, recording, or otherwise, without express written permission of the publisher.

No part of this book may be reproduced in any form or by any electronic or mechanical means, including information storage and retrieval systems, without written permission from the author, except for the use of brief quotations in a book review.

Edits by: Owl Eyes Proofs & Edits

Cover design by: D'Arte Oriel

Printed in the United States of America

Dedication

To those who found themselves once they were free:
not with a sword, but with empathy.

Content Warnings

Dear Reader,

This book contains some heavy topics that are discussed or experienced on the page by more than one main character.

Those topics include:
Verbal and Physical abuse and assault
Character Trafficking
PTSD Flashbakcs/Nightmares
Panic attacks
Self doubt
Death Idealization
Toxic and Dangerous Sibling Rivalries
Cliffhanger ending

Please note that this book also deals with the FMC learning how to be herself while trying to come to terms with all the new information and experiences she's being given. One of these includes the power of controlling her own sexuality. This book does feature MMFM Polyamory where two males are a mated couple, the female is an additional mate, and a third male is also courting the female.

There are also stylistic preferences in the writing of this book that some might not agree with, but please know that the lack of the possessive s for Nikaius' and Priamos' name as well as some instances of "head hopping" are written purposefully and are not errors or a lack of editing.

Glossary

Characters:
Morrigan Aegean (More-ih-gen Uh-jee-un)
Delaney Aegean (Dee-lay-nee)
Malin Aegean (May-lin)
Amara Ayrden (Uh-mar-uh) (nee Aegean)
Elijah Aegean (Ee-lie-juh)
Mae De'Lyon (May Day-Lee-on) (nee Aegean)
Nikaius Ayrden (Nik-eye-us Air-den)
Bastian Ayrden (Bas-chin)
Waric Cavanaugh (War-ick Kav-uh-naw)
Aslin Hawthorne (Az-lin H-awe-thorn)
Hawke Corviana (Hawk Core-vee-ana)
Aquila Corviana (Uh-quee-La Core-vee-ana)
Santiago "Santi" De'Lyon (Saun-tee-ah-go Day-Lee-on)
Imriel Gorlassar (Ihm-ree-al Gore-la-s-are)
Cadoc Kaan (Kay-dock Kahn)

"Primal" (animal) changelings:
Rekru'e (Reh-crew-ay): Mammalian changelings (wolves, bears, lions, etc.). Also the primary changeling language.

Clan/Pack/Family Names:
Ayrden: Panther Shifters

De'Lyon: Lion shifters (both Large and Mountain Lion)
Corinth: Nearly extinct Wolf shifters
Caan: Nearly extinct Bear tribe
Kitzira (Kit-zee-ra): An extinct tribe of Fox shifters
Kyilzar (Keel-zar): Avian changelings (Crows, Ravens, Owls, Eagles, etc.)

Flock Names:
Corviana

Velamo (Vel-uh-mo): Reptilian/Amphibian/Aquatic shifters (Dragons, Vipers, Mermaids, Sirens, etc.)

Nest Names:
Gorlassar

Rekru'e vocab:

Atce' (At-see): Alpha/superior
Logar (low-gar): Water
Ie (EE): I
Ae (ay)-- you
Ie amar ae (EE ah-mar ay): Term of affection that loosely translates to "I adore you" but can have other meanings.
Aeonie (Ay-own-ee): Literally "You and I". Typically used for some kind of union/relationship (Can be used to describe marriage or sex)
Koen/Koea (K-oh-en) (K-oh-ah): Savior
Kumnei (Koom-N-eye) God of Mischief

Places:

Cav'Sara (Kav-sar-uh): The continent on which Empathy takes place.
Be'Sala (Beh-sah-lah)- The Northeastern province of Cav'Sara. It is bracketed by the sea to the east and the Be'Sala mountains to the west and south.
Qu'tar - The town in which Morrigan lived closest to.
Kunmei (Koon-May) Southeastern province of Cav'Sara. It's the most central of the habitable areas nestled neatly between Be'Sala and the Pridelands.
The Pridelands: The largest territory that takes up much of the western half of the continent.

Contents

1. Morrigan — 1
2. Morrigan — 7
3. Morrigan — 13
4. Nikaius and Priamos — 22
5. Morrigan and Nikaius — 27
6. Nikaius and Morrigan — 33
7. Morrigan and Nikaius — 41
8. Nikaius and Morrigan — 47
9. Morrigan — 56
10. Morrigan and Nikaius — 60
11. Morrigan and Nikaius — 69
12. Morrigan and Nikaius — 80
13. Morrigan and Nikaius — 87
14. Waric — 93

15.	Morrigan	103
16.	Nikaius	113
17.	Morrigan	120
18.	Nikaius and Morrigan	128
19.	Morrigan	141
20.	Morrigan	151
21.	Morrigan	160
22.	Nikaius	167
23.	Morrigan	177
24.	Morrigan	186
25.	Morrigan	194
26.	Nikaius	199
27.	Morrigan	203
28.	Nikaius	214
29.	Nikaius and Morrigan	219
30.	Morrigan	229
31.	Nikaius	237
32.	Priamos	243
Afterword		247
Acknowledgements		248
About the Author		250

Chapter One

Morrigan

Aegean Manor

"I wonder how much I could sell you for?"

Lord Elijah Aegean's high-pitched arrogant voice was like the sound of nails on a chalkboard. It stirred Morrigan from her thoughts, scattering the daydream she was having of dark hair and stormy eyes belonging to a handsome man she had met once. He visited her dreams often, but she didn't know his name and doubted she would ever meet him again.

Being *thaber* (marked as non-magical) Morrigan had limited time outside of her home, and she knew that someday her mother would decide she was no longer of use to their family. The fact that she hadn't been sent away upon being marked always confused Morrigan, and on the worst days, she wished she hadn't been kept. Despite the knowledge that her mother could give her away on a whim, the suddenness of Elijah's question was jarring. "Mother is looking for you."

Morrigan's stomach sank as she looked up from where she carefully rolled out the dough for biscuits. Elijah stood in the doorway, his hands shoved into his pockets, and his upper lip curled into a scowl.

"Immediately?" It was rare that their mother called for her explicitly. The fact that she had sent Elijah to collect her raised Morrigan's concern even more.

"Of course," Elijah responded so plainly, his annoyance at the fact that he had been sent as an errand boy to retrieve her was clear with the roll of his eyes.

Morrigan knew he preferred to be anywhere but in the kitchen where she spent most of her time. Brushing flour from her hands and skirt, she nodded and stepped away from the table to follow.

"Mother has decided today is the day," Elijah snickered as if he knew some inside joke, "not your day, mind you. There is nothing beneficial that you will get out of this. I don't know what you've done to displease her, but I can't wait to see what she does with you."

Anger rose within Morrigan, but she knew better than to argue with him.

Ever since she had been marked, she had learned what her place was, and arguing was out of place.

Culling was a process that had been implemented decades ago to decide the magical worth of children once they hit the age of thirteen. Elijah, the eldest and only boy, had proven adept at creating and controlling ice, a prominent power for House Burgess. Mae had discovered her ability to heal when she was young. Like Elijah, Amara, Morrigan's twin sister, was capable of ice manipulation. Morrigan, however, had failed every test that had been tried on her. All records dictated her to be powerless, as did the horned, antlered deer brand that had been pressed on her shoulder.

Her life changed the moment the hot iron brand touched her skin. Mae assured her that their father would have fought for her, but he had died during a territory dispute when they were young. With that mark, she was no longer the youngest daughter of the last living heirs of houses Aegean and Burgess. Morrigan Aegean died that day according to her mother, but Lysandra Compton, daughter of a housekeeper, had come to stay. The tutors who had known Morrigan as a child of the Aegeans had been fired and new ones were hired to continue Amara's and Mae's education while Morrigan was forced to be educated on her new role in the family. The new staff took Lysandra under their wing and taught her to keep house.

Any indiscretion Morrigan committed was used against her, Amara, Elijah, and Delaney, her mother, constantly reminding her that they didn't have to keep her and what an embarrassment she was to their family. She was lucky they kept her, they said, because if no one knew she existed, then no one would know of her failure.

The Farm was a crude name given to the local compound where *thaber* were sent once marked because they held no real value to society after that point. Some were rented out as servants with their families receiving half the pay, others were used for more nefarious means, such as broodmares or studs for higher-born lords and ladies whose partners could not produce heirs. Morrigan often wished she had been sent there instead of being kept. She knew nothing about life at the Farm beyond rumors, but she did know that at home, any perceived indiscretion was punishable to the extreme. The scars on her back were a constant reminder of the lack of leniency her own mother had shown, treating her as a whipping girl until Morrigan had learned her place. Quiet and obedient kept the belts away.

Elijah and their mother often complained about their displeasure at the size of their home, always lamenting it wasn't as large or as grand compared to the homes high in the mountains above the valley in which they lived. Morrigan had never been anywhere other than Be'Sala, but in her opinion, Aegean Manor was perfect.

Their location was in a prime spot, owning access to one of the major freshwater springs in the area, and she knew that the neighboring houses did not have the expansive land theirs did. The house itself was stately. The upper floor housed enough rooms for the parents and all four of the Aegean children to have their own since birth. The upper floor also held their parents' room and a vast library. When she didn't have tasks to attend to, she could lose herself in the library for hours. Sciences were her favorite to read, something special she had shared with her father before his passing. The books they had read together were carefully tucked away in the bottom of one of her trunks after having been saved from one of her mother's attempts to cleanse their home of anything written by anyone other than the fae.

The lower floor housed a large kitchen, a dining room, a sitting room, and a sunroom that held its own small garden of herbs and spices that were rare in the area. Some had come from as far north as the scorching Pridelands, and though her mother wouldn't admit it, even a few different plants from the mortal realms were contained there. Morrigan loved the smell of the spices and would spend extra time carefully tending to them and selecting which ones would be best with whatever she was preparing for their meal.

Morrigan's favorite spot in the entire house was the kitchen they were now exiting. No one complained when she cooked something because she was stressed or upset. Peeling and cutting potatoes were rhythmic and needed focus that soothed the panic attacks when Mae would be unable to stay long for visits. Baking bread and biscuits in the early morning hours soothed nightmares and allowed some frustration to be released without injuring herself. Neither her mother nor Elijah ever came to that side of the house, so it became her own special haven away from anyone else.

Staff members who had once lived near the mortal realms told her of stoves and ovens that were powered by magic instead of flame and showers that had a never-ending supply of hot water.

"Hurry up, you useless thing." Elijah shoved Morrigan through the door of their mother's sitting room and she sighed, stealing a glance at her mother before dropping her eyes to the floor as she stood.

Delaney Aegean-Burgess was beautiful, even at her age. She was the last living member of House Burgess, a family that had been renowned for producing powerful fae. Despite being sixty years of age, she looked just as elegant as she had when she married Malin Aegean in her early twenties. Her hair was longer, but just as dark and straight as Elijah's and Amara's. A few lines graced her face and her caramel eyes still glistened when she smiled. Unfortunately, that smile was never given to Morrigan anymore.

Another glance around the room allowed Morrigan to find the portrait of her parents' wedding that rested above the fireplace. This portrait had always made Morrigan smile. It also reminded her that she understood part of the reason why her mother treated her with such disdain. Morrigan, like her older sister Mae, was the spitting image of her father, with deep red hair and jade eyes. Despite Mae and Morrigan being nearly identical, Delaney had always held a particular disdain for her youngest daughter.

Upon their father's death, Elijah was given the title of Lord Aegean as the last male heir to their family's fortune. That fortune, Morrigan knew, had been squandered years ago between their mother's need for extravagant things and Elijah's obsession with the gambling halls. As Morrigan grew, she heard whispers that the money dwindled. Yet Delaney looked as regal as always, dressed in a bright pink gown made of the finest silk available in their area, and Elijah wore a rather dashing suit.

Realistically, Morrigan had received the title of Lady Aegean when Amara had married six months ago, but that detail was greatly overlooked.

Both Mae and Amara had married shortly after their selection nights at age twenty-one. Selection Night was supposed to be a beautiful time in a woman's life when she would hopefully meet her mate, but that was rarely the case anymore. True mates were about as rare as seeing the sun in Be'Sala. Morrigan didn't expect to be presented because, to the outside world, she no longer existed.

Morrigan swallowed, her mouth and throat dry, as Delaney cleared her throat. She stayed silent as she dipped into a curtsy, knowing that Delaney's temper was just as wild as the freckles on Morrigan's face.

"I believe the time has come for you to leave us, Lysandra." The name grated on Morrigan's nerves, but she nodded. After all, Delaney's word was law, and Morrigan had to have permission to speak. "You've been invited to the Selection Night at Atce' Plaza. I heard Lady Ayrden was looking for a handmaid and was willing to pay a handsome price for one." Morrigan's stomach churned with anxiety. Had Lord Nikaius Ayrden taken a wife? Or was she referencing Amara, who had married Lord Bastian Ayrden, shortly after the summer solstice?

Morrigan knew better than to ask, not that Delaney gave her the time to come up with a response. Delaney had hardly taken a breath before turning to address Elijah. "Elijah, are you confident he will pay for her? I would hate to waste time on something so useless. If he doesn't pay, surely the Farm will."

At this point, even death will do. The warmth that settled in Morrigan's chest at the thought startled her a bit, but Elijah's next words pulled her from her internal monologue.

"I've been assured that he is expecting us, and he has promised one hundred gold as payment." One hundred gold? Was that all she was worth to them? While it was a rather large sum of money that they could live off of for years, Morrigan still felt ill at the thought that she had been reduced to their property to be sold.

"I'm sure you could talk him out of more money once you highlight her *special* skills." The fact that Delaney now referenced the magic she did hold as 'special' almost tore a laugh from Morrigan. Her father had believed her powers to be special, but Delaney had hardly believed they even existed.

"I've already informed him of such. He said he had many ways in which he intended to use those skills."

Oh.

Of course, they weren't talking about the magic Morrigan possessed that no one believed she had, but the *skills* she was forced to learn when she came of acceptable age.

"Either way." The motion of her mother's hand shooing them away made Morrigan cringe. Delaney laughed, and Elijah joined her.

Prickles of ice-cold indifference spread across Morrigan's jaw as Delaney grasped her chin and lifted it so their eyes met. "You will behave tomorrow and listen to Lord Ayrden, or you will go to the Farm. Either way, you will fetch us a nice sum, won't you?"

Morrigan's bottom lip trembled. "Yes, ma'am." The response seemed to please Delaney, and she shoved Morrigan away, making her stumble as Delaney reached for Elijah.

"Make sure she is dressed appropriately; we want everyone looking at her. If you can get a better offer from someone else, take it. Lordship be damned."

"Of course, Mother." Morrigan could hear the grin in Elijah's response and could feel his glee as he wrapped his fingers around her upper arm and tugged her after him

Chapter Two

Morrigan

Aegean Manor

Morning came too early and with it, a flurry of commotion that started with Morrigan being readied for the future ahead of her. The dress she was forced into wasn't even a dress but one long piece of mostly sheer fabric twisted and draped across her body. The light, smoky blue color was pleasing, but that was the only positive thing about it. It barely hid the color of her skin underneath it. Fates, she felt so exposed and uncomfortable. Typically, Delaney would try to taper the fullness of Morrigan's hips, but they had wanted them on display. Men of Lord Ayrden's caliber preferred women with childbearing hips according to Elijah. The comment had made Delaney scoff, but Morrigan was glad they had dropped the topic, not sure how she would breathe well as it was, much less with something trying to bind her hips.

One of the other housekeepers had been instructed to help Morrigan with her hair, not that there was much to do with it in the state it was. Most of the ends were braided together, permanently sealed by some magic Delaney had bestowed upon her in a fit of rage. While the ends of the braids reached her backside, only half of the length was manageable, and she had been beaten when she was caught trying to cut one free. Mae had been banned from the house that day as well. The only thing Morrigan could do every day to keep it from getting too damaged was separating the locks of hair by braiding and then twisting them up out of the way.

Esme, Delaney's helper, by some magic, and a lot of painful pins, managed to make Morrigan's hair almost presentable. She had taken most of the length and twisted and tugged, poking at her head until most of the braids were hidden underneath the rest of her hair in a chaotic bun at the nape of her neck. What few braids she left out were twisted together to make a simple crown secured around her head with more pins.

Unlike her sisters on their selection nights, Morrigan didn't receive jewels or crowns made of gold, the family color, instead had gold makeup forced upon her. The moment Esme walked out of the room, Morrigan frowned into the mirror. The color did not suit her like Delaney or Amara, instead, it brought out the yellow in her skin and made her look ill. Trying to scrub it off was fruitless, only leaving Morrigan with a sore face, the makeup magically unmovable.

By some blessing of the Fates, Delaney allowed Morrigan to pack her own things, but only enough for one trunk.

The trunk she chose was given to her by Mae. It looked old and was one of the trunks that had been in Mae's possession for years, but she and her husband Santi had used magic to give it several inches of extra space in the bottom, hidden by blood magic only they and Morrigan could open.

Picking at the scab on her thumb, Morrigan let the cut bleed for a moment before pressing it to the centermost design. The bottom clicked, and she wiggled it open. Carefully laid there were her father's books that she had rescued so long ago and had hidden in Mae's room for safety. When Mae had left with Santi, they were stored in the trunk and had remained there for the last year. Picking up one of the books she flicked it open, letting her eyes scan over the words on the page.

Ironically, the story was her favorite one her father used to read to her every night. It was about the exact event they would be attending. It was fabled that one would find their true mate on the winter moon. It had happened for Cinderella and been so for Mae, but Morrigan knew that because she was marked, no magic like that would work for her. She only hoped the plaza would look as lovely as it did in the photos on the page. Footsteps in the hall reminded her that she didn't have time to read the page, because if she did, she would get sucked into it and be caught. Taking a deep breath, she tucked it back inside and traced her fingers over the velvet case that held Mae's pearls. They were a courting gift to her from Santi, not that she ever wore them. Their courting was so short, Mae had never gotten the chance, and when Morrigan had been helping her pack, Mae insisted she keep them safe until she could retrieve them both.

She wondered if Mae would be able to find her wherever she ended up. Santi and the Ayrdens were close, so surely if she ended up there, they would cross paths at some point. The thought of that and what Atce' Plaza would look like had her quickly tucking undergarments into the space left.

Once she was sure no harm would come to the books and her sister's jewelry, she closed the compartment and looked around her room. What else did she want to take with her? The fact that nothing else came to mind made her bottom lip tremble.

The things she cherished most weren't even hers.

Quickly wiping away the tears that fell, Morrigan's head snapped towards the door as it opened.

"Are you ready yet?" Elijah's voice preceded him into the room, and Morrigan nodded as she caught sight of him. Walking over, he looked into the empty-looking trunk and frowned. "There's nothing in there. Do you plan to walk around your new home naked? It would suit the only use you're good for, but we'll look bad if we don't send you with something. Why must I do everything for you?" Without batting an eye, Elijah stalked over to her armoire and opened it, tossing a handful of dresses, corsets, and undergarments into the trunk. On top of it went the only two pairs of shoes Morrigan owned and then Elijah slammed it shut.

"There." Snapping his fingers, the entire thing disappeared. Morrigan's heart hammered in her chest. Despite knowing that he had just sent the chest to their carriage, she still feared the worst because this was Elijah, and it wouldn't be the first time he had destroyed her things because he could.

"There. Let's go." As he reached for her, Morrigan jerked away, not wanting his hands on her. The motion drew a dark grin to his face and before she could react again, he was behind her, snaring the back of her hair in his hand.

"You're going to behave, aren't you?"

The twist he gave made her whimper as the pins scraped her scalp and flared pain along her neck. "Yes!" She gasped high and loud, knowing better than to move.

"Good, perhaps you'll actually be useful." Instead of letting go as Morrigan had hoped he would do since he had earned her compliance, Elijah shoved her forward directing her down the stairs and into their mother's sitting room.

Delaney was unbothered by the way Elijah held Morrigan. Instead, her eyes glanced over every part of her before giving a low, noncommittal hum.

"She looks good enough." From Delaney, that was a high compliment, but the reason behind it kept Morrigan's pride silent. Delaney didn't care how Morrigan felt about the whole thing, just that she deemed her appropriate for the task at hand.

"We should arrive at Atce' Plaza shortly after sunset, which is when Lord Ayrden usually makes his entrance to things like this." Elijah sounded bored and finally released her.

Taking a small step away, she didn't bother trying to adjust anything and tried to let her mind wander. Despite the situation, a small bubble of excitement welled within her. She was going somewhere new, even just for a short while. It had been so long since she left the house that she was sure a trip to the next town would be all the excitement she needed for the rest of her life. But to walk the last known steps her father had walked before he disappeared felt like something important. Mae had been there as well. Even though she didn't have either of them in her life at that moment, they would still be with her when she needed them.

Morrigan had learned young that anticipation and excitement for things often bred to disappointment. She knew to expect that disappointment now because either way, she would not be free. Where her cage was located would depend on how the night went. She would either enter a new life as someone else's slave or return home to her quarters after a fierce lashing for having failed in her one task for the night.

Delaney's words drew her from her thoughts. "Get whatever you can for her. I don't care who it is."

"Absolutely." This time, when Elijah reached for her, Morrigan let him, deciding that letting his greed sink into her skin was better than the ache in her neck from his tight grip on her hair. Looking presentable might be her only way of possibly attracting someone kind. It was unlikely, but a girl could dream.

The clouds in the sky looked nearly black as they stepped from the house, the marble stairs were damp and cold under Morrigan's feet. She hadn't been allowed shoes for this event, something about making her look more vulnerable, a complete opposite notion of Elijah worrying people were going to judge them for not sending her with proper clothing. Some of their logic didn't make sense and Morrigan had stopped asking.

Fae didn't typically travel by carriage, but because of her mark, teleporting her was too much of a drain on Elijah's magic, and they hadn't had time to petition for a direct portal to Atce' Plaza. Morrigan thought it was a little weird that they didn't already have a portal, but as with everything else, she assumed it was because they were so remote and that had an effect on their connection to innate magic.

She was relieved to see her trunk settled on the back and the moment of distraction cost her. Her knee hit the step as Elijah shoved her forward, but he didn't give her time to properly recover before hoisting her the rest of the way in, making her crawl on her hands and knees to her seat as he laughed. Quietly, she settled herself down as far into the carriage as she could and remained silent as Elijah talked to the driver; his words were muffled, and she didn't try to make them out.

As he entered, he threw a wadded-up cloth at her, making her cringe as it hit her chest before settling in her lap. "You forgot something. I know you're eager to be a whore but do try to be modest *little sister.*" He rolled his eyes as Morrigan quickly untwisted the fabric to realize he had given her a cloak. Quietly, she tucked the cloak around herself. She was glad for the warmth but wouldn't tell him as such, keeping her eyes low as she covered what skin she could. Turning her eyes to the window, she wondered if Atce' Plaza truly looked as it did in the photos in the book. She hoped they would get there before the sun set just to see. While she loved the greenery of their home, she was eager to see if the sun really was as bright and the colors as vivid as what her books had depicted.

Despite her best efforts to stay awake and see all she could, the jostling of the carriage made her head hurt, and sleep followed soon after.

Chapter Three

Morrigan

Atce' Plaza

The carriage stopping some time later stirred Morrigan from sleep. She lamented the fact that she hadn't been able to see much of the world that they passed, but being able to see a clear sky was worth missing everything else. The sky outside the window was alight with the fire of the dying day. The mountains they had left behind looked blue, giving way to the purple of the sky and the red and orange blur of the sun that had not quite set. She was envious of anyone who got to see something like that every night. In her distraction, she hadn't heard the door open, but the snap of Elijah's fingers had her looking up, still trying to blink sleep from her eyes. "Come along, we mustn't keep anyone waiting."

Quickly as she could, she made her way out of the carriage and into the cool night. Curling the cloak around her shoulders, she held the part closed and followed as Elijah bowed, talking to the nearest guard.

Morrigan stared, tipping her head up and up to try to understand the vastness of the rise that stood in front of her. The entire thing was made of stone and stretched as far as she could see on both sides as well as high up as she could see. If there was a gate for the open arched entry, Morrigan couldn't see it. People dressed in all different colors came and went without so much as a glance from the guards, but none of them were as fair as Elijah. Was everyone in attendance a changeling? The light was fading fast and still Elijah spoke quick and low to the guard. A short moment later, another guard met Elijah, bowing slightly, before one gestured them forward.

"I'm Captain Hawke Corviana." His dark wings flared as he bowed, and Morrigan stepped back. They were large and wide but the rest of the people around them didn't even flinch as they moved. "I've been sent by the High Lord to make sure you arrive where needed."

"Ah, good. He knows we're here." Elijah grinned up at Captain Corviana, rubbing his hands together. "I knew arriving this way would get his attention." Captain Corviana gave a curt nod before he turned to Morrigan.

Giving her a bow, he held out his gloved hand to her, "My lady?"

"She's not worth a title." Elijah sneered.

Despite Elijah's words, Captain Corviana's hand remained outstretched, his eyebrows raised expectantly. His eyes were like bright amber against his dark skin. The light from the surrounding lamps made the color dance in a way that matched his mischievous smile. He knew what he was doing.

Tentatively, she offered her own, keeping Elijah in her peripheral vision just in case he decided to reach for her. She dipped a small curtsy in return. Instead of letting her go, Captain Corviana pulled her forward, grasping her elbow. "There's a step there, my lady." Elijah scoffed as Captain Corviana helped her step over a gap in the road she couldn't see until they were upon it. Something about him seemed familiar, like she had met him before, but she couldn't place it, and with his gloves, there was no skin contact so she couldn't pick up what he was feeling to see if she knew his energy either.

When he finally released her, she offered him an appreciative smile. Offering her a nod, Captain Corviana turned to address Elijah again. "Yes. He's known since before you arrived."

"Great man he is!" Elijah crowed. His self-satisfied smile returned to his lips as he strode forward, leading them through the gate and into the plaza as if he knew where they were headed.

The light inside the gates of the plaza was brighter and a bit overwhelming compared to the outside, not helped by the fact that she had only woken up shortly before. There was light everywhere, but it wasn't a firelight. There was no source. Some of it hung in the air, dancing along to the steady sound of soft music.

It was a lovely sound, paired with a guitar and a soft lilting voice whose words she didn't understand.

Other lights were strung up in the trees and across the streets from pole to pole of the stalls that lined the path. Though she desperately wanted to know what they were, to touch one just to see if it was some form of wickless fire, she knew better.

The laughter of people dressed in varying shades of blue and the sounds of children playing brought a smile to her face. So many voices surrounded her in a way she had never felt before. She enjoyed it, even though most of the conversations that surrounded her were in a language she didn't comprehend.

So many stalls spread out before them, each nearly an identical setup of a wooden frame and fabric cover, but the wares inside varied from what she could tell. Silver seemed prevalent throughout, especially in the jewelry pieces in the stalls closest to her. The jewels and adornments reflected the firelight of torches in a manner that made them look as if they each held individual balls of dancing flames within them.

Her attention was only drawn away by the hand that grasped her wrist and pulled her forward. The warm palm against her skin was anything but reassuring. Greed and malcontent seeped into her skin like prickles of poison from the point of contact that caused each nerve-ending to spasm. Taking in the frown on her brother's face, she shook the thought of questioning him out of her head, refocusing on the events around them.

She already knew why they were there.

Drawing in a grounding breath brought the savory scent of cooked meat and wonderful aromatic herbs. Samples of braised lamb, roasted boar, and various fowl were offered at stations they passed but each was denied by her guardian and Captain Corviana, who followed a few paces ahead of them. Another booth showcased a variety of loaves of bread and pastries that were lovelier than any she could ever have hoped to make. The smell of baking sweet spices filled her with warmth.

The sun-heated cobblestones underfoot changed to cool marble when they stepped into one of the long hallways that lined the pavilion. A shiver curled itself down her spine as they entered. Brighter than the market outside, the interior hall was just as wondrous. Large portraits of dark-haired men lined one wall. The other was inset with open windows decorated with the ruling lord's colors: dark blues that faded to purple and black like the night sky on the full moon's rising, she had been told. It seemed fitting for the night that approached.

Near the end of the hall, five breathtakingly beautiful studies of landscapes were spread out in a gallery for all to see. Each was a different place with vivid colors and immaculate detail. Morrigan marveled at the skill held by an artist who could capture things so lovingly and make them look so realistic. One of the five scenes she knew. Her home, Qu'tar, in Be'Sala province, was captured perfectly, the greens of the forest shimmering as if the artist issued personal drops of water to each leaf on every tree. Fog rolled off the river in the valley. The view was a glimpse of the end of a sunny day, one Morrigan had rarely seen. The vantage point of this one was curiously familiar, as if the person had sat high on the stairs and painted it from her home.

The next one she thought might be the Pridelands. She had never been but had heard some stories from Mae at their last visit. The sand rippled like waves, resembling a stormy, choppy sea. When she tilted her head just right, she could barely make out the shapes of buildings far in the distance, but when she righted herself, they disappeared. Santi had told her of heat mirages and how the heat warped the view of the world, but how this artist had captured it was beyond Morrigan's scope of understanding. Perhaps it was magic that made the dew in Be'Sala and the mirage of the Pridelands so realistic. Motion to her left made her jump, but when she realized it was Captain Corviana, she relaxed just a bit. He was intimidating, but he wasn't Elijah.

"These are lovely." Her voice cracked a bit from lack of use, and she cleared her throat as she looked at her hands clasped in front of her.

"Yes. They were done by a great artist. I never had the pleasure of meeting him."

Morrigan was pleased he agreed and gave him a small, shy smile. "I know Be'Sala. It looks like it was painted from our yard."

Captain Corviana opened his mouth to respond but snapped it shut, his eyes darting over her head. It was the only warning she had before the fiery jolt of annoyance spread through her as Elijah's hand returned to her upper arm again.

"This is where I leave you, my lady." Captain Corviana inclined his head before stepping around them to wade his way through the crowd. Initially, she would have thought he would be hard to lose being as tall as he was, but her attention was pulled from him as Elijah gave her a tug. When she looked again, he was gone.

"Come." Not having much choice, Morrigan allowed herself to be herded away from the gallery. Longing spread through her as she pulled her gaze away from the landscapes.

Improperly dressed for the cooler southern climate, Morrigan shivered as they stepped into the open-air courtyard and Elijah pulled off her cloak. She tried to ignore the sudden chill and the dread that sank through her by taking in their new surroundings.

Long stretches of tulle and shimmering lengths of satin twisted overhead, strung between the rooftops of the halls. Each piece of fabric faded from one deep shade to another until the very last one blended into black that encompassed the entirety of the wall at the end of the terrace. Small points of light shimmered throughout the wall, the moon painted against the backdrop, a beautiful ode to the night sky.

As they stepped through the crowd, her attention fell on the people around them. Some looked normal, but others were like the Avian guards that lingered nearby and possessed wings. Fangs flashed unhidden in smiles, and someone could change from one person to another in seconds.

Changelings.

Time seemed to speed up the moment cold fingers touched her chin, forcing her attention back to those her brother talked to. Cold lust sparked against her skin and made her bottom lip tremble while her face was turned from one side to the other. The conversation around her was quick and low, but she understood none of it in her attempt to fight the haze. She didn't want to let the emotions assaulting her with every touch sink too deeply into her. She didn't want to lose herself. The cold hands dropped away and the fingers of another took their place.

These fingers told of greed as they traced along the curve of her collarbone and down between her breasts. The gesture was shocking and distress curled through her, but she couldn't pull away.

Before she could gasp or protest, another set of hands turned her, trailing over her waist in a way that made her face heat with embarrassment. This person did not touch her skin, so she could not tell his real intentions.

Fingers touched the pins in her hair as another set of sneering lips took the place of the ones before. The hands that brushed her cheek told of dark malice and darker intentions that churned the acid in her stomach. Forcing her eyes closed, she tried to center herself with a deep breath. Her bottom lip trembled as she fought back tears. Another set of hands tugged her by the elbow, plunging more dark greed along her skin.

It was disorienting to have so many different hands on her, so many emotions sinking into her skin at once. She wanted to cry out, to shove the hands and faces away, and plead with everyone to let her breathe. Despite this being her only possible bid for freedom, she just wanted it to stop.

A warm, gentle hand caught her elbow as she was pushed aside. She whimpered before another touched her chin.

These hands were different.

Calm soothed across her skin, and the tremble of her bottom lip slowed. "Breathe." The voice was low and soft, and her lips parted of their own accord as she took a deep breath in and let it shudder out. "Look." The hand fell from her chin to hold her shoulder.

As she was turned, she opened her eyes and noticed how close she was to the rail she had thought was just a decoration. The last length of fabric didn't fall across a wall as she had thought but ended overhead. The wide black space behind the dais was the night sky. Her breath caught in awe.

How was it possible to see so much of the sky in one place?

The deep midnight hue spread across the wide horizon from the Be'Sala Mountains in the north and to the Cobalt Sea in the south. Morrigan had to turn her head from one side to the other to grasp the vastness of it. Like crystalline jewels, stars shimmered overhead, and the moon glowed behind the platform where the lords would sit. The chairs remained curiously empty.

As she turned to thank whoever had given her a reprieve, Elijah's stifling anger crawled up her wrist as he took hold of her again. "Don't wander." His breathy, adenoidal voice was a stark contrast to the one that had whispered in her ear moments before.

By some miracle, or just will alone, the calmness that had sunk into her remained. She didn't feel as intimidated as before and even the burn of Elijah's grip on her didn't feel as fierce. The next person Elijah introduced her to was a rather large man whose red hair blended so well with his beard that Morrigan didn't know where one began and the other ended. He wore a wide grin, fangs glinting as Elijah introduced us.

Morrigan already knew Lord Luca De'Lyon, second in lordship over the Northern Plains. His cousin was Morrigan's eldest sister Mae's husband. Lord De'Lyon's disinterested gaze heated Morrigan's skin as she watched his eyes focus on her barely covered chest, down to her corseted waist and then hips before returning to her chest. "What talents does she have?"

"Huh?" The response slipped out before Morrigan remembered her place and slapped her hand over her mouth.

The sudden connection of Elijah's hand on her elbow was near bruising, and she gasped as she tried to pull away. "Forgive her," Elijah's tone was flat, his frown deepening as did the sting of his ire on Morrigan's skin. "She requires a bit more training." Elijah gave the man a raised eyebrow, his lips splitting into a devious grin. "A bit of taming if you will. I'm sure a man of your legacy and renowned hunting would love the challenge of taming her?" Morrigan quickly covered her snort of laughter with her hand, feigning a coughing fit that she knew was hardly believable.

Lord De'Lyon's eyes traced over her again before he shook his head. "I haven't the time for that." His dismissal was short, and Elijah's face pulled into a frown once more.

"I apologize for wasting your time then, sir." Elijah bowed before turning away.

Morrigan stumbled as he pulled her along with him, his grip so tight it made her wrap her hand around his wrist to try to pull herself free. His anger flooded through her, spiraling from the connection on her arm to her fingers and back up her arm to her chest.

Pain sparked across the back of her head and down her spine, her vision spotting for a moment when her head collided with the stone wall she was suddenly pressed against. Her fear flooded through her as his hand found her throat, barely overpowering his desire for death in her mind. His hand wedged higher, tipping her head back and forcing a cry from her before restricting all air.

"Listen here." His voice was cold and dark, sending a chill through her as he pressed again. "If you don't get sold tonight, you'll be nothing. You'll be worse than nothing, you'll be nothing more than an animal at the Farm."

Though she couldn't show it with the way he had her pinned, Morrigan was more afraid of his hand than his words. She was more afraid of giving him the satisfaction of causing her death than being sent to the Farm. Struggling only made him press harder against her windpipe and tears sprang to her eyes while she fought for breath. Her fingers clawed at his hand, trying to get it to relax from her throat.

Footsteps nearby pulled his attention away from her and a woman's voice whispered something she couldn't hear over the roaring of the blood in her ears. Whatever was said, Elijah seemed to understand because he drew away just enough. Morrigan heaved a deep breath of air and lashed out to kick him in the knee. Before she could get steady on her feet and reorient herself, his hand caught the hair at the nape of her neck, and she cried out. Pain seared her scalp from the pins being ripped from her hair.

His voice was devoid of any emotion as he pulled her close, and she couldn't fight the fear that flared to life once more. "I tried to do this the nice way. Let's see how you fare being thrown to the wolves." The air was suddenly cold around her, and she realized he had shut down his emotions.

Before she could think too hard about it, he turned to her and shoved her forward. Caught off guard she stumbled, crashing into someone in a black suit. The wine-colored sauce he was serving spilled down her side, over the front of the server, and on several other people who loitered about. When she tried to back away from the commotion she had accidentally caused, her heel caught the back of her gown, and she fell backward. Catching herself on someone's arm, she tried to right herself, but the man looked her over, scoffed, and forced her grip off his arm.

When she was released from his grasp, her foot caught on a step as she turned away. Faltering, her balance failed, and she fell hard to the floor. Pain laced through her palms and up her arms, sending the aches from before into full throbbing pain as she caught herself; the slap of her hands on the glistening black marble echoed as the vast room fell silent.

Chapter Four

Nikaius and Priamos

Atce' Plaza

Selection Night.

It was rare that he attended, preferring the quiet of his home to huge festivities such as the ones that marked the end of the harvest. The Winter Moon was often foretold to be the makings of a great fated romance. Nikaius had heard the story of how his parents met many times over the years and the tale never changed. Everyone in his family, as far back as anyone could remember, found their true love upon the setting of the Winter Moon. Even Bastian, Nikaius' brother, had found someone during the summer solstice. Although he questioned how much they loved each other with how they behaved so cold and distant towards one another.

Nikaius knew that he had found that true genuine love in his mate, Waric. They had been inseparable from their first meeting when they were young teenagers. Their marking had been an accident, one brought upon during a high emotion moment when they had both turned fifteen. They had been skeptical at first, but when his father had sent them to separate sides of the country to train, the bond had snapped into place. He had been surprised to hear Waric's voice in his head, but after eight years, they had learned how to use it to their advantage but also how to block each other out.

While they were committed to each other, something always felt like it was missing, both hoping that the luck of the Winter Moon would provide them with what they needed.

Nikaius chuckled as he watched Waric entertain others by changing his shape from the carpenter's playful little girl to his normal self again. The woman beside him, Aeshira, was one that Waric had been trying to get the attention of for months, but she always seemed just out of reach for him. Nikaius encouraged it all the same. Once Waric stopped chasing, she would turn the tides and strike like the Valkyrie she was.

From Aeshira and Waric, Nikaius' gaze wandered to Aquila and Hawke, who lingered by the northernmost doorway, always within his line of sight. The twins had come to Nikaius' father's court when he was fifteen. Hawke had risen through the guard rank quickly, his second form making him quicker than most and his skill in changing quicker than the best swordsman's throw. Aquila had been assigned as a lady's maid, but Nikaius had caught her watching every training session she could.

When Nikaius took over Kunmei's court at twenty, he had chosen Hawke to be the head of his guard and allowed him to train Aquila as his second. Together, the twins were unstoppable. Nikaius often wondered if some sort of telepathic connection made them even more so. Twins were rumored to have bonds like mates, believed to be two halves of the same whole.

Letting his gaze wander once again, the peculiar feeling that had plagued him for most of the evening returned. It was something he had never felt before and almost made him feel too large for his body, earning him looks whenever he rolled his shoulders or rubbed the back of his neck. Paired with it was an odd, subdued scent that lingered in the air. The wolf within him growled when he caught a trace, and his chest tightened whenever he got close, but no matter how hard he tried to track it, he couldn't place its source.

There. The wolf's voice grumbled, and Nikaius' skin prickled with goosebumps.

Priamos, down. The unsettling feeling returned and with it, Priamos shifted under his skin, drawing their attention to the people around them.

His target looked quite young from where she stood surrounded by men who were surely twice her age. One man talked to the others while she was passed off from hand to hand. Nikaius didn't like the way she was being handled or the distress she seemed to be in.

The crowd parted a bit, but people either didn't recognize him or didn't care about his sudden presence among them. As he approached, he noticed more about her. She looked as if she was holding back tears with her bottom lip between her teeth. Her face was flushed, and her eyes squeezed tight as her breath jittered slowly through her nose. She smelled distressed. Sighing softly, he caught her by the elbow and tugged.

The pitiful whimper that escaped her made him pause to catch her chin, his thumb halting the tremble of her lips. "Breathe," his voice was low and slow, and her breath shook as she obeyed. Turning her face away from the crowd that seemed displeased that he had snagged her from them, questions flew through his mind as he tried to commit her to his memory.

What is her name?

Red hair.

Who is she?

Why does she smell the way she does?

Freckles cross the bridge of her nose.

Does she belong to someone?

Scars interrupted the freckles on her shoulders.

Was she being sold?

He needed to distract her long enough to learn more about her.

"Look." Nikaius had always been taken by the bright night sky, maybe she would enjoy it as well?

Nik. The word was soft, but he could hear it, and he turned his gaze to find who was trying to reach him. Waric. With a sigh, he released the beautiful girl and stepped away.

"This better be important, Waric."

"It seems people are trying to *sell* again." Waric's voice was hushed as he pulled Nikaius away from the crowd.

For the last few months, Waric and Nikaius had been trying to stop the trading of people who were deemed less by societal standards. While Nikaius wasn't surprised by this turn of events, he was concerned that it was happening within these walls.

"Who?" Nikaius turned to look over his shoulder, watching as a dark-haired man snagged the beautiful redhead by the elbow. She looked lost, but not scared, and he wondered if it was his doing that made her look less distressed. Had he been right? Was she the one being trafficked?

"I haven't gotten a name. Hawke told me it was some fae from Be'Sala." Nikaius' gaze pulled away from the girl to turn to Waric again.

"Fucking Be'Sala." Nikaius spat. While he had sway with those in his court, Bastian, his older brother, was another story. There had been talks of unrest within the planes Bastian oversaw and Nikaius could hardly blame them. Selling people was a line Nikaius refused to accept being crossed. "I'll talk to Bastian." It was the last thing he wanted to do with his night, but it was the more important thing to focus on. Someone's life could be saved.

He turned as if he was going to seek out his brother but instead, he searched the crowd for the female and her companion to see if his suspicions were correct. A glance brought nothing to his attention. They had disappeared.

Stepping away, he shifted slightly, rolling and straightening his shoulders to make himself look larger. People stepped away as he took a slow, deep breath trying to pick up her scent again.

It took a moment, but he caught it again, the curious mix of sunshine and rain. A commotion to his left made him pause. Something broke against the marble floor and people grumbled and shoved before the crowd parted. Turning once more to seek out the owner of the scent he had been dreaming of his whole life, a hush befell the crowd before the sound of flesh hitting the floor echoed through the room. His eyes flew to the small, disheveled female who now knelt at the edge of the marble dais. It was *her*.

Nikaius stepped closer only to notice that his brother had taken his seat in the silver chair. His heart ached for this unknown person. He could smell her embarrassment and a bit of fear curled with that sweet, soothing scent. He could also see the tears as they dripped onto the back of her hands, the way her fingers curled against the floor, and the shiver of her shoulders. He had embarrassed himself many times as a child, tripping over things and fumbling with his too-large frame when he was but a pup. He knew some of what she felt, kneeling there, a mess for all to see.

It only took a moment or two for people to start talking again in low whispers, and Nikaius looked at his brother, unsure what he would do. Where Nikaius was kind and calm, Bastian was not. Nikaius often thought it was the pressures of their family that had made his brother so hard and cold, but he had been in the meetings with their father and knew that those pressures were ones Bastian took upon himself.

Signaling Aquila, Nikaius stepped forward. He had to know why she smelled the way she did. As he reached for the golden fastening of his cape, Bastian held up a hand and stood, giving Nikaius a dark look.

Bastian's footsteps across the floor made the room fall silent once more, everyone's eyes now on the elder lord. He paused in front of the still-kneeling girl and cleared his throat, but she didn't look up at him. The way Bastian straightened pulled all attention to him once more before he impetuously slammed his foot onto the floor only a hair away from one of her hands. "Contemptuous thing. Look at your lord when you kneel before him."

Chapter Five

Morrigan and Nikaius

*Atce' Plaza
Pavilion*

The sudden hush that befell the crowd was deafening as Morrigan knelt there, looking at her reflection in the shining dark marble. It wasn't a clear image, but she knew she was a mess.

Not being a stranger to tripping over herself or falling into things, Morrigan knew that grace was not her forte. It was one fact that Amara and Delaney had constantly teased her about as a child. To be so thorough in drawing attention to herself in front of so many people though was humiliating. No matter how badly she tried to shove the hurt and embarrassment aside, she was too overwhelmed to reign in her tears as they dripped onto her hands.

She thought brothers were supposed to love and support their younger siblings, but she knew why that wasn't the case with Elijah or her sister Amara. She knew her place and the burden of her existence, but she had wished he would care for her the way Mae had and the way their father did before he died. Even Santi, Mae's husband, who was mostly a stranger to her, treated her with more kindness than those she had grown up with. Yet here she was, soaked from shoulder to hip, kneeling on the dais before the entirety of a foreign court on the eve of the Winter Moon.

It was said that the Winter Moon would bring great change; however, tonight, that change would probably be her death. It only took a moment or two for people to start talking again in low whispers, but she didn't move. The hushed voices curled around her, but she still couldn't understand, the heat in her face and pulse too loud in her ears.

After a few moments, her heart calmed but the loud steps of hard-soled shoes on marble silenced the voices again. Dark polished boots came into her line of view. Another set of footsteps shuffled nearby, but she didn't dare to look up. The foot closest to her rose and then slammed down onto the floor barely a breath away from her hand, but she was too numb to flinch, a small part of her hoping the pain would follow and clear the dark thoughts from her head. "Contemptuous thing. Look at your lord when you kneel before him." The lord's voice was harsh and inflected lower, but it didn't sound quite right.

Then Morrigan straightened, moving to sit back properly on her knees, but as she looked up at him, the word that came from her mouth was not respectful.

Nikaius watched curiously as she moved. She didn't appear as afraid at that moment as he had anticipated her to be.

"Asshole."

Nikaius choked back a laugh at her word before clearing his throat when Bastian's dark gaze turned to him, eyes narrowed. When Bastian looked away, Nikaius had every intention of grabbing the girl before she could fall victim to his brother, but Bastian was closer and quicker.

Morrigan's gaze briefly followed the lord's glance. When she looked up again, she knew she was in trouble before the lord even moved. Like before, with Elijah, she was snatched up by the hair at the back of her neck, and she gasped as he pulled her to her feet, grinding her teeth against the pain. Amusement and anger were often not felt together from what she could remember, so to feel those two emotions seeping off the lord was a bit disorienting as he turned her to the crowd.

"Who stakes claim to bringing this feral thing into my court?"
Silence.
Nikaius rolled his shoulders.
Priamos grumbled.

The lord turned them. "No one? Pity. Five gold to the highest bidder? Look how lovely she is, gentlemen." Fingers trailed down Morrigan's neck, down through the red sauce that stained her skin and dress. Following the trail of his fingers, malice seeped in, causing fear to flare through her again.

Bastian looked up at the crowd, and he scoffed when not one person came through with the barest desire to bid for the girl.

"Then, perhaps we should make an example of what happens to people who ruin my night." Bastian's face turned devious.

Shit. I'm going to die tonight. The thought of struggling was fleeting. Morrigan couldn't muster the strength to fight, nor did she want to give the lord the satisfaction. Plus, this was what she wanted, wasn't it? She was already exhausted even though the night had barely begun.

Morrigan didn't feel him move to pull the blade.

Nikaius wasn't quick enough to prevent the knife from nicking her skin, but he stopped his brother from slitting her throat. "I'll take her." The dark look that Bastian gave as he swung himself and the girl around to face him was one Nikaius had only received a few times before, but he knew there would be hell to pay for it later. Locking eyes with Bastian, Nikaius raised his chin, wondering how long it would take for Bastian to break.

Morrigan took in the appearance of the other male. The look on his face was one of open defiance, a challenge. She wondered who he was to be willing to fight the lord for her.

It felt like an eternity and the weight of what was going on crackled through the air as if lightning was being traded between the two of them.

Predator versus predator.

Bastian's teeth ground together as his eyes narrowed. There it was. Finally, Nikaius pulled his gaze away. He had made his point.

With a scoff, Bastian shoved the girl away and stepped from the platform with a wave of his hands. "Shoo!" The people scattered.

Nikaius rushed forward to catch the girl by her elbows, steadying her before she fell again. "I've got you."

His voice was soft and soothed some of the anxiousness that fluttered through Morrigan's chest.

Then their eyes met.

His were a deep shade of blue that reminded her of lightning-illuminated storm clouds. The depth of his gaze felt as if he was peering into the very pit of her soul. A flash of recognition curled within her, and she wondered, briefly, if they had ever met before.

Her eyes were a stunning shade of jade. Nikaius wondered how she had managed to be gifted with a color so pristine and bright. They matched the warm springy scent she gave, and he stepped closer, taking a slow breath to sink her entirely into his memory. He smiled at the surprised look that lit up her face.

Nikaius signaled to his guard as he worked the cloak free from his shoulder.

Morrigan jumped as warmth spread over her shoulders, a large tremble curling itself along her spine even though her gaze never left him. She hadn't realized until that moment how cold she was until the fur settled against her skin. His fingers worked at the buckle, securing it tight across her collarbones. The two edges of fabric met completely in the middle, and she realized he no longer wore his cape.

Did... Did he just give me the cape off his shoulders? Up until that moment, she had thought the cape was simply an adornment. Usually, the red fabric rested on one shoulder, secured diagonally across the chest and back by a thick leather belt. But now she knew it was functional as well.

Nikaius watched the emotions play across the girl's face for a moment before he turned to address Aquila and Hawke who waited nearby. "We have a bit of a situation."

"We saw." Aquila raised her eyebrows as she looked from Nikaius to the girl and back.

"What do you need from us?" Hawke asked, running a hand through his hair before elbowing his overzealous sister in the side.

"Ouch." Aquila elbowed back and the tension within Nikaius eased.

Morrigan stepped back, her bottom lip quivering as she looked down, fingers playing with the buckle. What was an appropriate way to thank him? Something else occurred to her then. He was out of uniform. The panic that welled in her chest made her step back again.

Tracking her out of the corner of his eye, Nikaius tried to hold his attention on his guards for only a moment longer before giving the command: "Go follow Bastian. He and I need to talk." Both guards bowed before stepping away.

"You're out of uniform." She seemed unsettled by that fact as she tried to pull the leather free from the buckles. Nikaius pulled her hands away from fidgeting with the buckle.

"It's not a uniform."

"I don't care what you call it here. You shouldn't get into trouble because of me." She stepped back again, wrenching her hands from his so she could try to work at the bindings again.

Ooh, feisty. Priamos purred.

He looked at her hands for a moment before looking up at her from under his lashes, lips parting into a grin that showed off white teeth. *"**I'm always in trouble.**"* He looked her over, his fang dragging over his bottom lip. Her breath caught.

Nikaius and Priamos preened over the way her breath caught.

"I..."

His eyebrows pressed together as he tipped his chin down, his dark gaze still locked on hers. "***Don't.***" His voice had dropped, and he could feel Priamos' power pulling from deep within him, lacing the words with it.

Morrigan huffed, slowly becoming frustrated with him cutting her off.

"But..." She took another step back.

"***No.***" He followed. Morrigan's heart fluttered at the sound of his voice.

"Sir?" Aquila's voice cut through Priamos' hold, and Nikaius was suddenly in control again, feeling as if a bucket of ice water had been dumped on his head. Quick change always left him a bit disoriented.

The distraction of the Avian guard's return lost Morrigan the freedom of her hands.

"Yes, Aquila?" Catching her hands was easy once she was distracted. He carefully wrapped his hands around her wrists. He pulled some energy from Priamos, just enough to be soothing and to will calm to settle through his touch. Being an alpha had its perks.

Calm settled through Morrigan, and she relaxed a bit, forgetting why she was fighting with him to begin with.

The curious look Aquila had as she glanced at the girl made Nikaius want to chuckle. "Bastian wishes to have a word in the War Room."

Morrigan frowned. She had addressed him as sir. Was he her superior? Maybe that was why he wasn't so concerned about being out of uniform.

Annoyance itched against her wrists as he switched to hold both in one hand and ran the other through his hair. The breath he let out was slow and measured and the annoyance faded just a bit, the calm returning.

"We'll go there now. See if you can find this one's chaperone." Nikaius wiggled his 'captive's' hands, and she huffed, a cute noise that settled somewhere deep inside him as she tried to tug her hands away again. To Aquila, he said "He's the dark-haired fae I pointed out earlier."

With a click of her boots and a bow, Aquila took her leave. There were many curious glances, but everyone seemed to know how to give them a wide berth. "Come, let's get this over with and then we can go home. Don't worry about the cloak," Possessiveness sparked through him as he looked her over in her disheveled state. "Unless you were enjoying walking around in a dress that leaves very little to the imagination."

The shock of his words and his assessing gaze made Morrigan gasp, and she shook her head at the insinuation.

Chapter Six

Nikaius and Morrigan

Atce' Plaza: The War Room

The War Room was usually meant for conversations regarding issues with outside forces and hadn't been used in several decades. The landscapes and figurines were covered with a thin layer of dust that evidenced their lack of use. No place in the room was untouched by the dust, and Nikaius wondered why Bastian would want to meet here of all places. This room hadn't been used in any memory that Nikaius held of Atce' Plaza. The room was only half-lit; most of the light came from what appeared to be a hastily lit fire in the fireplace. The magic that was the primary lighting source would typically have brightened the room by the time they entered; however, the chandelier overhead seemed to struggle with connecting to the magic grid, flickering in places as if it was alight with flames instead. The dark, unkempt environment only seemed to accentuate the air of the angry lord who prowled back and forth along one side of the table as if biding his time.

Nikaius could only assume the state of the area and his brother's actions were to emphasize his displeasure for the scene that they had caused.

Morrigan startled as her new companion leaned one shoulder on the wall, just inside the door, facing her. She giggled softly as he rolled his eyes, tugging her closer by the hip. The action, typically, would have made her jittery and hyperaware, triggering her habit of playing out every dark scenario she had experienced in the past. Was it because he was a changeling that she felt drawn to him instead? Nothing about him sent up red flags. Instead, she felt as if she could stay close to him for an indeterminate amount of time and still feel safe.

Snagging one of the braids that had come free from the knot at the base of her skull, Nikaius gave it a gentle tug, earning him a giggle that made Priamos purr.

"You shouldn't threaten to kill people in the plaza, Bastian. It sends a bad message." Green eyes widened and Nikaius frowned, giving her another smile that he hoped was reassuring.

"You, little brother, shouldn't undermine me in front of my court." Little brother? Morrigan frowned. If the enraged older brother was indeed a lord, that would make Morrigan's dark haired knight a lord as well.

Holy shit. A lord had pulled her away from her brother's antics to give her a reprieve!

A lord had claimed her when his brother threatened to kill her. The sense of safety vanished at the realization, like cold water dropped over her head. Morrigan's heart leapt into her throat as she thought back to everything that had happened within the last few moments they had been alone. Her behavior was unbecoming of someone who was in the presence of a lord. What would happen when this power play between the two brothers would end? She had never wanted to have a word with the Fates about their plan more than she did at that moment.

"This is the neutral territory between our courts, Bastian. You can't be killing people here. Especially girls who did nothing to warrant such an event." Nikaius kept his voice low, torn between keeping the girl calm while not rising to his brother's bait. Bastian knew better than anyone how volatile Priamos could be when angered and would often use it against Nikaius. Since being given his court, however, Nikaius had learned better control, and he could tell it bothered Bastian. His voice rose as Nikaius reached out to begin picking pins from the girl's hair.

"I don't care! You shouldn't undermine me, Nikaius!" Bastian slammed his hand down on the table and Nikaius' hands stilled when the girl jumped, her pulse elevating as she tucked herself a bit closer to the wall. Something dark curled in Nikaius' chest. Bastian was being unnecessarily rough and purposely trying to scare her just to see how Nikaius would react. He was probably hoping to force Nikaius to act against him in neutral territory.

He would not allow that. *Priamos* wouldn't allow that.

"I'm not your slave, Bastian. As much as you hate it, I'm your equal." Nikaius rose to his full height, and he let Priamos take over, rolling their shoulders as they lifted their chin higher.

Bastian huffed and rolled his eyes before dropping into the chair at the head of the table, his ease nothing more than a power play. Anyone who knew him knew this game.

Morrigan, however, was nervous as she watched him. The energy in the air twisting her stomach was something she hadn't ever experienced. She couldn't remember a time when she had been so nervous. Her stomach churned as if she might be sick if she had been allowed to eat, and her hands shook at the realization that neither brother owed her any form of kindness. There was a high possibility that she was just a pawn being used as a power play between them. Despite the younger lord seeming to be at ease and intrigued by her presence and the nonchalant way he kept touching her, Morrigan was unsure he was even going to keep her. The eldest had made it clear that he had no contention with killing her and it made awareness spread through her at the possibility that she might still end up in Bastian's care. Her life hung in the balance of two warring brothers.

"This is why you keep losing people, Bastian." Nikaius stepped forward to block Morrigan from Bastian's gaze.

"I keep losing them because they are traitors, and you are soft."

"You keep losing them because you don't care about them."

"Gentlemen, My Lady?" Aquila dipped a bow as she entered followed by Hawke.

"Yes?" Priamos retreated and Nikaius turned away from Bastian to address his guard.

"I found the fae. He claims that he was invited here. I think he was trying to sell her." A harsh breath left Nikaius' chest and Priamos growled low in the back of his mind.

"Why her?" Waric followed close behind and affection surged warm and pleasing through Nikaius, along with soft appreciation. Waric was always the best at keeping Nikaius and Priamos under control when Bastian was around, despite the group's overall disdain for him. Waric had been trained to handle social and political events more than Nikaius had and having him to lean on in times like that was one of the reasons he was sure the Fates had put them together.

While the newcomers spoke with Nikaius, Morrigan had a chance to really take in Hawke's appearance, as well as Aquila's. It was clear that they were twins, nearly identical with dark hair and umber skin. Morrigan allowed herself a moment of bubbling acidic jealousy over Aquila's complexion, betting anything that it did not flush to show her every emotion or mottle in the cold. The smattering of freckles across Hawke's nose definitely suited him better than her as well, as if the Fates had lovingly pressed each one to his skin. Their pattern was nothing like the stippled chaos of her own.

They had wings that were larger than she was tall and were an interesting mix of flesh tones that faded into a deep, rich onyx. The wings were beautiful, made even lovelier by how the flickering of the chandelier overhead hinted at sapphire and emerald notes that weren't seen to the naked eye at first glance.

Aquila's wings flared a bit as she spoke, shifting with the motion of her hands as if an extension of her. Hawke was the complete opposite. Aside from his slow deep breaths and the flick of his eyes around the room, he was nearly motionless by the door. The only motion of his wings were minute twitches of the feathers that she could only see due to her proximity to him. Morrigan wondered if there would ever be a chance to touch them.

"You look as if you have a question." Something about her must have caught his attention, and he frowned as he looked at her.

Morrigan's cheeks burned with heat as she looked at her toes, nervous about the sudden silence of the room. She could feel all eyes on her.

"No... I mean... I was," She licked her bottom lip nervously before turning her attention to Aquila, who looked at her curiously. Posing her thoughts to Aquila was less mortifying than admitting she was admiring a male she didn't know. "I was admiring your wings and wondered about them."

The room fell silent as they spoke. It was interesting for Nikaius to note that she didn't seem afraid of those who were changelings, even though she wasn't one herself.

"What about them?" Hawke asked.

Morrigan sighed softly. She knew asking to touch them would be rude unless explicitly offered. "How do you keep them protected?"

"What do you mean?" Aquila asked.

"I imagine the weather wouldn't affect them because of oils and other natural barriers, but what about in combat?"

"I try to avoid situations where that would be necessary." Hawke laughed. When he crossed his arms over his chest, Morrigan had to resist the urge to step back. He was rather large.

"But you're a guard, aren't you? What if you get attacked?" Logic should have dictated her brain but somehow had decided to leave her as she mirrored Hawke's pose, lifting her chin.

Hawke scoffed. "It's never happened."

"Hypothetically, then?"

"We can phase them out. My brother is just posturing because there is too much testosterone in the air." Aquila stepped between Morrigan and Hawke, throwing an exasperated look at her brother over her shoulder. "I'll show you sometime if you'd like."

"Oh yes, please!" Morrigan gave an eager, childlike bounce on her toes as she smiled, forgetting that they were in a room filled with prominent people.

Something fluttered in Nikaius' chest, and he rubbed the spot vacantly. Her curiosity was endearing and her eagerness to accept Aquila's offer to show her how changeling powers worked made Nikaius smile. Maybe she'd be eager to meet Priamos.

A throat cleared in the hallway and the girl's exuberance died away, panic replacing it. She knew who the newcomer was and feared him to some degree. Aquila raised her brows as Nikaius watched the girl shrink back against the wall. This displeased both him and Priamos, who grumbled in the back of his mind. His instinct to step in between the girl and her chaperone was strong, but Aquila moved before he could. He watched as she turned, settling against the wall to block the girl from view.

"Gentlemen." Elijah stalked into the room unbothered by the Avian guards and glaring lords.

"What do you have to say for yourself?" Nikaius' voice was low and harsh.

Elijah went straight for Bastian, easily side-stepping Aquila to snag Morrigan's arm on the way. She gasped as his anger sank into her, chasing away the calm that settled into her while they had been separated. Her wide eyes caught Nikaius', and she watched his jaw flex as if he was grinding his teeth.

Priamos had only settled for a minute before he caught the girl's alarm. Something was wrong.

"We had a deal, sir."

All heads snapped towards Bastian in disbelief. What plan did they have?

"If you had claimed her, maybe you would have had your deal." Bastian stood and crossed his arms, gaze nasty but disinterested.

Waric stepped between the girl and the fae, severing his hold on her wrist.

"***You invited him to this court because you had intentions of buying this girl from him?***" Priamos snapped before Nikaius could control him, whipping around to face the girl. "***Who are you to him?***"

The fiery look in Nikaius' eyes gave Morrigan little time to think, and she blurted her words out without a second thought. "Youngest sister."

Priamos had startled her. Rolling his shoulders, Nikaius shook him off, but the deep grumble of alpha didn't recede. "Sister? I didn't even know Amara had another sister. How old are you?" It didn't escape him that he knew nothing about this girl, but somehow, she had enraptured Priamos.

Nikaius' face turned thoughtful and Morrigan realized the truth she had just told.

Oh no. This was when the tides turned. But up until then, Nikaius had been kind to her so Morrigan felt as if she owed him her honesty. "Twenty-one."

The girl seemed so unsure of her answer, but Nikaius didn't give her time to rebuke it, his gaze flicking from the fae to her and back. "Amara was given at the summer solstice Selection Night, right? So, you're here for yours?" Something about that didn't feel right to Nikaius. Bastian had taken Amara on her Selection Night four months prior, and the eldest Aegean daughter had been mated to Santiago De'Lyon six months before that. The Aegeans only had three children that he knew of.

"You misund—" The sound of the male's hand as it made contact with Morrigan's cheek echoed through the room. "You speak out of turn" were the angry words that followed.

That was the wrong move. Nikaius stepped between them with a low growl. "***Touch her again and you will leave without that hand.***" Elijah stepped back as Waric pressed Nikaius away with his hands. Their attention turned to the girl again. Priamos wanted to rage at the reddening mark on her cheek and the split in her lip. Something dark and possessive took over for a moment before Nikaius shoved Priamos down and reached out to touch her chin, wiping the small trace of blood from her lip. Elijah would pay for that.

"You said I misunderstood. Please explain."

"I..." Morrigan knew her admission would be her death sentence, but her choices were limited.

Nikaius dipped his head down to catch her eyes. "You're safe. You can answer freely." The twist of ice blue that lined the stormy eyes settled something soft and kind into Morrigan and she nodded. She would rather die at the hands of a kind, gracious lord than be sold to the Farm by her brother.

"I... I'm Amara's twin. I was marked." The scarring Nikaius had seen on her skin now made more sense but still. Nikaius had always been told twins were as rare as second sons and should be coveted; however, there seemed to be exceptions to that belief.

"You knew, didn't you? That's why you invited him here." Nikaius refused to look at Bastian. He knew there would be no guilt. He knew Bastian's game.

Nikaius' voice was tense, but he carefully trailed his fingers along Morrigan's stinging cheek before they dropped to adjust the cloak across her shoulders. The kindness of the action made tears burn in Morrigan's throat.

"I was going to buy her as a present for Amara." Bastian's tone was light, almost teasing.

"A present or a pet?" Nikaius had seen the things that Amara did to her 'pets.' They never survived a fortnight, and he wouldn't let this woman fall to the same fate. "We both know what she does to her 'pets,' Bastian."

"Don't make this about me," Bastian's voice rose. "You," he gestured at Elijah, "you watched as I tried to pawn her for you and didn't even step in on her behalf when I was going to kill her. So, no. We have no deal. Now that she is in my brother's possession, you have also lost your money. Get out of my court." Elijah gasped as Bastian stalked by.

"My lord?" After the door shut, the fae turned his attention to Nikaius who raised a brow in disbelief.

After the things he had put his sister through, Nikaius and his pack owed him no kindness, but Nikaius wanted to know more about the girl before he sent her home with the man attempting to sell her.

"You may stay the night at my home, but in the morning, you will leave with whatever punishment I decide to issue with no complaints. No man should bring a woman dressed like that," he gestured towards her, watching as she tugged his cloak self-consciously closer to herself, "into a court and abandon her. You're a cruel and despicable man." Seizing the girl's hand, Nikaius nodded to Aquila and Hawke before stalking from the room.

Chapter Seven

Morrigan and Nikaius

Atce' Plaza

Morrigan followed Nikaius, her eyes flicking to find Elijah's before dropping them down to where Nikaius' hand held hers. The tranquility that he gave off was such a transition from every other touch she had received that she wasn't sure if she should let go for propriety's sake. Selfishly, she didn't want to let go. Doing so might also insult him, she rationalized as well, so she was content to cling to him, wrapping her other hand around his wrist to keep up with his quick pace.

As they stepped out into the hall, she felt as if she could breathe again, the air cooler and fresher than the musty room they had just exited. A hand found her lower back, and she gasped, stumbling as she tried to twist away.

"Nik." The brunette spoke up, grasping Morrigan's elbow to keep her upright. "There's no real reason for us to stay. I'm pretty sure she's who we were looking for."

Looking for? Why had they been looking for her? Nikaius didn't seem to hear him, keeping up their pace even though Morrigan had stumbled.

"Waric's right, Nikaius." Hawke caught Nikaius by the shoulder. Nikaius turned on him with a snarl, and Morrigan watched his eyes flash ice blue as hot rage pricked her palm. Gasping, she jerked away, which threw her back against Waric who stabilized her. She gave him a small, grateful smile, confusion flooding through her as he gave her a quick smile back before stepping around her to place his hand into Nikaius'.

Taking Morrigan's elbow, Aquila pulled her aside, away from where Waric and Hawke talked softly. Waric's head was pressed against Nikaius' temple, and Hawke had both hands on his shoulders.

"What's happening?" Morrigan asked Aquila, turning to the Avian. Though her dark brows were set in a frown, Aquila's attention was solely on her.

"Rekru'e the — the primals — sometimes struggle with big emotions and lords are no different. He's just really close to the edge right now and is trying to not let it consume him."

"What happens if it does?"

"The animal comes out." Aquila gave her a partial grin.

Oh. She knew that changelings actually changed, but she hadn't realized that it wasn't by choice. "That must be scary."

"It can be the first time. Most children are ready for it to happen by the time it does though."

"That's good." Morrigan looked over her shoulder at where the men were talking. It was good that they had each other. She knew Amara's tantrums were dangerous and she would lose control of her ice, but Morrigan was convinced that it was done on purpose. The only time it ever happened was when Morrigan was in the room.

"What about Avians?"

"Hmm?" Aquila turned her attention back to Morrigan. "Oh, well, we're called Kyilzar. We have more control over our animals and typically meet them at a young age. I think I was six, and Hawke was seven, maybe? Rekru'e are predator-based: big cats, wolves, bears, and that sort of thing. They've got bigger animals and the ruts, so their emotional regulation is a bit tricky, which is honestly why you will never see a Rekru'e as the solitary head of any major force. There's typically a Kyilzar or Velamo with them to help keep them rational. The magic balances itself out somehow."

Morrigan had forgotten Elijah was with them until he spoke. "What about the fae?" Surprise chilled her, and she looked up at him in confusion.

Aquila rolled her eyes at Morrigan before turning to face Elijah, flaring her wings a bit as she crossed her arms over her chest. "What about them?"

"Surely they're better suited for that type of thing?"

"Most of the time no." Hawke's sudden appearance at her side had Morrigan looking up at him curiously. "Your type are too frail to handle the physical ramifications of a Rekru'e strength." He looked Morrigan up and down, raising his eyebrow a bit before resuming his words. "I don't think you're bright enough to keep up with the emotional load." Morrigan wasn't sure if the comment was a dig at her or at fae in general, but the way he had looked at her made it feel personal.

While Morrigan had been paying attention to where Hawke's gaze was, Elijah had been solely focused on Aquila. Always needing to be the center of attention Morrigan almost laughed when he turned to Hawke looking insulted. "How dare you speak to me like that?" Elijah's head whipped around to search out Nikaius, but he wasn't paying attention and Waric was gone.

"We're not even on the same level, you and I." The bravado from earlier had returned to Hawke's words, making him even more distant from the man she had met earlier in the night.

Elijah's brows dipped and the temperature around them dropped. While Morrigan was content to watch Elijah dig his own grave, she didn't want to be in the middle of a fight between anyone and her brother.

In an attempt to diffuse the situation, she blurted out the first thing that came to mind. "My sister is married to Santi De'Lyon, surely they're alright."

"From what I've heard she's fine, yes." Nikaius' voice from behind her was stronger than it had been and Morrigan turned to offer him a shy smile that made her bottom lip throb as her cut split again.

"My lord, your Avian —" Elijah whipped around to face Nikaius and Morrigan was sure his intent was to get Hawke and Aquila in to trouble with the lord, but Nikaius cut him off before he could speak another word. "My Avian nothing. Please keep your mouth shut or we'll do it for you."

Waric appeared out of nowhere, smacking his hand onto Elijah's shoulder and using it to shove him forward. "I think it's time to go."

Nikaius nodded and gestured Morrigan to follow Waric and her brother.

With Nikaius' hand a constant presence between her shoulder blades, Morrigan felt more settled. The members of Nikaius' court were kind, even though Hawke's demeanor had changed for some reason between the beginning and the end of the night. She wondered what had happened. Was it because he had found out she was marked? Her heart ached a bit at the thought.

As they stepped out of the eastern exit, Morrigan blinked up at the moon over them, her breath catching again at how clear and bright the sky was.

Nikaius looked around at the collected group before turning a smile to the girl at his side. He felt more settled having her and Waric close to him. "I believe this is all of us. Should we head home?"

Aquila and Hawke chimed in their agreement and a fierce joy curled through Morrigan when Elijah said nothing, hoping that Nikaius' threat would keep him silent until they reached their destination. "How are we getting there?" she asked.

Someone, Hawke probably, chuckled, and Morrigan frowned. It was a good question considering they were in a walled-off garden.

"There's a portal through there that we had set up for the evening." Waric gestured toward the darkened corner of the garden.

"Portal?" Unease curled through Morrigan. She had never taken a portal before.

"Yeah, you've never portal jumped before?" Hawke looked like he could laugh again when Morrigan looked up at him.

"Hawke." Aquila admonished, smacking him on the shoulder before shoving him away from Morrigan with a confused look. "What are you doing?" Clearly, her brother's behavior was alarming to her as well.

"What?" Hawke gave her that look again, the one that started at her head and trailed to her toes before flicking upwards again. Was he trying to memorize her? Assess her as a threat? "Who hasn't been through a portal before?" Hawke looked over his shoulder at his sister before raising an eyebrow at Morrigan.

This look pulled the air from her lungs, and she crossed her arms over her chest. Standing before her was a complete turn from the man she had met earlier in the night, and she didn't really know how to respond to his sudden blatant disrespect for her. Anger at herself was at the forefront of it. She had known better than to try to forge a connection with anyone, but he had treated her with kindness in the beginning.

Frustration burned through her as the feeling of inadequacy grew. She had started out the night as a possession for her family, then became a pawn between two warring brothers and now she was having her inadequacies bared without remorse by someone who had only known her an hour. The entire night she had been treated as nothing more than the extension of someone else. She knew she should keep quiet and would gain lashes if Nikaius sent her home, but exhaustion seeped into her bones, and she just wanted everyone to stop talking about her as if she didn't have thoughts or feelings of her own. "We've established I've got limited experience with most things. Yes, I've never been through portals or to Atce' Plaza or seen changelings with wings, but that doesn't mean that you need to constantly point those things out. I know it. You know it. Everyone here knows it. You're just the only one being blatantly rude about it."

Nikaius would have laughed watching the small stature of the girl straighten her shoulders so she could go toe to toe with Hawke. Frustration rolled off her, and he stepped closer, wondering why his commander was acting the way he was. That would be a matter for another time because selfishly, Nikaius wanted that fiery attention for himself. Glaring at the captain, Nikaius reached out and tugged the girl's chin to face him again, brushing his thumb over the split in her lip again.

Needs clean. Priamos grumbled, displeased that she had been hurt when they had been right there.

We'll clean it when we get home. Nikaius mentally shoved at the wolf's power.

Priamos shoved back. ***Now.***

Nikaius trembled a bit, earning him a curious look from the girl, but refused. *With what? We're not licking the split in her lip.*

It would be easier.

And cause infection. No. Priamos huffed but backed down, and Nikaius felt like he could breathe again, turning his full attention back where his fingers touched chilled skin. "The sooner we get home, the sooner I can tend to your lip."

Morrigan's heart gave a flutter at the way he spoke the words so quietly, like an intimate promise against her lips. His words were hushed, and his thumb brushed carefully under her bottom lip, his focus solely on her. He was so close; she could almost kiss him if she wanted. A large part of her did, but the other knew that there was no way in any strand of Fate that would happen. Pleasure at having the attention of someone like Nikaius warred with worry that Morrigan was taking up too much of his time.

Nikaius could hear her pulse hiccup and Priamos stirred within him again. *Not now.* They needed to get home and get everyone sorted.

"Nik, it's cold." Looking at Waric, Nikaius hummed gently before he nodded, leading their group deeper into the garden.

Even with the moon overhead, the garden was darkened by the leaves of the trees. Morrigan had once seen drawings of gold-lined portals that held entire galaxies on their faces, but the one they approached just looked like an endless black void against the wall of the garden. The energy it gave off felt weird, and the butterflies from earlier melted into anxiety that turned acidic in Morrigan's stomach as they got closer to it.

"Portals are easy. You just step in, then step out into wherever it's connected to." Waric's voice was soothing like Nikaius' and Morrigan nodded but watching him actually perform the step and disappear had every instinct in her rioting.

Surely, they would be locked in the void forever if they stepped through that. It was nothing like she had seen or expected. While she had wished for death for a moment earlier in the night, walking directly into it hadn't been part of the plan. Who knew what awaited them on the other side?

When Aquila and Hawke stepped through with Elijah, Morrigan made her decision.

Breaking away from Nikaius, she turned and ran.

Chapter Eight

Nikaius and Morrigan

Corinth
Manor: Kunmei

She didn't get far. Nikaius' arms snagged her around the waist before she moved more than two steps, and she thudded against his chest at the force.

"Hey! Woah, no. No, we're not going to do that." Turning her, he lifted her chin so he could look at her. Tears streaked down her cheeks and her bottom lip trembled. Why was she so scared? "You can't run here. There are far worse people than me and your brother in those halls." Like his own brother. Priamos growled, and Nikaius let out a low breath. He needed to figure out how to soothe her. To just get her back home with him. They could figure out the rest tomorrow.

"I can imagine it's scary doing something you've never done before. Let's go together. I won't let anything happen to you, okay?" As they took a step closer, she curled her fingers into his shirt, and he chuckled. Once she was through, she would be fine, but her readiness to sink into what comfort Nikaius was trying to offer was reassuring for him. She hadn't tried to run because of him. They hadn't scared her away just yet.

She didn't know why she trusted him as deeply as she did, but she couldn't fight the way she nodded. As they took a step, she curled her fingers into the front of his shirt. "It's just one..." The wild current that engulfed her was startling, like the static tingling feeling when one's foot falls asleep. Morrigan gasped and slammed her eyes shut, turning into him. "Step." The contrast from cold to warm made her shiver and curl closer. Nikaius' chuckle rumbled against her cheek.

"You can look now, we're through." Pulling her face away from him, Morrigan wavered, her head spun as her pulse suddenly roared in her head and beat against the back of her eyes.

On instinct, Nikaius banded his arms around her shoulders and lower back, holding her steady as she trembled, her nails scraping against his chest through his shirt as she clung to him. "Take a deep breath, you're okay. You're safe." His hand slid up from her shoulders to card slowly through the hair at the nape of her neck.

Pressing her forehead against his shoulder, Morrigan took a deep breath, matching hers to the slow rhythm under her hands and his warmth sinking into her chest. She had never been this close to anyone before. The steady stroke of his fingers back and forth along the nape of her neck soothed her nerves and another breath eased the pounding in her head.

"At least she didn't puke like you did, Hawke." Aquila teased, and Morrigan peeked up just as she elbowed her brother.

"Hey, I was a kid!" Hawke glared at his sister as he shoved her away grumpily. A frown was set in his brows, and he looked away when Morrigan met his eye.

"That's enough you two. Why don't you show our unwelcome guest to his rooms? I'll take..." Nikaius' warmth dissipated when he stepped away, holding Morrigan at arm's length for a moment. "I don't believe we caught your name."

With Priamos' sudden infatuation with the girl, Nikaius was embarrassed to realize he had never actually asked her name.

Her cheeks reddened into a delightful blush, and she stumbled over her words trying to answer. "It's Mor—"

"Lizzie is what she's called, or Lysandra." Elijah's eyes caught hers, daring her to object.

"Hmm." Nikaius turned and Morrigan looked up at him. She watched as he assessed Elijah before turning his attention back to her, catching her gaze.

"Mor and Lizzie sound very different. Ignore the scum who brought you here. You're safe and allowed to be who you are here." Her brother was going to be a problem they were going to have to work out of her system, Nikaius decided.

Something about his request made her shy. "Morrigan."

"Greatness," Both Morrigan and Nikaius looked up at Hawke in surprise. "Morrigan means greatness."

"I... Is that what it means? It's what my father called me."

"Is that what you would like to be called?" Hawke asked. Morrigan nodded again, and Priamos hummed softly. Morrigan.

"Well then, welcome home, Morrigan." Nikaius gave her a squeeze before gesturing around with a smile. "This is Corinth Manor. There's more to it than what meets the eye, of course. It's getting rather late though, so let's get you cleaned up and settled. I can give you the grand tour tomorrow."

"I don't think that's appropriate!" Elijah had found his voice again, but Hawke shoved him away, through the door.

"Neither is trying to sell your sister."

"It's going to be a long night." Aquila pinched the bridge of her nose before giving Nikaius a look that Morrigan couldn't quite interpret and stalking through the door.

When the hall was silent, Nikaius led Morrigan out with Waric following close behind. "Glad to see you made it." Waric's voice was soft as he reached out to adjust the cloak on her shoulders a bit. "I've made and jumped through so many portals that I didn't remember how daunting they can be the first time."

Waric chattered as they walked and Morrigan only half listened, exhaustion seeping into her bones. "Aslin should be home in the morning, so you shouldn't be without female company for long. I'm sure she'll be overjoyed to have a friend in the house aside from Aquila..."

Morrigan knew that receiving so much input from other's emotions would leave her drained for a while. She hoped the fatigue wouldn't last long enough to turn her into an inconvenience.

After passing a dining room and what appeared to be a study, Waric pat Nikaius' shoulder and stepped away to enter what Morrigan assumed to be his room. A few doors down and across the hall, Nikaius paused. "This is your room. I'll let you explore it a bit, but let's get you cleaned up first. I'll start the bath."

Unsure what to do, Morrigan followed him through the room that was to be hers into a large bathing chamber. The room was mostly occupied by the tub that sank into the stone floor. Against one wall was a vanity of dark wood with a mirror. Against the other wall, flanked by two doors, was a matching dark wood armoire. She wondered where the other doors led but knew exploring would be better kept for another time. Her mind wasn't quite able to focus on one thing for too long, her pulse fading in and out of her head as she sleepily watched Nikaius work. He collected a jar from the vanity and poured its contents into the tub before murmuring *logar*. Amazement shot through her as the tub began to fill with clear water on its own, no sort of spigot or knob to be found. The rumors she had heard were true!

While the water ran, Nikaius moved to the armoire and pulled out a towel and a robe. Setting them on the bench beside the tub, he looked up, his hair falling into his eyes as he gave her a smile.

She shivered a bit and Nikaius wondered, briefly, if it was because of the weird attraction he felt, or it was simply a chill. Offering his hand to her, he tried to give her a reassuring smile even though his brows dipped in worry. "Take a bath. It will warm you."

Morrigan stared at his hand for a moment, puzzling over the time they had spent together. The only other time a man had drawn a bath for her had been one of the countless situations she could not refuse. She didn't believe Nikaius was that type, but the memory still flared uncertainty through her, burning like acid in her chest.

The primary feeling she had gotten from him throughout the night was calm and kindness. She knew that people, changelings in particular, could shield and change their emotions, and now that they were alone in his domain, no one could step in on her behalf even if they wanted to. "What are you going to be doing?" Her voice broke as she stammered over her words. "Y-you're not going to…"

Nikaius watched as jade eyes flicked towards the running bath and back to him. "I'm not going to hurt you, Morrigan." The feisty creature from earlier was gone, and in its place was someone who had been hurt. He could tell by the way she curled into herself, clutching her hands to her chest as she kept her eyes low, that she expected the worst from him. Something bad had happened to her, beyond just being used as a servant. Part of him, not just Priamos, wanted to turn and find her brother and tear into him. The need to rip into his mind and find every dark thing that he had ever allowed to hurt the small cowering woman in front of him was so fierce that he had to take a deep breath.

That dark part of him warred with the almost overwhelming need to reach out to her, to soothe that pain and the distressed scent that scattered around them. To promise no more pain would come to her and no one would touch her without her permission. He would vow to rip the tongues from those who spoke against her and end the lives of those whose actions disrespected her.

Breathe, Nik. Waric's voice flashed through Nikaius' head, and he shook himself, looking over his shoulder briefly, expecting to see his mate standing in the room. Turning his attention back to Morrigan, he shook his head. "No. I'm going to find you some clothes that hopefully fit and a salve for your lip. Are you hungry?"

"You… you won't…?" Morrigan's focus was centered on the one possible event and not the rest of the words he spoke. Nikaius sighed and reached for her again, but she took another jittery step back.

"I'm not going to hurt you." Hands held up in front of him, Nikaius took a step back, then around her back into the bedroom. "I'm not going to prey on you, Morrigan." He took another step back, towards the main door. "You're safe here. Get in the bath. I'll be back." He turned, and when he exited the room, Morrigan let out a trembling breath.

Time seemed to slow once he was gone, and the headache throbbing behind Morrigan's eyes made her ears ring. She just wanted to sleep. It was quieter there, and as she took a deep breath, she sighed. The entire room smelled like freshly fallen rain. Was it whatever he had put into the tub before somehow starting the water?

A flurry of thoughts flashed through her head. How had he started the water? Was it something only the members of his house knew? Would she be allowed to stay with them past ridding her of Elijah?

Nikaius said he wasn't going to prey on her, but was his word good indefinitely? What about the others?

When his face reappeared before her, Morrigan blinked. When had he come back? She couldn't find it in herself to be startled that time, the weight of the evening numbing everything to a dull ache.

"Let me get you warmed up." Something happened when Nikaius took her chin carefully in his hand and lifted her eyes to meet his. Warm fingers touched the tender spot on her mouth before tingling spread across it. She stepped back, startled.

As she reached up to touch her mouth, Nikaius' hand caught hers, and he hummed gently. "Don't touch it, let it work. Don't lick it either. I assure you, it tastes terrible." The way his nose wrinkled as if remembering the terrible taste made her breath catch. How normal he looked with such reactions on his face. Morrigan could forget that he was a changeling.

Her chin was caught in his hand again, and he smiled as his gaze locked onto Morrigan's once more. Warm fingers tracked over the spaces where Elijah's hand had wrapped around her throat. She hadn't realized he left marks, but Nikaius coated her neck with the same salve nonetheless.

"Morrigan, come." His voice was a dark mellow timbre that sank rich comfort and contentment over her in a simple wave. Not remembering bidding herself to move, suddenly she was bare and stepping into the water of the tub. It was warm, warmer than she had ever experienced, and she gasped as she jumped back. The fog in her brain shifted when Nikaius' bare hand pressed against the skin of her stomach. She trembled.

"Are you alright?" Nikaius trembled with her. Beneath his palm was skin that felt like ice. Something about touching her so intimately shocked him. Priamos grumbled in his mind, displeased at how cold she still was, and Nikaius had to remind him that her kind were slower to warm and didn't generate as much heat as changelings did. Instead of agreeing, Priamos settled on admiring the dip and fullness of her waist and hips.

Oh, Fates. Now definitely was not the time. He needed to get her into the bath. Mentally shoving Priamos aside, he cleared his throat and reached up to stroke his fingers through her wine-colored hair.

The fingers of his free hand found a spot at the back of Morrigan's neck, and he ran his nails over it, earning a soft unburdened hum from her before he helped her step into the water. She whimpered a bit with the large chill that ran through her as the water crawled up her skin. The initial shock of the heat had faded and the warmth that now surrounded her was comfortable. Nikaius kept soothing his fingers along that spot on her neck, and she didn't want to disobey.

"I'm going to check on the food. Stay here and warm up a bit." It took everything Nikaius had in him to step away. Morrigan seemed skittish, but he understood from her questions that she probably hadn't had a good experience in a bath. The way she had looked at the tub was curious, and Priamos purred at the thought of allowing her to bathe every day if she desired.

Was the water too hot? No. The tub was built out of the same stone as the house, the magic imbued within it would keep the water at a perfect temperature.

Nikaius stiffened as he shut the door behind him, the hair on his neck rising as his skin prickled. A low growl escaped as he turned quickly and grabbed the perceived intruder by the throat, yanking him off his feet.

"You know," Waric wheezed, "no matter how many times you do this, you're not going to kill me." Waric's dark hand wrapped around Nikaius' wrist. The matching stars spread across their hands danced silver before Nikaius sheepishly set him down properly on his feet. "Oof. The new girl has your hackles raised. I know you're a bleeding heart, Nik, but not every person needs to be treated like a delicate pet." The sarcasm laced words made Nikaius roll his eyes. Of course Waric would give him grief about something that they both knew he had limited control over. Priamos was too close to the edge for Nikaius to assert control over at all times, and if that meant a new member to his household, then so be it. This outcome was certainly better than others.

"Where would you be if I didn't treat you like a delicate pet, Waric? We both know your sister would have happily kept trying to drown you if I hadn't come by." Even though it was now a running joke between the two of them, there was still a deep well of sadness over how Waric and Nikaius had met.

"I wish she would have with the way you're all moony eyed right now." Waric's hands straightened his shirt, and he raised an eyebrow at Nikaius.

With a roll of his eyes, Nikaius huffed and turned away from his mate, his eyes skimming across the hall. "I'm not moon-eyed. I'm a wolf. My eyes are naturally like this. I can't help it any more than you can be a whore."

"I'm your whore though." Waric laughed and shoved Nikaius' shoulder as they made their way into the hall. "How did this happen??"

"Remember how I mentioned I kept catching a strange scent?"

"The sunshine?" Waric pulled a pipe from somewhere within his jacket and flicked a match to life.

"Yeah. It's her." Nikaius rubbed his sternum with a soft sigh.

Red-brown brows rose as Waric puffed at his pipe. "I get that. She just smelled of magic to me." Nikaius didn't usually tolerate any sort of dangerous vices within his household, but what Waric smoked was a nonaddictive leaf that created a mild high. It mostly just made Nikaius sleepy.

"That's weird right?"

Waric blew the smoke away from Nikaius, coughing gently before turning his eyes to Waric again. "I mean, unless you've randomly come across our mate after eight years and no one realized what she is to us."

"Be serious, Waric." As Nikaius' best friend and mate, he was one of the few people who could openly tease Nikaius without extreme irritation. Being part of Priamos' pack had that advantage.

"I am. You're almost twenty-three. Your father will probably start hounding you to marry soon. Why not give the girl a try? I know the odds, but it's worth a shot."

"She's not a pair of shoes!" Nikaius ground out from between clenched teeth. Waric choked out a laugh, but Nikaius ignored him. "I don't want her to think I'm taking advantage of her."

Waric hummed as he took another puff from his pipe. "I get that."

"Do you?" Nikaius stepped over to the door across the hall. He knew Aslin would have little issue with him borrowing something from her guest closet for the night. She'd probably give him grief for whatever fashion choice he made for the girl.

"Yeah, but what if she was our mate? That'd be one hell of a fuck you to them, wouldn't it? They'd lose it if both their sons ended up marrying fae women."

Nikaius paused at Waric's voice, looking up from the drawer he was sorting through. "We're mated though." She wasn't as slim as Aslin, so borrowing clothing directly from her probably wouldn't work.

Waric knew where Nikaius' mind wandered, and he sighed, stepping over to rest his hand on top of Nikaius'. "I love you and nothing can ever take that from me. But your father won't accept me as your mate because he's archaic. What if it's her, and we just haven't figured it out yet?" Waric raised his eyebrows as he pulled a garment from the closet. It was magic so it would mold perfectly no matter how Morrigan wanted to wear it.

"I don't know." The way the fabric fluttered slightly made Nikaius swallow nervously before he snagged it from Waric's hand and shoved it into the drawer. Absolutely not. He didn't know if showing that much skin was something she was comfortable in and while he was a gentleman, Priamos was not.

Waric blew out a puff of smoke, licking his bottom lip. "She smells like magic and not the type that's bound in her hair or binds powers. Just like natural magic." He paused for a second, tilting his head. "Huh."

"What?" Gathering a random shirt and a pair of trousers that he hoped fit, Nikaius stepped out of the room, waving his hand as he stepped through Waric's smoke.

"You're right, she does smell warm and light like the first sunny day after winter."

"Told you." He shot Waric a look before pulling the door to Aslin's room shut.

"I think she's got something others can't see. Let's keep an eye on her and see how it goes."

"Yeah." Nikaius definitely wanted to see where this would go...

Chapter Nine

Morrigan

Corinth Manor

Soaking was delightful, something Morrigan hadn't done since she was a child, and whatever Nikaius had poured into the bath had soothed away all the aches and pains of the day as it washed the red sauce from her skin. She heard his footsteps in the hall and figured it was time to get out. Standing, she made her way to the lowest point to try to step out but slipped, smacking her knee against the floor as the towel she had been reaching for tumbled on top of her.

She must have made a noise because Nikaius' hands were suddenly on her upper arms and lifting her, helping her stand. He kept his eyes on hers as he collected the towel and offered it to her. His cheeks were as red as Morrigan's.

"There, sit and dry off." His voice still held that soft and low tone, but the brush of his fingers against her hinted at shyness and embarrassment.

The lord was just as shy as she was. A thrill of pleasure curled down her spine at the realization. No male had ever reacted to her like that before.

"Thank you." Morrigan gave a little smile and Nikaius nodded, stepping away.

"There are clothes in the bedroom for you. They might be a bit big, but they're dry. I'll take this," he gestured to the dress on the floor, "and have it cleaned."

"Burn it, please. I'd rather go naked than look at those clothes again." The laugh her comment earned her made Morrigan flush again and her heart flutter. Never had she been so affected by someone just because of their kindness. This wasn't the first man to be genuinely kind to her, but it had been so long that it felt like there was something different about him.

Sitting next to the vanity, she began to towel off her tingling skin as she listened to him in the bedroom next door.

It was so strange. He had let her have her privacy and only returned when she almost fell. That was... new. He was right about the bath. She did feel warmer but still a bit chilled. She thought she would never be warm again. The South was colder than the North, but it felt warmer in the house than it had ever felt at home. She would have thought it to be cooler, with changelings having such high body temperatures.

Once sufficiently dry, she stepped into the bedroom. Nikaius' steps paused, and he turned to face her, giving her a once-over before clearing his throat. "I'll be in the hall."

How could one person sound so nice? Something about his voice soothed every ache stored in her body after years of abuse from the emotions of others. She felt like she could breathe here.

When he left, she dropped the towel and pulled on the garments. The underwear fit well, but the clothing was like nothing she had worn before. The top was soft as a kitten and fell to her knees when she pulled it on. Pulling on the tight black pants, she frowned at herself in the mirror. She looked like a child playing dress-up in clothes belonging to someone else. The shirt was baggy and ill-fitting, almost swallowing her whole, and the pants needed to be rolled at the leg so she wouldn't walk on them.

Once she sorted herself out, she cautiously opened the door.

A chill ran down her spine as she took in the man, the alpha, leaning against the wall. She knew, without having to ask, that he was an alpha, one of the stronger changelings. If it hadn't been for the compulsion he had used earlier, then just how he looked would have given him away. He was tall and broad with a strong jaw and a determined lift to his head.

Even though he wore a dark Henley and simple dark pants, he commanded the air around him. Morrigan imagined that even in a crowded room, all the attention would be on him. It was hard to imagine she had missed him in the plaza.

Realization dawned on her. At any point during their time together, he could have taken advantage of her, but here he was, tending to her instead. Something warm bloomed in her chest, and she cleared her throat to get his attention.

Nikaius turned a cautious smile towards her. Relief flooded through him. "There's color in your cheeks again." Something he said must have startled her because she jumped and he laughed, offering the tray in his hands. She stepped from behind the door and pulled it open so he could enter. Once inside, Nikaius paused for a moment. She would need a better table to have meals on if she decided to stay.

"Why are you being so nice to me?"

Her words were like ice dumped on him and he frowned, remembering some of what she had experienced earlier in the night. Setting the table, he turned to pull out a chair for her. "I told you earlier, you're a member of my household. Just because you were treated poorly before doesn't make that the standard." He gestured for her to sit, and she obliged.

"In every other court, it is." As she sat, Nikaius was distracted by her again. Her contentment was warm in the air, mixed with the cautious expression he could see on her face. Something was settling her even if she was still scared. That was good to know. Pushing her chair the rest of the way, Nikaius moved to sit in the other vacant chair.

"Not in mine." He watched her pick apart the food with delicate fingers. In what way could he prove to her that the experiences she had in the past weren't how life should be lived?

"Why not?" *What makes you so different?* Morrigan wanted to ask.

His dark eyes caught hers in a gaze that sent a thrill down her spine, like prey caught in a predator's eyes. That's what he was, after all, an apex predator in both physical and social aspects of life. "Not everyone thinks in black and white, Morrigan. As much as my brother hates it,

I think that everyone should be treated with kindness until they are proven to not be worthy of it." His voice was different from earlier, no longer as deep, but still soothing. It was obvious that his learning was exponentially better than hers, simply by the way he enunciated his words.

Nikaius reached across the table to gently take her hand, his heart throbbing at the contact. Fates he was in trouble. "You had no control over the hand you were dealt, and I can hardly hold that against you. I don't know you." *I desperately want to.* "Just as you don't know me." *Please say you want to know me.* "How can I know how you deserve to be treated," *like a goddess,* "if I don't give us the chance to know each other yet?"

Their gazes locked in a moment. Did she feel what he did?

"I..." Morrigan couldn't fathom a response, her attention drawn to their hands and the emotions he was giving, mostly the curiosity and some other pleasant feeling she couldn't place but enjoyed.

"Eat, then rest. We can talk more in the morning." Nikaius rose from his seat, a touch of hurt flaring before he pulled his hand away. The way he looked at her made Morrigan almost ask him to stay.

Almost.

Chapter Ten

Morrigan and Nikaius

CORINTH MANOR

The golden light pulled Morrigan from sleep, and she was confused when she opened her eyes. This was not her room. The night sky painted on the ceiling was a beautiful contrast to the slate gray of the ceiling of her room back home. The stars seemed to glisten in the sun, and for a moment she wondered what they were made of to be shimmering the way they did. The bed was soft and warm and more than anything, she wanted to doze off again. Shaking the thought from herself, she crawled out from under the heavy blankets.

Standing was a mistake, she realized with a gasp. The floor was like ice and there was a terrible draft. Climbing back into the bed, she curled back into herself, tucking one of the furs around her feet while snuggling the blanket to her chest. Fates, it was cold. As she curled her toes into the warm blankets, she looked around. The size of this room was at least three times the size of what she had been afforded in her mother's house, and she was awestruck. The bed itself, made of some light wood, wouldn't have fit back home. The matching dresser and armoire was more than she could have ever had before.

Her eyes wandered to the large standing mirror next to the armoire but snagged on the pants hanging haphazardly at the foot of the bed. Then was when she realized why she was so chilled. At some point during the night, she had shed the pants she had been given. The shirt she wore only reached her knees, doing little to protect her from the chill of the room. When she turned her attention to the balcony doors that stood open, her lips parted in wonder.

"Really?" It had been years since she had seen direct sunlight. Her home in Be'Sala rarely had sunlight, the warmer coastal area was mostly hidden under a near-constant state of rain.

If the buttery golden rays that spread across the floor were some figments of her imagination, she never wanted to stop dreaming. Getting up, she tugged one of the large furs from the bed and wrapped it around her shoulders. Ignoring the icy floor, she stepped around the table and chairs where she and Nikaius had sat the night before and made her way to the balcony door.

Despite the brisk wind, the sun felt warm, and she let the fur dip so that the rays could spread across her chest and shoulders as well. It was almost like drinking tea that was too warm, starting at one point and then spreading across her skin. Her skin prickled at the contrast until she was shivering, but she didn't want to move from the beautiful space.

"You best be up, you useless thing." Elijah's voice preceded him into the room and when his eyes fell on Morrigan, he scoffed. "Looks like you're getting practice walking around half-naked like the whore you're going to be. I'll send for a maid to bring you clothes and then we're going to see the lord." No sooner had the words left his mouth then a young woman with chin-length auburn hair poked her head into the room with a smile.

"Good morning! I'm Aslin, and I was told you might need these." Morrigan held back a laugh at the look the newcomer gave Elijah. It was unpleasant, her brows dipping down as her upper lip curled in a scowl.

"If you'll excuse us, it's improper for a man to be in the rooms of a lady without her permission."

"She's no lady." Elijah scoffed.

"And you are no gentleman. Get. Out." As if summoned by Aslin's tone, Aquila appeared at the door. Elijah scowled but left, slamming the door shut behind him.

Morrigan stared at the girl in wonder. "I wish I could do that."

"Oh, you absolutely can now that you are here. You're to be treated just like the rest of us while you're in this court. Would you like help dressing?" Morrigan nodded, shutting the balcony doors before moving back towards the bed where Aslin laid out some clothing.

It didn't take much to help Morrigan dress, although she felt rather naked in the pants Aslin had brought. It had been so long since she had worn anything that fit properly, nonetheless something so well-fitted, the entire curve of her legs and backside was visible. The shirt Aslin offered was warm and thick and fell to her thighs, covering some of her figure. Elijah's words rang in her head about how she looked the part of a whore.

Was that what she was to be for Nikaius? He could have easily taken advantage of her the night before, but he hadn't. Despite knowing it would only bring disappointment, Morrigan dared to hope that Elijah was wrong.

When she had finished tying the boots, she gathered the cloak Aslin has offered in her arms. The boots and cloak were both lined with soft, white fur. When she was finished, they met Elijah and Aquila in the hall. The angry conversation that was happening between them stopped as they stepped out, and Elijah rolled his eyes and turned to walk away.

Aslin frowned up at Aquila, who only shrugged and gestured for them to follow Elijah.

"I will be having words with the lord about his staff. I hope you'll all be met with swift justice at the treatment I've received. I came on his brother's command, surely that word stands for something."

"Hawke said that Lord Ayrden has stepped out, but you're welcome to wait for him."

"As if I'm going to accept the word of a woman." Elijah snickered and shook his head. "He's just refusing to accept the truth of what he knows."

"Elijah!" Though Morrigan typically tried to remain out of her brother's fights, he had crossed the line by being blatantly disrespectful to the guard of a lord.

"Your worry is kind, my lady, but I assure you I've heard much worse." Though Aquila had a smile on her face, her words were clipped as if she was reining in some form of anger.

"I—" Aslin seemed speechless. "I'm going to go work on lunch." Pausing in her step, Aslin turned and disappeared. Morrigan envied the ability of those who could easily teleport, but because she was marked, she hadn't been taught.

Elijah turned on Morrigan. "You dare try to admonish me?" Morrigan cringed back as he raised his hand as if to hit her again, but Aquila stepped between them before he could.

"I should remind you that Lord Ayrden did say you would lose your hand if you touched her again. He's a patient man, but not with members of his household." Before Elijah could respond, Aquila turned to Morrigan with a smile.

"There's a courtyard through that door." Though she smiled, her words felt like a dismissal, and Morrigan was grateful. While she was worried about what Elijah might do, she selfishly didn't want to be caught in the middle. To distance herself from Elijah for another short while would be a blessing from the Fates that Morrigan couldn't refuse. Giving a nod, she eagerly obeyed.

There was something so simple but pleasing about snow in the South. This was not the harsh ice that her home received during the winter. It did not encase branches and grass in hard crystalline sheets that snapped when you touched them or crackled loudly when you stepped on them. No, this was softer, almost serene in how the soft white fluffs lazily fell from the sky to collect on every available surface. The cold didn't immediately bite at her face or send a chill down her spine when she stepped out onto the carefully carved path, she didn't know whether that was because of the enclosed nature of the space or the woolen cloak that covered her shoulders.

Breath curled out in front of her in a cloud of white as she took in the view of the courtyard that was larger than any she had seen before, being confined to her mother's house. Against her better judgement, Morrigan stepped further down the path, into the tree line.

Time fell away as she wandered along the path, deeper into the wooded area of the courtyard. The air was cool in her lungs, but it was refreshing. Even though everything was softly frozen, she could hear running water nearby and decided to seek it out, wondering if it was a hot spring that she had read about or if this part of the world was just not as cold as she had thought it needed to be for snow.

She briefly wondered how long it would take for someone to find her if she wandered off the path and lay in the snow. Would Elijah even care? Would anyone? It was amazing that she was still standing the morning after being threatened by a lord, draped in borrowed clothing and boots.

"Good morning." Morrigan's foot found a nearly invisible patch of ice just as a male voice behind her spoke and a loud surprised squawk escaped her as she slid hard to the ground on her backside.

"Holy Fates! I didn't mean to frighten you!" Nikaius had assumed Morrigan had heard his footsteps as he had heard hers when she walked past the bench he had settled on to work on correspondences. Dropping to his knees, he offered a hand to Morrigan to help her up. Something was endearing about the surprised noise she made as she had fallen, but Nikaius shook that thought off as he helped her up. "Are you alright?"

"I-I was lost in thought, I guess. I didn't hear you approach." Morrigan accepted his hand and stood. When their palms met, Morrigan had expected the mask from the night before to have fallen and for something vicious and cruel to crawl up her arm. However, his delight, the warmth of amusement, and curiosity snaked into her very soul like a balm to ease the abrasions Elijah's endless rage left. Her gaze traveled from their joined hands up his arm to his face. His jaw was defined, lips hitched to one side in a half smile as he looked down at her, his wide, short nose wrinkled a bit as he grinned. . His narrow dark stormy eyes danced with mischief while strands of his near-ebony hair fluttered around his pale face. His complexion was warmer than hers, hinting at more golden undertones than her stark paleness.

Awareness hit, pulling a gasp from her as if one of the now swaying branches struck her in the chest. His face was the one she had seen in her dreams so many times before. She knew she had met the Ayrdens once before, on her culling day eight years ago. She knew she had met the high lord and one of his sons, but she couldn't remember which it had been.

Had Nikaius been the one to wield the brand? She couldn't remember, but she knew she could never forget those eyes.

This was Lord Nikaius Ayrden, holder of the Kunmei Court. He... he wasn't as Morrigan had imagined a lord to be. She wondered how much of it was an act. She pulled her hand away, stepping back to dip into a quick bow. "Forgive me, my lord! I wasn't thinking —"

Nikaius reached out to touch her elbow. It didn't feel right to have her address him by his title. She startled, looking up at him with those wide jade eyes. "Like I told you... Wait... I didn't introduce myself, did I? Nikaius is fine. I hate formalities, especially in my own home."

"You-your home?" Morrigan looked shocked by this realization, and Nikaius had to fight back a laugh. Something was interesting about how her every emotion played across her face. She must have been so tired and overwhelmed the night before that she forgot they were in his personal home.

"Yes, this is my home."

"I... it's lovely, especially this courtyard."

"Mm. This one is my favorite." He was pleased she liked the landscape he had chosen today. Watching her, he had noticed she was completely enraptured with the snow before he had spoken. Perhaps he should have waited a bit longer, but her sweet scent had drawn Priamos into pushing him into action so they could be near her again. Looking over at her, Nikaius smiled. "I'm glad the cloak and boots fit. I wasn't sure if I had anything that would fit. You're rather small."

"And you're rather rude!" Nikaius laughed at the shocked look that crossed Morrigan's face at her own words. She must have anticipated something worse to happen to her besides Nikaius' laugh because she remained tense as she looked down at herself. "You arranged for these to be brought to me?" Why did she seem so unsure of every action he took, Priamos wanted to know, but Nikaius knew that she hadn't been treated the best.

"I did. I like to ensure the needs of the members of my home are met. For you, it seems you don't have any acceptable outerwear for our winters."

"That's a large kindness to give to someone who is visiting." Despite her words, Nikaius caught a bit of a hiccup in her breathing. Priamos purred. She was pleased to have been given something, even if she was unsure about it.

Her words registered. "Visiting? You're a member of my household now. I acquired you last night, do you not remember?"

"What?" The air left Morrigan's chest so fast it felt as if Elijah's large palm was pressed against her chest, right between her collarbones. Luck was against her, it seemed, for when she stepped back, away from him, her foot slipped off the path.

"Careful!" Nikaius' hand tightened on her elbow and the other caught her around the waist before she could fall. Looking back at the icy creek below the roll of the hill, she saw what might have happened. She swallowed hard as Nikaius steadied her.

She stared at him, her breath catching in her chest as she realized how close they were. There was hardly any room between her and her hands that were pressed flat against his chest. She could feel each breath that flowed through him and the warmth that radiated off him even though he wore no cloak. His height was impressive and the wide breadth of his chest and shoulders made her hands look small in comparison. When she dared look upwards, she froze, and her face heated when their eyes met again. His ears and nose were a bit pink and being so close to him felt so different, more intimate than when she had been close to her sisters.

The thought of her siblings jarred her from that moment, and she gently pushed away from him, hyperaware of the pressure of his hand as it slid from her back and across her hip before falling away. "What do you mean you acquired me?"

The moment was broken by her words and Nikaius cleared his throat. "Last night. My brother condemned you to death, and I bought you instead." She looked confused, and he sighed. "When you fell. Surely you heard the entire exchange, you were right there."

"I thought you were joking!" Her voice jumped an octave, high and surprised, and Nikaius laughed.

When she remained silent, he frowned. "You're serious?"

"Yes." A mix of emotions flooded across Morrigan's face, and he watched in fascination, hoping her reaction would be a pleasant one. Suddenly, she let out a laugh that seemed to startle her as well. This reaction was a bit better, but he was desperate to know what was going on in her mind. "My lady?"

Morrigan blinked at him. "I'm hardly a lady."

"Both of your sisters are married, correct? That would make you a lady to compare with your brother's lordship."

Nikaius never thought he would ever find someone rolling their eyes as attractive, but the way her eyelashes fluttered against her pink cheeks made his mouth dry. "I'm *thaber,* my family's titles don't apply to me."

"A lady is a lady." She wasn't wrong. That was how it worked in the rest of the world, but he and Waric had decided there was more to this woman than what was seen to the naked eye, and Nikaius wanted to know her more.

"But you bought me?" He could tell she was trying to process.

"No money actually passed hands." A devious smile spread across his face, a fang tracing along his bottom lip as he wondered if he could get her to snap at him again. Something about her feistiness made Priamos purr.

Her eyes dropped. "He just left me?"

"Do you want to go back?"

"No."

"Then you're now a lady of my court."

"Be that as it may, I'm also fae. We're below changeling merchants, are we not?"

"What?" It was Nikaius' turn to be surprised. What in the Fates' names had she been taught?! "A lady is a lady. All courts hold the same titles. It's a lateral transfer. What you were there, you are here. You were a lady there, albeit not treated as one, and here you are a lady and shall be treated as one."

"I know nothing about being a lady!" Did she really stomp her foot like a child? Nikaius laughed.

"Would you like to learn?" Shoving his hands into his pockets, Nikaius turned. It was about time to help prepare lunch.

"What?"

"Would you like to—"

"I heard what you said!"

"Then why did you ask again?"

Before she could formulate a response that wasn't something angry or petulant, the crunch of snow gave away someone's approach.

"That fae fucker has a good hook, Nik. Swung on me when I told him he couldn't meet with you." Nikaius turned at the sound of Waric's voice and frowned, taking in his mate's appearance. It looked like the split bottom lip was the worst of it.

Priamos grumbled low and deep. Someone had hurt what was his.

"Your face!" Morrigan's startled gasp settled Priamos' desire to shred the male who had touched Waric, but a bit of jealousy flared as well as she reached for Waric, gently touching the bruising that was blooming on his cheek.

Guilt welled cold and acidic within Morrigan as she carefully touched Waric's cheek. He had been hurt because of her. "He shouldn't have hit you. You both have been too kind to warrant such an act."

"It's nothing darling." Waric's hand covered her freezing fingers, engulfing them with his warmth. "He thought he could take me fae to fae but that doesn't really work when you're outnumbered, and changelings don't fight by fae rules." The connection between them, forged by her fingers under his hand tingled, but only gave her hints of pride and pleasure. Nothing that showed he was upset.

"Outnumbered?"

"Mmm. I think you've made quite an impression on our Hawke. I can't remember the last time he took a swing at anyone."

"Why would he do that?"

"You're a member of our household. We protect each other." Nikaius' warmth against her back made her tremble. His hand on top of Waric's joined the three of them together by touch, and his feelings mostly matched Waric's. Pride and pleasure were at the forefront, with soft caring and peace underneath.

Morrigan felt like she was imposing on an intimate moment, but before she could try to pull away, the door to the courtyard opened again and Aquila called them in.

Chapter Eleven

Morrigan and Nikaius

Corinth Manor

"Here you are! Took you long enough. That fae bastard was quite adamant about seeing you, but we..." Hawke's words died away when he poked his head out of one of the doors up the hall to see that Nikaius and Aquila weren't alone. Shock shot through Morrigan at the fact that he seemed to feel bad about his words. As he cleared his throat and dropped his eyes, Morrigan's attention turned to Aslin who approached.

"You two," she pointed between Waric and Nikaius with raised eyebrows, "are supposed to help me with lunch today." She shoved Waric into the room, earning her an indignant "Hey!" from him. Opening the door more, she stepped aside to allow Morrigan and Nikaius to enter. Morrigan paused when she stepped through the doorway. She had expected a dining room, not the kitchen. And even though it was a kitchen, only Aslin and Waric were there.

Without a word, Hawke turned and left. Morrigan watched him go before Waric drew her attention away again.

"I could use help with the rabbits." Waric tugged an apron over his head before offering her a knife.

"Rabbits?" Morrigan looked from the knife to Nikaius and back in confusion.

"We're making rabbit stew for dinner," Waric explained, wiggling the knife expectantly.

"Am I to be kitchen staff?" The entire situation confused Morrigan as she watched the three interact.

"There's no regular staff here right now." Nikaius accepted the knife and reached for his own apron.

"No staff?" Morrigan's shock must have been written on her face because Aslin laughed gently.

"We're self-sufficient in this house," Aslin explained, kneading the dough under her hands. "The Mountain's Edge manor is the more formal residence used for parties and balls and events that need formalities. There's a staff there, but here we don't require a large one with only five... six of us living here. Most of the staff have time off after large events anyways, like Selection Nights and the Moon Festivals. We're pretty good at working together. Hawke and Aquila join us often if their duties don't run over."

"I thought they were personal guards?" The way things ran in Kunmei was so vastly different from her own territory that it left Morrigan reeling.

"They are, but Aquila is also the captain of my guard and Hawke her second. They oversee guard training on the days when I don't intimately need their service." Nikaius threw a grin over his shoulder at Morrigan who smiled in return.

"You're not worried about attacks while at home?"

"The magic that guards this place doesn't let just anyone in, and they're rather difficult to break. Those of us who live here are blood bonded into the wards." Like the trunk Morrigan so eagerly waited to be delivered. "Those who aren't part of the wards have to be touching someone who is." Waric responded as he turned to shuck the innards of the rabbit he had just gutted into a bucket. The sight of the viscera in his bare hands and the squelch it made as it hit the rest turned Morrigan's stomach and made her gag. Embarrassed, she stumbled away, clipping her hip on the table and tumbling to her knees.

"Shit! Are you okay?" Aslin's voice startled Nikaius, and he flung off his apron before wiping his hands down and following Morrigan to the floor. He shot a look over his shoulder at Waric who cackled and took over the rabbit Nikaius had been working on.

He could tell she was more embarrassed than anything else, and he shifted, reaching out to touch her hand. "It's okay. No animal processing for you. Got it." His mind turned as he tried to think of things to take her mind off it. "Do you eat meat at all?"

Her head shook, hair falling to hide her face. He reached for her, tucking the hair back, but she jerked away, eyeing his hands. "It's fine. I'm clean, see?" Turning his hands front to back, he reached out again, grasping her elbows and helping her stand.

"It's okay. We can make something else." He locked eyes with Waric who nodded. "We usually put the meat in last so we can portion out some of it with just the vegetables before the meat."

"No, please don't do anything differently because of me." Her protest was soft and Nikaius smiled, reaching out to twist the stubborn lock of hair away from her face again.

"It's honestly not even an extra step." She looked so pitiful staring up at him that he gave a gentle smile.

"I've just never had it. I don't know if I'll like it."

"Never?" asked Aslin.

"We lived near the Corviana territory." Waric gave a loud laugh at Morrigan's explanation, his eyebrow raised at Nikaius when Morrigan turned to look at him curiously.

Though Waric saw humor in Morrigan being from the same area as Hawke and Aquila, dread sank through Nikaius.

"Small game wasn't readily available, and any other meat had a high price." She cleared her throat, turning her attention back to Nikaius as his mind turned. Was Waric right? Was she the girl that Waric thought was possibly their mate?

"Being marked, I kind of just stuck to the kitchens and baked. I can't remember the last time I ate any meat at all." Priamos let out a low grumble of displeasure, and Morrigan frowned in confusion. "Are you okay?" She reached out as if she was going to touch him and Priamos purred, hoping she would, but her hand paused, and she frowned at it before pulling away.

"How about this?" Nikaius snagged her attention back with his hand catching hers. "We'll make it like normal and let you taste the meat before it goes in." Her eyes searched his, her face still pink, but she gave a nod. "That way, it'll be the same and you can try it if you want and if not that's okay. We're not going to be upset if you don't like something. We just want you to be fed."

"I... Okay." Her face paled again as another handful of innards hit the bucket. Nikaius glared over her shoulder at Waric who was pointedly ignoring him.

"Here, why don't you come help me?" Aslin chimed in, snagging Morrigan's elbow and leading her over to the other side of the room. Morrigan nodded, giving Nikaius a small smile before allowing herself to be pulled over and set up with carefully cutting apples.

Returning to his mate's side, he frowned at him.

That was a dick move. Nikaius began working on the final rabbit.

Waric's response was instant in Nikaius' mind. *As if you don't think that little tremble her bottom lip does is cute. Face it, Nik.*

I will face nothing.

Apparently, cooking a stew with meat took longer than a vegetable soup in the fashion that they did. Their lunch was a salad of surprisingly fresh, springy vegetables. Though they were in the height of winter, everything was crisp and crunchy, as if it had just been harvested from a garden.

"Do you freeze your vegetables?" She asked after her second bite.

"No. The courtyard, the one with the snow, can change seasons on a whim depending on what the first person who entered wanted or needed. We utilize the farmlands in the spring and summer, but during the winter, the courtyard is a large help."

"And only the members of the household can use it?"

"We typically open the house to visitors once a week to allow them to utilize the gardens if they have a need."

"How do you prevent that from being abused?"

"Magic has its ways."

"It always does it seems." As she ate, she took in the dining room. She had noticed a pattern throughout most of the house that it was built with dark stone and decorated with dark woods. The only exception she had seen was the bedroom she had been given. The dining room was no different from the rest. The table they sat at was a deep red wood with eight matching chairs. The wood was smooth under her hands and held no ornamentals like the tables at home had. Despite being a lord, it seemed that Nikaius' home was decorated very simply. There were no portraits on the walls or any form of decoration on the fireplace, and she enjoyed the cleanness of it. It seemed he had no desire to flaunt his worth like her family had.

"Waric and I have some things to attend to before supper." Nikaius' voice drew her attention back to him, and he gave her a small smile. "If you would like to explore a bit, you may."

"I could give you a tour if you'd like?" Aslin offered as she cleared away Nikaius' and Waric's plates with her own.

"I would like that." Finishing the last few bites from her plate, Morrigan followed Aslin to help with the dishes. They worked in silence, Aslin humming to herself as Morrigan dried what was handed to her. The silence was comfortable and allowed her to gather her thoughts a bit.

She enjoyed the leisurely pace at which they seemed to exist in Kunmei. Aside from the morning's chaos with Elijah, she hadn't been hurried or shouted at for taking her time. She hadn't been alone for very long, but when she was, she hadn't felt too stressed about not doing anything. There wasn't a list of things for her to do just yet and so she assumed free time was expected.

"I know you're good at baking," Aslin turned a smile to Morrigan who returned it shyly. "Do you have any sort of hobby? I like to sew. Making something with your own hands is enjoyable."

"I can knit a bit. It's not a strong skill, but I can learn better if it's required of me." It was the only task she could think of that she had learned when she was young to bide her time, but she had rarely had time to perfect it, focusing more on baking instead.

Aslin dried her hands and tossed the towel onto the counter before linking her arm through Morrigan's with a smile. "Having a hobby is not required. I know Waric likes to read. Hawke and Nikaius like to scrimmage a bit. They've always been rough and tumble. I sew and Aquila plays cards." Only Aslin's hobby seemed to benefit anyone. Morrigan hummed.

"I also enjoy reading."

"You and Waric will have to share the library then." Aslin smiled as she tugged Morrigan along for what Morrigan assumed would be the tour she promised. "I don't have the patience for reading. I have to have something to do with my hands or I'll get bored. Holding a book while sewing isn't possible, so I just don't." Aslin's laughter eased Morrigan a bit. While the men in the house were one thing, Morrigan had a mixed view of what women could be. Would Aslin be kind like Mae? Or territorial and mean like Amara?

So far, signs pointed to the former, and Morrigan felt at ease with her even though she hadn't had any physical connections to her to know for sure.

"So we'll start with a tour."

Stepping out of the kitchen, Aslin gestured towards the room across from them. "This is the main entrance room, it's where we came in last night. It's also the main entrance and exit for the house. To the left is a guest room, the one on the end is the study, we won't go in there right now, I think Nik and Waric were having a meeting, but I'll show it to you later." On the other side of the kitchen was the dining room and another bathroom. Across the hall from both were large picture windows that looked out into the courtyard she had spent time in that morning. Could it really change seasons depending on what the first person wanted?

"I know we came from there, but can I see the courtyard again? I wonder what it thinks I need." Aslin had shown Morrigan how to use the stove and an oven with the simple command of *Atior,* but the innate magic of the courtyard was something Morrigan didn't think would be so easy.

"Absolutely. You put your hand on the door and take a deep breath. It will know what you want." Morrigan eagerly pulled away from Aslin to stroke the handle of the door and closed her eyes, taking a slow deep breath.

What did she need? She needed some direction, some knowledge of how things were going to go and what Fate had in store for her. Taking a slow deep breath, she pushed the door open and paused. It was still snowing the thick serene fluffs as it had before. It hadn't worked.

Of course it hadn't, why did she think it would? It wasn't as if she had learned any magic. Perhaps her mother was right and the powers she thought she had were just a figment of her imagination. Letting her hand drop from the knob, she let out a soft, dejected sigh. She had gone from one magical household to another, again the only one with no magical access.

"I love the snow like this." Aslin smiled as she stepped through the door to hold out her hand, giggling as the snow touched her skin.

"It's very nice."

"Come on, I'll give you the rest of the tour and then we can see if the study is free so you can find a book."

Morrigan looked over the snowy courtyard again. At least it was pretty.

Settled at the dining room table sometime later, Morrigan ate quietly, enjoying the conversation around her. Their topics were vast, from tomorrow's meal ideas to idle gossip about the goings-on in the court. Part of her wondered when the other shoe would drop, but at that moment, she was being treated as normal as any other guest in any other house. The only difference was that house belonged to a changeling lord she had just met.

She mulled over her previous encounters when a thought struck her.

"How do you do that thing with your eyes?" The conversation between Waric and Aslin paused as both of them looked at Morrigan and then at Nikaius.

"What thing?" He blinked at her as he tried to think back to what exactly she was referring to.

"The thing you did last night when you were coaxing me into the bath." Surprise shot through Nikaius as Waric choked on his drink, the red wine dripping down his chin as Aslin patted him on the back.

You had her in the bath? Waric's voice flicked through Nikaius' head, but Nikaius ignored him in favor of offering his hand to Morrigan. "May I?"

Morrigan's eyes flicked down to his hand curiously, taking in the muscle and veins of his arm and wondering how nice they would feel.

That was absolutely not the point of this. Focus Morrigan. Shaking herself, she nodded and leaned forward a bit so that he could slide his hand into her hair. When he found the spot at the nape of her neck and stroked, she sighed softly. "This thing?" Nikaius' voice had settled into the soft dark tone from the night before. It sent a curl of pleasure through her.

"Yes." Her response left her lips in a cooed sigh, and her head automatically tipped back against his fingers. The tone of his voice made her blood turn sluggish, and her mind filled with static. Everything was blank and empty except for him. All she felt were his fingers where they made contact with her skin. He was warm, and the feeling of contentment lurched in her chest, reminiscent of that feeling between wakefulness and sleep. Was she content, or was he? Had he overloaded her so that she couldn't read him? That was a worry for another time. Letting out another slow breath, her eyes slid closed for a brief moment.

When he pulled his hand away, she wanted to cry.

Nikaius shifted uncomfortably. Exercising those skills always brought Priamos a little too close to the surface. "That's an alpha response. Well... For you, it's an alpha response. For me, and others, it's a natural occurrence. When an alpha needs control of a subordinate, they find the most sensitive spot for that person and stroke it while lowering their voice to the most non-threatening tone they can manage." Morrigan blinked up at him sleepily, and it made his heart flutter. Priamos also wondered if that look was one he would get if he woke beside her every day.

He cleared his throat. "It's for soothing though, not for like... There are different command responses for different situations though, not just that one." Picking up his mug, he took a sip before turning to his stew again. "I'm not the type to do it randomly, but I thought you were about to go into shock on me or something, and I didn't want to physically haul you into the bath. That would have been traumatic and the exact opposite of what I wanted to accomplish."

Morrigan nodded slowly, the fog clearing at a crawling pace as she resumed eating.

She was surprised at the fact that she had enjoyed the meat enough to stomach a few bites of it, but as Nikaius promised, there was a small plate set aside for her to pick it out if she didn't want to eat it. She hadn't noticed what was happening at first but the meat had disappeared after several minutes, and in its place were carrots. Cautiously, she picked another piece out and set it aside as she had been, but this time watched, expecting magic or something to change it into carrots. Instead, she caught Nikaius snatching the meat away and replacing it with the carrots from his stew. He didn't even seem to notice she had caught onto him, but she decided not to say anything, glad that no food was going to be wasted.

"How did you end up in Atce' Plaza last night?" Aslin's question was soft and when Morrigan looked up, a spoon full of carrot halfway through her mouth, she blushed, realizing that all eyes were on her. Waric and Nikaius knew, didn't they?

Setting the spoon down, Morrigan cleared her throat. "I was unexpected. I'm sure you're aware twins are really rare amongst our kind. It's even rarer that one of them doesn't present and gets marked. My father died before my marking, which I'm thankful for, but my mother kept me for the money. They started calling me by another name, saying I was the daughter of a maid to hide their shame."

"That's why he called you Lizzy," Waric asked, and Morrigan nodded.

"I fought it for a few years, confused because I didn't understand. No one had prepared me for the chance that I could be *thaber*. My mother told me that I should just be grateful they didn't haul me away when I was marked. I started living the lie." Nikaius refused to look at her and so Morrigan dropped her eyes to her hands.

"And you didn't want to keep living that lie when we asked last night?" Waric seemed slightly confused.

"I don't really know what happened. I thought I was going to die regardless of who I ended up with at the end of the night." She lifted her head to glance at Nikaius who stared at the spoon in his hand. His knuckles were white as he gripped it. Her blunt response seemed to startle Aslin, whose spoon fell into her bowl as she looked up with wide brown doe eyes. "I decided that I would rather die as myself than with the lie. There wasn't any other option for me at that point."

"There is now." Three simple words shouldn't have so much effect on her, but when Nikaius finally looked at her, jade eyes meeting blue, she trembled, lips parting a bit as she watched Nikaius nod. It felt like static was being shared between them, and it took her breath away. Did he feel it too? If he had, he didn't mention it, holding her gaze for a few more moments before turning away to ask Waric a question she didn't hear.

The way he said *there is now* muddled around in her head for way too long. What had he meant by that? Did she have options now? Even though she had been in Kunmei for only a brief time, Nikaius' court had exceeded all her expectations for the better. The outfit she wore wasn't a uniform, nor was it something that indicated Nikaius intended to use her as Elijah suggested. Aslin, Nikaius, and Waric had been welcoming and kind, and even Aquila and Hawke seemed to treat her the same. Though they were curiously absent from dinner. Tucking her fingers into the sleeve of the sweater, she rested her chin in the palms of her hands, watching the others interact.

They behaved more like a family than just friends and she briefly wondered if she would have had that if Mae had been able to take her when she married. She remembered how she had begged Elijah to sign her over to Santi, Mae's husband. She had so badly wanted to go, but she assumed that was probably why Elijah had said no.

Morrigan missed her sister, the longing she felt taking over every other feeling and opening the painful pit inside her chest. Closing her eyes, she took a deep breath. She couldn't let that feeling linger. It would break her. Without knowing Nikaius' true intentions, she wasn't in a position to break. She let out a slow breath and pieced the aching edges back together before shoving them away.

Her breath must have been louder than she thought because when she opened her eyes again, Nikaius was looking at her. "Are you finished?" he asked softly, gesturing to her empty bowl, and she nodded, passing it over to Waric's waiting hand.

"I'll help."

"It's his turn to do the dishes." Aslin's touch on her elbow made Morrigan pause instead of following Waric back into the kitchen. "Let us see if I can find you something to sleep in. Hopefully, your brother will send your things sooner rather than later. Until then, you can borrow whatever you like from our guest collection, or we can go out and get something new if nothing is to your liking."

"I'll make do with whatever you have, thank you. I wouldn't want to put you out." Morrigan turned her attention to where Nikaius and

Waric were clearing the table before being tugged along behind Aslin to find suitable clothing for the night.

Chapter Twelve

Morrigan and Nikaius

Corinth Manor

While Aslin dug through an entire closet worth of clothes to find something that would fit, Morrigan remained quiet, sitting where Aslin had put her and taking slow deep breaths with her eyes closed. A lot had happened in a short amount of time and while Morrigan buzzed with the energy that prickled through her, she tried to let her mind blank, not thinking any one real thought except to focus on her breathing. She liked the ease with which everyone acted towards each other. Though she hadn't really had too many moments alone, she didn't feel crowded or as hurried as she had at home.

Since Elijah had left, Morrigan had gone almost an entire day without negative energy prickling her skin. It was refreshing.

"Here we go. I think this will do. Hopefully, your brother will send your things soon. I imagine you'd be more comfortable in things that were fitted to you. I know I am." Aslin smiled and offered the clothing for Morrigan to try on.

Aslin had a good eye, and Morrigan agreed. Even though she would have been alright with anything they cared to provide. She was grateful that they wanted to provide at all. Looking at herself in the mirror, Morrigan nodded. The top she wore was soft and flowed to her hips but the only reason it fit was because of the thin straps and the skimpy back. The two sides of the top met in a twist of fabric just under her shoulder blades but left her shoulders and low back exposed. The leggings she wore were made of the same soft fabric. She felt less exposed wearing them, but the attire was a lot less than what she was used to wearing. She wasn't naked or in a dress like the night before, so the feeling that Nikaius hadn't bought her for pleasure was becoming more of a reality. "This is perfect. Thank you." Morrigan returned Aslin's smile with one of her own.

As soon as Aslin left, she bundled up in one of the large soft furs that covered her bed and headed into the bathroom in hopes of doing something about the wild nature of her hair.

The vanity was nearly identical to the one Morrigan's sisters had shared. This one, however, had a top that matched the house's floors: shining black stones with streaks of gold spread across it. She had never been one to know things like stones and wood types on an intimate level but part of her wondered if it was marble. The temple she had been to when her father died had been made of marble, but it had been white and silver to represent the peace and serenity of Fate.

Turning her attention to the sink, she frowned at it. Back home, they had simple plumbing where one could turn a knob and get water from the faucet, but here, the sink seemed to have no dial or handle to turn. Waving her hand under and around the faucet proved futile and even looking under the sink in the cabinets didn't give her any clue as to how to make it work. Crossing her arms over her chest, she let the fur fall to the floor and stomped her foot in frustration. Washing her hair was now out of the question, even though she knew the magic that bound her hair would not be washed away.

Turning, she plopped herself down on the vanity stool and started pulling out drawers, surely there was a pair of scissors in one of them.

She didn't know how long she dug through the drawers or how loud she was until a throat cleared behind her and she jumped. Turning so quickly she had to stabilize herself on the bench, she frowned when she noticed Nikaius standing across the room with his head tipped to the side.

"I heard you grumbling quite crossly in here and figured I'd check in." It was almost as if she could feel his gaze as she watched his eyes trail down her form and back up, his ears turning a bit pink at the tips. She could feel her face heat, and she tossed her hair over her shoulder before turning to face away from him to look at *herself* in the mirror.

"I'm —" Fine was not what she was.

"Would you like some help?"

Their eyes locked in the mirror and tears burned her throat as she watched him approach. She hated feeling so helpless. "Would it be a bother if I said yes?"

"I offered." Nikaius insisted, stepping closer. "What exactly is it you're looking for?" He picked up a bottle of dark blue liquid from beside the sink.

"I... My braids. I can't get them out." Morrigan's sigh was heavy; she hadn't known she was holding her breath until he looked away.

Nikaius hummed before pulling a different bottle from beside the tub.

"When we were younger, Aslin had long hair. It was so pretty, but it was also really thick and would tangle very easily. That's why her hair is so short now. Once she was no longer under the pressures of her family to look a certain way, she cut it all off and found she liked it better that way." Taking a bit of the lotion from the bottle, Nikaius smoothed it over the ends of Morrigan's hair.

"The binding agent can't be soaked out. It has to be cut or some sort of magic applied, but I couldn't find scissors, and I'm not privy to that type of magic." Her voice was soft, and uncertainty rolled off her in waves. As he nodded, he rose, rinsing his hands before returning to his room to find the trimming shears he used for his own hair.

"Here we are. We'll nip the ends and try to work as much of your hair free as we can, yeah?" When she nodded, he settled down onto his knees on the floor behind her and started carefully clipping the ends of every braid he could find.

Morrigan sat nervously, picking at the skin around her nails while she waited. His hands were gentle, and he worked quickly too. When he parted her hair in two, he settled some of it over her shoulder to allow her to work through one side while he worked through the other.

"Why is your household so informal?" Morrigan asked after a moment, and Nikaius paused in what he was doing to look up at her in the mirror.

"What do you mean?"

"No other lord would be helping someone remove their hair from bonds from her previous home. Most would have accepted my fate as fact and not bothered, but not you."

Because you are worth more than you know. Priamos' emotions flared so Nikaius put them into coherent words. "No, I suppose you're right. However," he cleared his throat, "as I stated before, I don't want to be like the other lords on this continent. I think that if you allow people to know you and feel as if they can trust you, they will be more loyal to you when the time comes."

Morrigan let his words sink into her, contemplating the realness of them and how strange they were compared to everything she had previously experienced. The evidence behind his words was important. In Atce' Plaza, he had easily walked among the people, and no one bowed or cowered in his presence. Everyone in his company spoke freely, and no one seemed to fear him. *She* had spoken freely and had yet to be reprimanded, even when her words were not polite.

When Morrigan didn't respond, Nikaius breathed slow and deep through his nose, trying to scent anything that would give away her thoughts, but he only caught whiffs of sunshine and a bit of unease.

He let the topic drop as he continued to work his way through the braids and knots in her hair.

Nikaius' silence bothered Morrigan, making her wonder if she had angered him with the way his breathing changed.

"Our courts are so different." The need to fill the silence was overwhelming, and she blurted out the first thing that hit her.

"They are." He didn't look up as he worked, his voice distant as if he wasn't quite focused on what she was saying. She didn't mind his distraction too much. Something about the way he looked at her unnerved her at times because she felt like he could see into her soul.

"Why is that?" she asked. The need to know why their courts were so different outweighed her desire to observe him as he quietly worked.

"What do you mean?"

"I know we're not entirely the same, but we all live on the same continent. I don't understand how everything can be so vastly separate."

Letting out a soft hum, Nikaius thought. It was becoming more evident by the hour how much information Morrigan lacked.

"I do not fault them for it." He chose his words carefully because he didn't want her to get the wrong impression. He understood why her family was the way they were and didn't agree with it, but he didn't want her to think he was judging her for their choices. "Those in your court in particular meet certain advancements with great disdain. We're closer to the mortal realms, so we've learned how to integrate their things into our world. If it can be patched into the grid of magic, we've been able to accommodate it."

"Like the furnishings of your kitchen and your plumbing."

"Exactly. The fridge and stove were mortal devices that we've figured out how to work on the abundance of magic we have. Because we are not deep in the mountains, we have more access to the world's magic than those in Be'Sala so we can add more things to it without weakening it. We've embraced the things that mortals have created. I'm sure you've noticed our fashion is vastly different as well."

"I have. Your shirt is rather interesting. I only knew what it was because Santi wears similar fashion."

"He does. Most of the continent has reconciled with the mortals. It's been centuries since the fall, so it's the natural progression of things."

"My mother would disagree."

"Your mother is one of the ones who is trapped in traditional thinking centered on purist ideals." Morrigan watched his face change as he blinked up at their images in the mirror with confusion, as if he hadn't actually meant to say the words out loud.

His shock made her laugh. "My sister said the same thing the last time she visited!" A pang of sadness curled through her at the thought of her sister.

"You miss her." Nikaius' voice was soft at the comment and Morrigan nodded shyly.

He let silence envelop them as he thought. Surely, it wouldn't hurt to have Hawke bring a letter to Mae when he next visited the Pridelands. But he and Priamos were selfish, and neither wanted to let her go so soon. After a few more moments, Nikaius was able to pull a comb through the bottom of her hair with ease. "There we go." When he shifted up onto his knees, they both realized how close they were. Leaning forward a bit, Nikaius inhaled deeply.

A thrill ran through Morrigan.

Was this normal?

Did she care?

The heat of him sank into her shoulders, and she could barely feel the rumble of his voice in his chest. She jerked away, turning to stare at him with wide eyes.

"What was that?"

"I... Sorry. My wolf... He gets overzealous a-and you smell like sunshine."

"Sunshine?" How did one smell of sunshine? She knew that people smelled of the soaps they used, or things they were around. Nikaius smelled of vanilla and tobacco like her father had smoked, Waric of cinnamon and of freshly fallen cedar, and Hawke and Aquila smelled of fresh leather when she had been close to them. But sunshine wasn't a scent she knew could be put into a soap. Was it a changeling thing? Did she smell that way to all of them despite using plain unscented soap?

"Mhm. Like stepping outside on a sunny day after long rains." She couldn't picture what he meant, Be'Sala having been nearly constant rain, but before she could ask for more details, he nodded and stood, running his hands through the ends of her hair once more, his fingers brushing the back of her neck.

He was pleased with the result. "I believe we're through. Have a good night, Morrigan." Berating himself and Priamos for giving into the wolf's desire, he turned to leave.

Her breath caught then. For some reason, she didn't want to let him leave, so she didn't. Without really premeditating it, she caught his hand before he could make it more than a step. When he turned back to face her, she heard his breath catch.

Nikaius paused when she caught his hand and turned to look her over, struck by how different she looked now that her hair was free. She was pale, but a smattering of freckles covered the bridge of her nose and the high arches of her cheekbones. Her hair tumbled over her shoulders, covering her breasts and reaching her hips in a way that obscured most of the nightgown she wore. She was small, barely reaching his chest when she had stood earlier, but she wasn't obsessively thin like the fae women he had known before.

In fact, now that he studied her with her hair free, he could see the resemblance between her and Mae De'Lyon.

Not that he was complaining, he appreciated curves. Curves that he would love to trace with his hands... lips... tongue. Another grumble pulled itself from his chest and he shook his head trying to pull himself back from where the wolf had drawn him.

Another grumble pulled itself from his chest and Morrigan wondered where his thoughts had wandered to. Was it a good or bad place? Her eyes caught him, and she watched as his face reddened slowly. Shyness and embarrassment flooded her system through their touch. She couldn't tell whether it was hers or his.

He looked over her one more time before he stepped back again, but he looked down at their joined hands in surprise. Morrigan had already forgotten that she had reached for him. Lifting her hand slowly to his mouth, he pressed a kiss against her knuckles and an unbidden giggle escaped her throat.

"I'll let you rest." Dipping into a quick playful bow that elicited another giggle from Morrigan, he pulled away and exited the room.

"That was smooth." Waric's voice teased from the bedroom door, and Nikaius flopped himself facedown onto his bed with a low groan before chucking a pillow in his general direction.

Chapter Thirteen

Morrigan and Nikaius

Corinth Manor

Morrigan turned to stare at her reflection, noting that her face was just as red as it felt. Pressing her hands to her cheeks, she gave a giddy laugh before her attention was drawn away by a muffled thump and a groan coming from the way Nikaius had left.

Standing, she tiptoed her way across the floor towards his door but paused when she heard Waric's laugh and realized the door was slightly ajar.

"Did you actually just kiss her hand?" Waric laughed.

"Shut up. I don't know what I'm doing."

"What are you doing? You mean talking to a pretty girl?" Waric's voice was teasing. "Aslin's a girl."

"She's not..." Morrigan pressed her back against the wall, hoping not to be seen. "Aslin is Aslin. That ship sailed A LONG time ago. I don't know."

"You *like* her."

Morrigan really liked the way Nikaius laughed, and Waric's soft chuckle joined his in a sound that made her heart feel whole. The amount of shared emotion between all the inhabitants of the house was a vast change from what home had been the past year that Mae had been gone.

"Fates alive! You actually do! We talked about this, Nik. If you want it, go for it."

"I don't want her to feel obligated to like me just because she's..." Morrigan desperately wanted to touch him to tell how he was feeling, to know what was going on in his head even though her powers didn't work like that. "What would we even consider her? We know what she is, but I don't want to force that on her. I'm not going to tell people I won her or bought her, or whatever. She's not an animal — or an object."

"Let's start with just introducing her as Morrigan and let her take the reins on deciding what our relationship will be." Morrigan felt like her heart stopped. Let her be in charge of deciding their relationship. She knew nothing about relationships! Did she even want to be in a relationship? What if she was terrible at it?

Morrigan didn't hear what else was said as she turned and tried to make her way quietly to the vanity. A noise at the door distracted her, and she tripped, letting out a loud yelp as she tumbled to the floor. She had forgotten about the fur that she had been wrapped in earlier, but she was thankful for it simply for the fact that it dampened her fall, even if it had been the reason she had tripped.

Nikaius and Waric jumped at the sound of something falling in the bedroom and both were quickly at the bathroom door, looking around in concern.

"Morrigan?" Oh no. Nikaius... Morrigan hoped they hadn't heard her.

"Are you okay?" Waric approached, and she groaned softly, pressing her face into the fur. Concern rippled across her skin as a warm finger tracked up the scars on her back.

Waric frowned as he looked up from Morrigan, tracing his fingers along various scars, one leading up to the very obvious *thaber* brand on her left shoulder. Nikaius frowned at the mark. It was the council's mark: a stag with antlers as well as horns. Before he could touch it himself, Morrigan wiggled over so she could settle on her back with a groan, dragging the hair from her face.

"Are you okay?" Waric asked again. Morrigan let out a hard breath before nodding and opening her eyes. "Hello again," he laughed, wiggling his fingers in front of her face in greeting.

Both men laughed when she huffed and swatted away Waric's hand. "Did you trip or faint?" Nikaius asked softly. Morrigan rolled her eyes and tried to sit up, but Nikaius' hand on her shoulder made her pause.

"I tripped." Nikaius' concern crawled across her skin where his hand touched her shoulder.

"Did you hit your head?" His voice was so low and calm that it made her sigh.

"No." But she wished she had as embarrassment settled over her.

"Are you hurt?" Waric took one of her hands in his, and she felt his amusement.

"No." Just her pride. She sat the rest of the way up with Waric's help.

"Alright. Let's get you back upright then." They tugged her up with their hands at her elbows. The energies they gave off were a combination of kindness, concern, adoration, and amusement. It was such a significant change from what she was used to that it was overwhelming. She swayed.

Nikaius' eyes flashed to Waric's quickly. Something was off. Even if she hadn't hit her head, something was affecting her. Waric gave a subtle nod, and Nikaius swept Morrigan up in his arms with ease.

Morrigan's face burned and the dull roar of her blood in her head muted the world around her.

"Are you really okay?" It only took a couple of strides across the bathroom to enter Morrigan's room. Sitting her on the bed, he knelt before her.

She gave a small nod. Nothing ached. For the first time in as long as she can remember, she held no tension in her shoulder. She hadn't clenched her jaw once that day in anticipation of dark emotions crawling up her skin. It was rather disorienting to be thrown from one extreme to another but physically, she was fine. Emotionally, however, was another story.

"I... I'm confused and a little overwhelmed, honestly." Nikaius frowned at her, tilting his head a bit when she shyly lifted her eyes to catch his.

When their gaze caught, it felt like her heart had tumbled deeply into her stomach, forcing the air from her lungs as it went.

Those eyes were ones she had seen in her sleep so many times before. When she was young and still had dreams of finding refuge and tenderness and *love*. That feeling, those memories, made tears burn the back of her throat and her bottom lip tremble.

She hardly believed in soulmates, but something deep within her knew that Fate had brought her here for a reason. Even though they had only met just over a day ago, she felt like she had spent lifetimes beside him.

"How can I help?" His gaze searched hers, trying to get something, anything from her that would confirm that she was feeling what he felt.

"I-I don't know." Why was she whispering?

"Well, tell me where your confusion lies, and maybe I can assist in remedying it." He reached for her, slipping his hands in hers to hold them gently in her lap. Taking a deep breath through his nose, he pulled Priamos closer to the surface, allowing him the room to try to soothe her so that the rioting in his own heart would fade just a bit.

"Everything is so new, honestly. I'm afraid I'll do something wrong or mess up."

"That's not confusion but anxiety stemming from the lack of proper positive reassurance, Morrigan." Nikaius had felt it himself on many different occasions growing up and it had only started to get better because of his distance from his family and interaction with those who truly supported him.

Morrigan huffed. "Well, that is how I presently feel." Nikaius' hands tightened on hers for a moment, just a small squeeze before his thumbs started making slow trails up and down her knuckles. Her defensiveness settled.

"I didn't intend to negate your feelings; I was simply trying to explain. I promise that if you mess up or do something wrong, you won't be in trouble for it. I prefer having honest conversations rather than reprimanding for something that was most likely an accident or error."

Morrigan wondered how could a man as large and powerful as him be so kind. Never had she met someone who would willingly get down on their knees in front of a stranger and attempt to reassure them in the way he was doing then.

Hadn't she always wanted someone to treat her like that? Actions meant more than words to her, but she couldn't understand why his words, his tone, caused a small part of her to break inside. No, it absolutely shattered it into a million tiny frayed and painful pieces. Her throat once again burned with tears she refused to let fall, her chest tight.

"You're amazing." The words escaped before she had really thought about them, but before shock seeped in, he laughed.

Nikaius' chest warmed at the scent of awe that engulfed her, and he laughed again.

There was something about the way he laughed, so unburdened and carefree that it made her heart stutter moments before his amusement welled through their connection.

Nikaius' emotions tumbled through her in such quick succession that Morrigan hadn't had time to process what he was feeling before he surged up, cupping her face in his hands. Her breath was caught in her throat at the sudden movement, but all thought fell away when he kissed her.

This kiss was different from the ones she had experienced in the past. From others, she had experienced lust and desire and need, but from him, none of those took the forefront of his emotions. There was something soft and unnamed that warmed her, encouraging her to return the gesture in equal fervor.

Her hands found his hair, and she pulled herself closer. Priamos purred as Nikaius eagerly seized the opportunity to shift her head just enough to deepen the kiss. His fingers curled along her lower back, mapping all the places where scars interrupted the smooth skin, counting as he kissed her with the intent of inflicting twice as many on anyone who had dared to touch her in the past. He would allow her to have her revenge, or he would dole it out for her, whichever she preferred.

Catching her before she tumbled off the bed, he eased her down, settling her comfortably in his lap before his hand slid higher to curl around her neck. The sound she let out was delicious, sending a chill down his spine. The things he would do to her if she allowed it were vast, and each one passed in a flash through his mind as he pulled away, his lips trailing slowly over her jaw and down her throat.

Her pulse fluttered like a bird under his lips and by the Fates, he wanted to mark her, bring her crashing down into his life even deeper than where she was now. He had to have her.

When her hips rocked against his, he stilled. This was too fast. He pulled away, letting out a low groan as he pressed his forehead to her shoulder. Fates alive.

"*Nikaius.*" His name on her lips mingled with Waric's in his head and he paused, heat turning to ice in his veins. He couldn't do this. He was too close to the edge, and he needed to stop. He needed to step away.

He hadn't intended to leave so quickly, but his hold over Priamos was greatly slipping, and he needed to be as far from her as he could when the primal gained full control.

Morrigan pressed her fingers to her lips with a frown. That was some kiss, but why had he left so quickly? Did he regret what he had done? It was only a kiss, wasn't it? Her heart fluttered as she thought about it but could find no reason to be ashamed. He had kissed her first, and there was nothing wrong with enjoying it, right?

Something drew them together in a way that was different from the others she had been with in the past. There were a few instances of interaction between men that Morrigan had chosen, but for some reason, this felt different. More important. And it had nothing to do with him being a lord.

Chapter Fourteen

Waric

Corinth Manor

After leaving Morrigan, Nikaius seemed a bit off, but Waric didn't press. He knew his mate was struggling with the fact that there was a new person in their home, and that she had the potential to be the mate they had been searching for. Despite all the teasing he had subjected Nikaius to, Warichad been searching for her while Nikaius denied her existence; something Waric knew to be a product of his guilt. He just wanted Nikaius to accept the fact before making a move to get confirmation of his suspicions.

As they readied for bed, they hadn't talked much between the two of them and once clean and dressed for the night, they both elected to catch up on work that had fallen to the wayside with the preparations for Selection Night.

He watched his dark-haired lord flip through pages of a book in their personal library and sighed softly. That was the first time Nikaius had stepped forward and chosen someone for himself, but Waric knew he wouldn't have let Bastian kill her. Neither of them would have as decent people, but especially not when she smelled like she did. While their personal library was vast, it seemed to hold none of the answers Nikaius sought as he had browsed through the varying titles on the shelves.

Waric felt bad. He wanted to comfort his stressed mate, drag him to bed and find all the secret places he knew would make the other sigh and forget the world, but tonight was not the night for that. Nikaius needed to sit with his thoughts and feelings and that wasn't something Waric could do for him.

When Nikaius seemed to have found a book that was promising, he settled in the leather chair at the large main desk and flipped through it, sleepily resting his chin on his hand as he read. The desk was large and regal, solid mahogany that shined in the light. Most days, Nikaius looked every bit like the lord he was, but tonight, despite the severe look of the desk, Nikaius just looked like a tired young man. Tapping into their bond, Waric settled at Nikaius' feet, resting his head against Nikaius' knee. The book Nikaius read was about how the culling was carried out and what evidence was needed to be available to confirm whether someone did or didn't present.

Most of this Waric already knew. For Bastian, it had been easy to tell. Stormy eyes turned green before his entire body trembled, and he folded into the form of a large black panther. Nikaius' presentation was chaotic, and he hadn't even known what happened until after the fact.

Waric's heart hurt for his mate every time he thought about it. They hadn't been mated at the time, but he had been there when Bastian forced Nikaius to change. Since then, those who knew him best had all come to reconcile with the wolf that lingered in his head, a primal creature who functioned mostly on emotion alone. Waric hadn't known how hard it was for Nikaius some days, the struggle he went through to keep Priamos at bay, until they were mated. Waric ended up with a front-row seat to the chaos in Nikaius' head.

Waric knew from the way others glanced at Nikaius that they had all come to know something was up. It seemed only the people within his court trusted him, but Waric knew Nikaius was thankful for the lack of invitations to large lavish events because of it.

Setting aside the book, Nikaius sighed. "Have you ever heard of one of the fae not presenting but still having powers?" Waric looked up from his work and frowned. "There has to be more to this than what we've been told."

"I've never heard of it," Waric stated, setting aside his letter to shift closer, resting his cheek against Nikaius' leg to look up at him. "Maybe Soren has though. We're meeting with Silas tomorrow morning, so perhaps he could reach out to his brother for us?"

"I'll talk to Hawke and Aquila about it to see if they can spare him from training for a bit." The fingers of Nikaius' right hand slipped into Waric's hair as the left flipped back through the book. "Something just feels weird about this whole thing."

Waric gave a noncommittal hum and settled back into his work, knowing that Nikaius had to work things out for himself.

By the time a sleepy yawn drew Nikaius from his book, Waric had finished his work and had simply been enjoying the time with Nikaius' fingers stroking through his hair. The time they spent outside of their duties was always special to him. The study was one of their own sacred spots in the world where nothing else existed, just them.

"Mmm." Waric hummed as he stood, rolling his shoulders before shifting to lean over the back of Nikaius' chair to wrap his arms around his mate's shoulders, nudging his nose into soft, dark hair. "I'm about done for the night; you should turn in too. Don't let it weigh on you too much." He pressed a kiss to Nikaius' temple.

"Yeah." Nikaius stood, reaching out to tug Waric to him. Pressing their foreheads together with a soft hum, Nikaius seemed to settle just a bit.

"Let's go to bed." Waric stroked his hands through Nikaius' hair before pressing a kiss to his mouth.

Those words seemed to be magic as Nikaius' shoulders sagged and he blinked sleepily, giving a hummed "Kay" before making his way to bed.

Despite being a big strong alpha, and a lord, Waric not so secretly adored how adorable sleepy Nikaius could be.

Only a short few hours later, Waric found himself leaning against the frame of the kitchen door, watching Morrigan slowly knead dough under her hands. He knew he should feel guilty about going against Nikaius' desire for the slow approach with her, but Nikaius hadn't been really following his own orders either. Waric knew he really should be the one to hold back, after all, they didn't know what sort of things she had gone through in her home. Most *thaber* weren't treated with kindness. How Morrigan hadn't been sold to the Farm when she was marked was something Waric wanted to look into.

He had been searching since her culling day to find out what happened to her, because despite what Nikaius thought, Morrigan was their mate. She was the girl they had held for her culling those years ago and there was nothing Nikaius could say that would change Waric's mind. She looked and smelled the same as the day they had met her.

While Nikaius wanted them to take their time with getting to know her, Waric knew he was struggling on that front. He had initially decided to let them figure themselves out, but that didn't mean he wasn't curious too.

Despite not knowing her for long, he felt a kinship with her in a way that had nothing to do with the bond. That would need to be solidified by her before that sort of intuition would come to light between them. No, this was something less primal and borne more of trauma and a life that hadn't always been kind. She had nightmares. The night before, he had woken from his sleep to hear her soft cries from the adjoining room. Nikaius typically slept like the dead, but Waric was surprised his mate had slept through the night without trying to check on her. He would have thought that Nikaius would have been on high alert the entire night, but he also knew that he was close to drop, and Priamos had been riding him hard the last few days. The vacant looks as the two argued in his head were becoming more and more prominent as the weather deteriorated around them. The turning of the seasons was always the worst for the drop, especially for Nikaius in particular because of the split between their personalities.

Perhaps it was just their proximity and the fact that he had only woken a few moments before that brought her plight to his awareness. Her sobs were soft, not something a normal person would hear, but he had barely caught them as he stood to shake his own fears from his skin. The nightmare he had experienced wasn't one he could remember, which meant it wasn't as bad as others. The fact that it hadn't sent a wave of panic through their bond to wake Nikaius attested to that fact as well.

Tonight though, he woke to near silence, his heart a flight in his chest as he woke with the demons in his head. Once the pulse in his head slowed and then dissipated, he noticed the night wasn't silent. A soft humming roused him from the dregs of drowsiness enough that he decided to seek out the siren's song.

For all he knew, it could have been one of the Velamo who hummed softly from their kitchen, but the wards would have been triggered and the rest of the house would be awake. Neither thing was happening and Waric couldn't find any shame in seeking her out just to satisfy his curiosity.

The song she hummed was so soft, he was honestly surprised he heard it as he followed the sound to the kitchen. Maybe it was more of an awareness of her presence that had roused him. He wasn't super pressed to know as he stood in the doorway of the kitchen where he found her rolling out a sheet of dough. He took her in, a slow smile spreading across his face. A few red wavy tendrils had fallen from the messy bun she had secured her hair into. Those pieces of hair seemed to annoy her, and he grinned as he watched her try to brush them away, smudging flour across her forehead.

A timer went off, and she jumped, dusting flour from her hands before seeking out a towel to open the oven and pull out a tray.

"Is that bread?"

Startled, Morrigan dropped the tray and gasped high and loud as she pulled her hand quickly from the hot oven. Shit, he had scared her.

"Fuck, I didn't mean to scare you!" The water kicked on as he rounded the island to reach for her.

"Don't touch me!" She jerked back away from him, and he threw up his hands to step back.

"I'm not going to hurt you. You just burned yourself, and we need to treat it. I don't have to touch you, but you do need to get it under water. It'll help the pain."

"I know how to treat a burn." Her words were vicious, but she didn't turn to put her arm under the water like he instructed, instead she retrieved the towel.

"If you know how to treat a burn, you know that the worst thing to do is put something dry on it." He let out a low huff and snagged the towel from her hand, physically putting himself between her and the oven as she tried to take it back.

"I've got to get the bread out or it will burn."

"Or you worry about yourself and fuck the bread." Slapping the towel down onto the counter, he bracketed her against the sink. He wasn't going to allow her to injure herself further on his watch. Nikaius would be mad enough that he had been the reason she got burnt in the first place.

Her eyes dropped to her toes. "But it'll be ruined." He could hear the way her heart fluttered and could smell the fear that rolled off her. Fuck. He had scared her.

Was she afraid she'd be punished for letting the bread burn? That wasn't important. She needed to heal. "And you will be scarred."

"Wouldn't be the first scar."

Anger flared through Waric's veins as he remembered the lashes he had traced up her back earlier in the night. "But it would be on my watch and that's unacceptable." He had to remember that she wasn't the one he was mad at. Taking a slow breath, he took a hold of her upper arm so she wouldn't turn away and moved her to trade places. He easily scooped the bread from the oven and slammed it shut, setting the tray onto a rack before turning to face her again.

Her cheeks and nose were red, but she hadn't tried to pull away again. "There, now go rinse that. I'll get some salve." He kept his voice low, at a loss on how to show her that he wasn't angry at her, but at the situation as a whole. "You'll receive no more scars under my care. I'll fight anyone who dares, even if that means your own stubbornness."

When she didn't move, he sighed and led her over to the sink by the shoulders. What was it with this girl and water? "It won't be too cold, I promise."

"How do you know?"

"The house is magic. It knows the perfect temperature for anything."

Finally, she tucked her arm under the running water, gasping as it hit her scalded flesh. "If it's so magical, why didn't it stop being hot when I touched it just now?" Her tone was a new one that was full of sass and sarcasm that did a funny thing to his heart. The fear that he had sensed from her was fading.

That was a good question though. He had never once been burnt by anything in the house. It was another thing about her that was curious. "Perhaps it was because of your mark? We've never had a marked one like you, or any mortals here before so I'm not sure how the magic will work for or against you." Her cheeks flushed, and she turned to look away from him, her concentration turning back to assessing the burn on her forearm. It was only a few inches long, but he knew it had to hurt.

Reaching out, he pulled the salve from the bathroom through the ether and then opened it, stepping closer so he could offer it to her. "Here, we'll put this on it and after a few applications, it won't be visible anymore. Just like magic."

"Just like magic." She rolled her eyes at him but dipped her fingers into the pot.

"Oh, not that much. Hang on." When she pulled her hand back, eyes flicking to his in surprise, he swiped the cream from her fingers and returned half of it to the pot. "It just takes a little bit. Here." Setting aside the container, he stroked his fingers carefully down her arm, only focusing on the white areas within the red before swiping it out slowly.

"There. Too much will block air from getting to it, which won't be conducive to healing." Wide eyes watched him, and he gave her a smile before closing the container and sending it back to the bathroom, pulling out a roll of gauze in its place. "Most people aren't awake at this time of morning, everything alright?"

Morrigan hummed but nodded. "I'm fine." Her voice was soft as she watched him carefully wrap her arm, and it made something weird settle in his chest. Was she shy, or was her demeanor learned? Reaching out, he tipped up her chin with his forefinger and gave her a smile.

"We're equals here, you don't have to bow or lower your gaze."

Her cheeks pinked as he watched, and her gaze flashed to his for a second before dropping away again. "So everyone keeps saying."

"No one here is telling you a lie. You'll just have to learn."

"It's not a common practice, so it feels a little weird."

"Then I'll show you." A grin spread across his face, and he offered his hand to her. "Hello Morrigan, I'm Waric Cavanaugh. It's nice to meet you."

Morrigan watched him curiously, holding her arm to her chest as her gaze searched his before she looked down to examine his hand. He knew the smattering of silver stars along his wrist must make her curious, surely, she hadn't seen a mating mark before.

Tentatively, she slid her hand into his, and electricity tingled down his arm, confirming his suspicions. She was who he thought, and he couldn't wait to confirm it with Nikaius in the morning, but for now, he wanted to get to know her on his own.

"I'm Morrigan," Her voice was shy and unsure, and he remembered that her brother, and family, had been calling her by another name. If she was who they said, that meant that Santiago De'Lyon's wife was also her sister. That thought didn't add up though, because surely Santi would have done something knowing that his wife's family had kept someone captive in their home for years without following legal protocols.

The fact that the three of them, Waric, Nikaius, and Santi were actively trying to change those protocols was neither here nor there, especially if it meant that he had found the girl he had been searching for.

But that also meant that it was possible Nikaius had already known and failed to tell him. A flare of hurt surged through him, and Morrigan gasped before trying to tug her hand back. Pressing a kiss to her knuckles, he grinned up at her, curious about the timing. Despite there being a bond that she hadn't yet accepted, there was something simmering just beneath the surface, and Waric intended to find out what it was.

Letting out a low laugh, he stepped around her to collect the loaf pan and let out a soft sigh before taking a deep breath and inhaling the scent of warm bread.

It smelled like home. His mother used to bake, a favored pastime of hers, but it had been years since he had been in the kitchen with her. The practice had stopped once Waric became old enough to be groomed to be his uncle's heir. Everyone knew how well *that* turned out.

Well, not everyone.

Carefully removing the loaf from its pan, he set it aside and turned to her. "Can I help?" He felt like his knowing she had nightmares was a truth he shouldn't know and to compensate, he felt he should share one of his own, even if it was the same one.

"I haven't baked anything since I was younger. It's very unbecoming of a fine gentleman you know?" He puffed up his chest and tipped his chin, which gave him the desired effect. A giggle from Morrigan.

"I'm just making biscuits."

"Just nothing. I saw the tarts you made with Aslin. I bet you know how to bake pretty much anything. What is your favorite thing to make?"

"Biscuits." He washed his hands before turning to where the dough she had been working was still sitting.

"But biscuits are so boring." He had hoped she would have said something sweet like a cake or fruit tart.

"They're hardly boring. You can turn biscuit dough into anything if you add the right seasonings or ingredients. I know one that incorporates cheese that is wonderful."

"Cheese?"

"Yes."

"Can we make some of those?"

"You'll have to shred the cheese. I'm kind of down a hand because *someone* snuck up on me while I had my hands in the oven." The look she gave him was one that would silence a lesser man, but Waric laughed.

"You raise a fair point, milady." Dipping a bow, he grinned before seeking out the grater and one of the blocks of cheese from the fridge.

"Can I ask a question?"

"You just did." Closing the fridge door he turned to see her tilt her head, watching him curiously.

"How long have you had access to things like these?" She gestured around the kitchen. Nikaius had mentioned to Waric that Morrigan was suffering from a bit of culture shock, but he didn't quite understand the extent of it until she asked.

"You mean you don't have these things? How do you cook?"

"By fire."

Waric paused with a small handful of shredded cheese to his mouth. Shoving it into his mouth, he spoke around it. "That's so archaic."

"We're in the middle of the mountains. Nothing works out there except things that only require a small amount of magic to work, like the lights."

"So how did you figure out how to work our stove then?"

"Aslin showed me yesterday when we made the apple tarts."

"Ah. That's right. Well, we have all the best things that money and magic can afford." He finished shredding the cheese and watched her take a piece of the biscuit dough, roll it in the cheese and knead it before rolling it again and dropping it onto a waiting baking sheet. "We still go to the market frequently, though, don't worry about that." She raised her eyebrows at him but said nothing as she kept working.

He was amazed at how easily she worked with her nondominant hand, not that he knew which one was more dominant than the other at this point in their relationship. "With Nikaius being a lord and all that, social calls are forever on our lists of things to do. Perhaps we'll take you tomorrow."

"I would like that." Morrigan agreed, nodding before starting on another ball of dough.

Chapter Fifteen

Morrigan

*Corinth Manor
- Kunmei Plaza*

They worked in silence, Waric shredding cheese while Morrigan made the biscuits. It was a comfortable silence, and she didn't feel the need to say anything in particular. The experience was new. She hadn't ever spent time with someone in the dark hours of the night like they were doing. The last time had been with a stable hand that had been visiting and was one of the only times Morrigan had taken something she wanted. But with Waric, there didn't seem to be a reason why he was there.

"You don't have to stay up with me. I'm content to be alone." Her voice was loud in the quiet room, and it made anxiety twist her stomach. What would people think if they found them together like this? Nothing was happening between them, but she knew how people talked.

"I have nightmares." She watched him turn and pull the tray of biscuits from the oven, embarrassed by the tingle of want that trailed down her spine. Though he spoke again, she was distracted by taking in his appearance. In the chaos of her burning herself, she hadn't realized he was shirtless until that moment. Waric was a very handsome man. Though he wasn't as wide as Nikaius he was nearly just as tall. Being so close to him felt comfortable, nothing like when she had been near others, and it was a peculiar feeling to be curious about him just as she was with Nikaius.

But Nikaius was a lord and there was absolutely no chance he would ever be interested in her. Waric had been just as kind and open with her though, and she was curious what would happen if she actually told him her thoughts.

Embarrassment flooded through her as she shook herself from her thoughts. Hadn't she been worried about being used as some plaything? Why on earth would she want to initiate something like that in a place where she didn't know her standing with them?

Suddenly, his hand was cupping her cheek and tipping her chin up. As if he could sense where her thoughts had gone, he was daringly close. She could feel the heat of his body and smell his soft cinnamon and cedar scent. A tremble went through her as he gave her a smile.

"I lost you for a second. Are you alright?" He tilted his head, thumb brushing along the apple of her cheek as he gave her a curious smile.

Shit. changelings could scent changes in a person's body. There was no way he didn't know what she was thinking. "I—" She what? Words? She needed to figure out how to get out of the situation she had suddenly thrown herself into. Oh Fates. "I feel a little faint. Excuse me." Pulling away from him, she turned and fled, his chuckle following her down the hall.

Somewhere in between swearing at herself for being so foolish to basically handing Waric her interest on a platter and the rising of the sun, Morrigan had managed to find a dreamless sleep again.

Sleep didn't last long, and Morrigan woke to a knock at her door that stirred her into awareness. "Good morning!" Aslin's soft, sweet voice preceded her into the room, and she smiled at Morrigan as she set down a breakfast tray on the table by the balcony. A blond-haired man followed, and surprise sparked through Morrigan when she recognized him to be one of the men in Elijah's employment, though she didn't know his name.

"Good morning," she answered, watching the man depositing her trunk of belongings next to the armoire, tip his head and exit the room without so much as a glance in Morrigan's direction. She wasn't sure how she felt about the fact that not only did her brother know where she was but one of his men did as well. Even though she had started to settle into feeling comfortable in Nikaius' home that knowledge unsettled her. Would Elijah come back and try to steal her away in the night?

Morrigan's thoughts were interrupted by Aslin setting up the table for them to eat at. "I've brought you breakfast since Nik and Waric have already left for the day." The thought of her kiss with Nikaius sent a confusing throb of arousal through her, and she shifted onto her back with a soft sigh. She had kissed a lord and basically screamed her want for his friend all in the span of eight hours.

"Do they often leave early?"

"Not usually, but the court is held this week, so they will be out most of the day."

"Court?" Morrigan sat up, remembering that Nikaius held a position of power.

"Mmm. Nikaius is the lord of this court, so he oversees everyone here. During the week of the full moon, the people bring their concerns to him. I was asked to show you around. I thought we could start with the market?" Settling herself into one of the chairs at the table, Aslin watched Morrigan slowly extract herself from her bed. "Perhaps we should start with some better-fitting clothing." Her amused smile made Morrigan frown, but she nodded, looking down at the borrowed nightgown she wore.

"I don't have any money for clothing," she stated softly, digging through the trunk. Pulling out her underwear, she stepped into the bathroom to freshen up and change. Removing the wrap from her arm, she frowned. Waric hadn't lied about how quickly the salve worked. The worst of the burn was gone, only the deepest part still red and tender. It was as if she had only scalded herself with water, not touched hot metal.

"You're a member of Nikaius' home, we have accounts he settles at the end of the month." Aslin's voice pulled her from her thoughts, and she resumed dressing.

"Is there an allowance?"

"I mean, Nikaius doesn't mind as long as we don't go overboard, and I'm sure that none of this..." Morrigan could hear Aslin shifting through the things in her trunk, "looks even remotely weather ready. We could get away with a trip without Nikaius fussing too—" Morrigan huffed as she tugged on the laces of her corset before she exited the bathroom. Aslin's voice died away as she dropped the things she was holding, her mouth hanging open slightly. "What in Fates' name are you wearing!?"

Frowning, Morrigan looked herself over as she tugged the top of the corset tighter. "I know I don't have a dress on, I'm working on that. Can you tie me off?" Turning to face away, she adjusted herself again.

The lid of the trunk slammed shut, and Morrigan cringed as Aslin looked up at her in shock. "No. Seriously. You're not going to wear that, are you?"

Her question baffled Morrigan. "What else would I wear?"

"That looks like it hurts," dipping her fingers in between the back of the corset and the shift, Aslin clicked her tongue. "How can you breathe? Is this what that bruising was from?"

So used to the corset and other things she wore, Morrigan hadn't realized that her skin was bruised. "My mother—"

"Nope, not a chance. I thought the bruising was just from the events of Selection Night, but if this is the case, then we're going to remedy it now." Aslin cut Morrigan off before she could protest further and seized her upper arm.

Morrigan had nothing to compare teleportation to. One minute they were in her room, the next she found herself hitting the floor hard as her knees gave out from underneath her. Words were being exchanged that she couldn't quite understand as her head swam. The floor beneath her was carpeted in rugs of varying colors, the intensity making her stomach churn as she fully settled onto the floor, trying to regain her bearings.

Before she could do more than take a couple of breaths, she was hauled to her feet by Aslin who said something that didn't register. She pulled Morrigan through a door into a more private area where she was guided to stand on a platform as another woman entered.

This woman was tall enough to see over Morrigan's head, even with her standing on the elevated platform. Her dark hair was pulled back by a pair of knitting needles, and with her assistant a younger woman with pale blonde hair carried a basket of varying items including measuring tapes and pins.

"On Skadi's honor, child, who taught you to dress? They ought to be sent to Fate herself for this atrocity." Morrigan flinched at her words, eyes dropping to her toes at the tone.

"Be kind, Eda," Aslin cut in softly, "she came to us like this."

"Mmm." Eda stalked around Morrigan once before clicking her tongue again. "Take that archaic thing from my sight at once." Morrigan didn't know whose fingers undid her laces, but her head spun at the quick release. She gasped, pressing her hand to her chest as she righted herself on Aslin's shoulder when the cloth and bone fell away. They had just cut her from the binding.

"There's no need for things like this here. Only mortals dress their women so pitifully, and that was centuries ago. Your mother ought to be slapped." Eda's hands caught Morrigan under her chin and lifted her so that she stood straight again. "A lady holds her head high and shoulders back at all times." While Morrigan felt no maliciousness, Eda's displeasure sank into Morrigan's skin, and she trembled. "Let's get you measured first and then sorted with some basics."

More hands were on her suddenly, and she gasped as cold fingers pulled her shift over her head. She cringed. Eda's tongue clicked again. Morrigan held in her whimper. Her mind flashed back to Atce' Plaza and all the wandering hands that sank dark things into her as they felt her up. It wandered back further to her mother's birthday where she had worn barely anything as she served, being pinched and grabbed by the lords.

Further still to the winter moon when Mae had been married the year before. Chilled fingers found the scars on Morrigan's back, and suddenly she was neither here nor there. She was standing in a room with others being measured, but also fifteen years old in the snow after Mae's sixteenth birthday party.

Stop! She had whimpered as cold hands forced themselves places she did not want them.

"Please stop!" She whimpered as she was turned so her back length could be measured.

"Stop!" she screamed as blinding pain lit across her back, and she tried to jerk away.

"Please stop!" Cold fingers on her back jerked her between realities, and she wasn't sure which one she was in.

Warm arms engulfed her suddenly, and she felt like she could finally breathe. A deep rumble met her ears and a wide hand curled into the hair at the back of her neck. Warm tobacco vanilla reached her senses. Was she with her father again? Had it all been a terrible dream?

"Calm." Nikaius' forehead met hers as she clung to him. "Calm." His voice sank into her, his purr relaxing the muscles of her back, the knot in her throat loosening until the tears fell freely. She realized she was sobbing so hard she shook them both.

"Calm." Had his voice always been that deep? Breathing was easier the next time she tried, and he rumbled again as his fingers slid through her hair. "Good girl"

Her body felt heavy like she would fall away at any moment, but his hands held her tight to him. His movements were slow as he shifted to tuck her face into his neck as he swayed them from side to side.

"My lord?" Eda approached. Some dark, vicious sound tore from Nikaius' throat, but as she heard everyone step back, she did not feel afraid. The anger that prickled against her skin was not meant for her. It bubbled and twisted with other emotions, worry and calm at the forefront.

"Nik—" He cut her off, lifting her chin to look her over before humming softly again.

"Calm."

"I'm okay." And suddenly she felt okay. No one had ever come to her like that, had known how to quickly bring her back from the dark spiral of panic. "I'm okay." She reached up tentatively, brushing dark hair from his ice-blue eyes. Those were not Nikaius' eyes. "N-Nikaius?" She had never seen his eyes this color before. They were just as beautiful as when they were dark and stormy blue, but she felt like she was looking at a completely different person. She had only known him a short time, but this felt like something important.

"Priamos." They both looked up at Waric's voice.

"What's happening?" Aslin asked.

"We were in a meeting. He looked concerned and then suddenly he was gone." Waric sounded concerned, but all Morrigan felt from herself and Nikaius was confusion.

"Priamos?" Those light eyes turned to Morrigan once more. "I don't understand."

"Let's get home, and I will explain." Waric stepped forward, and Priamos looked Morrigan over before giving a low warning grumble. She followed his gaze and frowned, pulling herself closer to him before peeking at Waric around Priamos' shoulder.

"I... I'm not decent enough to leave." She looked from Waric to where her clothes had been discarded. He cleared his throat and nodded before turning to Eda. The shop matron had both of her shop helpers tucked behind her though they both watched with wide eyes.

"I beg your pardon, Madame. Aslin, please get Morrigan something quick and simple to wear." Aslin nodded before tugging Eda and her assistant out of the room.

"Fine mess you've gotten yourself into." Waric chided while stepping closer, ignoring another of Priamos' warning growls and giving one of his own.

Shock curled through Morrigan. She had forgotten that Waric was a changeling as well. She watched them for a few moments, noting that nothing about Priamos was concrete. His emotions flipped from annoyance to affection, to determination, and back in such rapid succession that Morrigan stopped trying to keep up after a few moments.

The next growl Priamos gave was different than the others, and at Waric's responding grumble, Priamos' hand left Morrigan's hair to slide into Waric's. "There you are your big idiot." Waric laughed as he matched Priamos' stance, gripping his shoulder and connecting their foreheads as Priamos had done to Morrigan.

"What happened?" Waric asked, and she assumed he was speaking to her since Priamos had yet to say anything other than 'calm'.

"I... I don't quite know. I was dressing and suddenly Aslin was here and there were hands on me and..." She felt embarrassed just explaining it, and Priamos made another soft sound. His hand trailed slowly up and down her back as she closed her eyes, resting her cheek against his chest. "I... I panicked."

"Hey, it happens. It's just really weird that he was so violently pulled to you."

"Waric?" Aslin returned then, stepping into the room without Eda, and approached cautiously, holding out a garment to Waric who turned to Priamos, gesturing to Morrigan.

"'Amos, you have to let her dress." Waric's tone was not unkind, and Priamos gave a soft grumble of approval before slowly peeling himself away from her. He didn't wander far but gave Aslin enough space to help her dress.

"I... I'm so sorry Morrigan... I didn't realize. I was just so mad that someone would put you in something that didn't fit that I didn't even think. I just acted." Aslin bundled the slip that she held and helped Morrigan pull it over her head. Once settled, it shifted, and a weird sort of feeling encompassed her.

The feeling reminded her of when they stepped through the portal at Atce' Plaza. The shift interestingly molded her body, providing support where it was needed but not being too tight or constricting.

"It's magic. It changes depending on the day and what you need. If you want more support, it will give it. It also changes color and style. It's the best thing to have in your wardrobe. Every other outfit can be worn with just this one piece. Eda is divine in mortal form."

"Aslin." Waric's hand tugged her elbow gently. "Now's not the time for fashion."

"Right. Sorry." Aslin frowned and looked around before tugging a dress from the rack. Looking it over, she nodded and helped Morrigan put it on and adjust it. It fit pretty well; a bit tight on the top, but she would take it for the time being.

"We'll come back when you're ready. Let's get home before they crash." Waric gestured to Priamos who looked rather grumpy but also suddenly very tired. "Shifting like that takes a lot out of him." Morrigan's heart ached for how exhausted he looked, and she stepped forward and reached up to gently touch his cheek.

"You should rest." Morrigan was whispering again. Every time they touched, it felt like an intimate moment shared between them. The feeling confused her, but she didn't feel up to picking it apart at that moment.

Priamos' eyes closed, and he pressed his cheek into her hand.

"Alright, here we go." Waric's words were the only warning Morrigan got before Priamos pulled her to him and they teleported again.

Back in the study, Morrigan sighed and pressed her forehead against Priamos' chest as her head spun again. Hopefully, she would get used to teleportation sooner rather than later. Priamos sat them down on the couch. Morrigan smiled softly as she settled against him.

As he stroked his fingers up and down her bare arm, Morrigan hummed. Adoration and weariness were his primary emotions, but they were soft, as if he hadn't quite decided how he felt, but had no other conflicting emotions within him. His chest rumbled softly as he pulled away a bit to assess her before stepping back a bit. Like a small child, he yawned, pressing his palms to his eyes before reaching for her hand. He looked so tired, dark hair falling across his forehead as he blinked sleepily around the room.

"I'm fine," Morrigan's voice was soft as she impulsively reached for him. "You can rest now." She tucked herself closer until his arms wrapped around her and his face pressed into her neck. He rumbled again before he shifted them so that when she was mostly laying down, his large frame settled over her. His head rested carefully on her chest, and he purred softly as her fingers slowly worked through his hair.

Morrigan carefully stroked her fingers through raven locks as Aslin appeared from thin air. "Again, I'm sorry for acting so quickly. I didn't think."

Morrigan's emotions were a bit chaotic at that moment, upset about having been put into a situation she hadn't asked for, warring with understanding for her situation. "It's not alright, but I forgive you. Maybe warn me before you throw me through the void again?" Aslin's eager nod made her hair fall into her eyes before she moved to settle at the table nearby.

The head on her chest didn't stir as she shifted, and she knew Nikaius was well and truly out, but she didn't mind his weight. It was comforting. Everything about him was comforting in such an odd way. She couldn't help but want to bask in him and the way she felt when he was around.

She should be scared, but fear was the furthest emotion from her mind.

She had just met this man and somehow, she was lying on a couch cuddling him.

A noise drew her from her thoughts, and she realized Waric had appeared.

"I don't understand," she whispered. Having Nikaius there, running her fingers through his hair, felt so natural and right that she didn't feel embarrassed to be so thoroughly wrapped up in him.

"It's not my story to tell, but most changelings, the primals anyways," he gestured towards Nikaius, Hawke, and Aquila who had just entered, "have animals within them that come out when they shift." Morrigan nodded. She knew this.

"Nikaius, and his wolf, Priamos, are separate entities."

Chapter Sixteen

Nikaius

Corinth Manor

Gentle fingers stroking through his hair pulled him slowly from the darkness. He hated it when Priamos pulled them so strongly. Nikaius had no control. Especially not as close as he was to drop. Quick shifting always left him feeling disconnected from his emotions and body for some time after Priamos gave control back. This was the first time he was drawn from sleep by the presence of someone other than Waric.

His mate often came through to him in thought long before Priamos gave up the reins, but the fingers in his hair did not belong to Waric. The fingers weren't as long and thin as his, the palm not so broad, but it was soothing, the fingers, as well as the scent of warm summer rain. Those fingertips carefully traced his ear before stroking up across his temple, along his eyebrows, and down his nose. He inhaled slowly, drawing in that smell deep into him. It drew a soft grumble from Priamos, but he seemed to be content with where he was. Nikaius dared to open his eyes.

"Is it not normal to be separate?" Morrigan's voice was soft as if she was trying not to disturb the calm that had settled over the room. Silence followed her question and Nikaius shifted, pulling his eyes open more. The overhead light was too much though, and he groaned softly, shifting to turn away from it.

Morrigan's soft laugh buzzed against his cheek, and he sat up, startled to realize he had been lying on her.

"Good morning." He was curious to know how she wasn't startled or upset by how close they had been, but he didn't ask about it, instead ran his hand through his hair and gave her a small smile.

Hawke lingered by the door, looking rather bored. Aslin and Aquila played cards at the small table to his left. Waric raised his eyebrows when Nikaius turned his attention to him. He tilted his head in confusion before their attention was drawn to Morrigan again. She gave a little chortle as she reached for him. "Your hair is quite wild, Nikaius." She didn't seem to be bothered by their closeness as she reached up to smooth the lock of hair along the side of his head.

"What happened?" He pulled away from her, carefully catching her wrist and dropping both of their hands onto the couch between them.

"I was hoping you could tell us." Waric frowned as he leaned his elbows on his knees, hands clasped between them as he looked up at Nikaius.

"I don't..." Nikaius let out a slow breath as he tried to think back to the last thing he remembered. "I was uncomfortable all of a sudden, then Priamos had taken over." He actively avoided Morrigan's eyes as he ran his hand through his hair again. "I felt like he was ripping me from existence for a moment. And now here we are." Had he and Priamos done something embarrassing? No one seemed exceptionally flustered. He was the only one making a big deal out of it.

"And now we're here." Hawke laughed darkly from the door and Nikaius frowned. Something was off with his friend. He made a note to speak with Hawke about it later on, once he fixed whatever Priamos fucked up.

"What happened in between?" Nikaius asked.

"I'm not quite sure, to be honest." Waric leaned back, ruffling his dark hair with one hand. "One moment you were in the library, the next you were in Madame Eda's, growling over Morrigan."

"Growling?" A flare of anger flooded through his memory, and he shuddered as he turned to Morrigan so he could look her over. "He didn't hurt you, did he?"

"Quite the opposite. I was having a panic attack." Her voice was soft, and a haze of embarrassment rolled off her as she picked at the skin around her thumbnail. "Everything was cold, and I couldn't figure out what was real or not..." Her voice trailed off, and he looked up at Waric in alarm.

"What do you mean?" Waric's head tilted and Nikaius couldn't help the flair of affection that surged through him when Waric tilted his head like a confused puppy.

Don't start drooling now. Waric's voice flicked through Nikaius' head, but Morrigan continued before he could respond.

"I don't... I don't know how to explain it." Morrigan whispered, her cheeks pink.

"It's alright. I think I know what you mean. I get lost sometimes too." He cautiously brushed his thumb along the back of her hand as she stared at the hem of the dress she wore. Taking a slow breath, he relaxed a bit, leaning his head over the back of the couch, eyes trained on the ceiling. "You asked if it was normal to be separate from our animals? It's not." Something was grounding about touching her as he talked.

"Is it an alpha thing?" The confident way in which she asked as if she already knew the answer made him laugh a little. She was so divine.

Waric's laugh echoed through Nikaius' head again, and he had to clear his throat and shake himself from where his mind had wandered to all the ways he would make sure she never fought those demons again. "Yes, and no. It was caused by an alpha, but it's not normal. I think I'm the only one."

"I heard that Imriel Gorlassar had a similar experience." Hawke was still holding vigil by the door, but his words surprised Nikaius.

"When did you hear this?" Waric shot up, but Nikaius held up a hand. He could smell the agitation that came from his mate, and he preferred to prevent any more chaos for the moment.

"Selection Night."

"Has he responded to the Solstice invite?" Aslin asked, setting her cards aside to turn and face Hawke.

"I don't know."

"I'll find out." Aslin stood and Aquila rose from her chair as well, following her from the room.

"I'm still confused." Morrigan's voice seemed to dissolve the sudden tension in the air as Waric settled back down into his chair and Hawke returned his attention to the door. Something put the captain on edge and Nikaius wondered what because it was so unusual.

"Ah... Right... Well." Nikaius stood and stepped over to the fireplace. "When we were children, Bastian, my brother, was stronger than me. He was bigger and older. He's got two and a half years on me. He was marked to be the future high lord when he presented early and as an alpha no less. I've mentioned that having two sons was rare in our line; having two alphas is nearly unheard of. My animal didn't present at the same age as Bastian's did. I hit ten, then eleven, and never hit a point where it came naturally. My brother thought it was the funniest thing in the world." Nikaius heard someone shift, but he kept his eyes trained on the landscape hanging above the mantle, bottom lip between his teeth.

Waric crept into his peripheral, offering a glass of brandy as he took over the story. "It was Bastian's fifteenth birthday. A huge thing was held for his coming of age. He and some of the older boys had been teasing me, and in came awkward and gangly Nikaius, tripping over himself trying to stand up to his big brother. Bastian had just come into some of the stronger alpha traits, such as compulsion and alpha commands."

It wasn't even lunchtime, and they had broken into the liquor. Today was going to be a day. Nikaius could feel it in his bones. He took over the story. "He held me by the throat and forced me to shift." He took a drink of the brandy, letting it burn down his throat and hissing out a breath through his teeth before continuing. "It was so painful." His voice broke at the memory, and he wiped the moisture from his drink from his bottom lip with his thumb.

"He took a lot of joy out of it once he realized he could do it. Whenever someone he wanted to impress was within hearing and seeing range, he would force it."

"That's how we became friends too." Hawke's voice was almost affectionate, the crinkle around his eyes showing Nikaius the smile on his face was genuine. Leaning back against the wall, he picked at one of the dreadlocks in his hair. "He was positively scrawny when I first met him. This tiny thing that was dragged around by his elder brother like a puppy on a leash." Hawke, Waric, and Nikaius all chuckled.

"You punched him in the mouth when he tried to make Nik shift in front of all of us gathered." Waric's voice was full of laughter, and Nikaius set the side of his lips kick up in a smirk.

"Six months later was my thirteenth birthday." He finally allowed himself to look back at Morrigan. His eyes wandered over her, face pale and jade eyes interested but holding a bit of sadness within them. "Something within me snapped when Bastian swung back. Priamos shifted us and almost took a chunk of Bastian's leg. Priamos took over for almost a week. The only people he would let near were my mother, Hawke, and Waric. We had marked them as part of our pack at that point."

"Then came Aslin." Aslin's sing-song voice preceded her through the door, and Morrigan turned to smile at her. It warmed Nikaius to see that she was settling in so well with his pack. "I was just a girl who got lost." She sat primly on the loveseat across from Morrigan, the picture of a well-trained lady her friends knew she wasn't.

"Got lost my ass." Waric plopped himself down next to Aslin, half throwing himself into her lap.

"His father decided to start setting him up once he hit marrying age." Waric laughed at the look Aslin gave Morrigan as if the other would understand her visual cues. "Guess who was the lucky girl who got to be dragged in front of the high lord to be courted by his son." Nikaius snickered at Aslin's tone.

Downing the rest of his drink, Nikaius moved to cautiously sit next to Morrigan once again.

"Unfortunately, for those of us who are so inclined, you prefer the fairer folk." Waric teased Aslin, poking her cheek.

"I hardly count Aquila to be fair." Hawke nudged his sister who tried to hide a shy smile as she looked away from them. She was used to the teasing but knowing how she and Aslin felt about each other made it sweeter somehow.

"So, you're his pack?" Morrigan's voice was soft as Nikaius watched her suck her bottom lip between her teeth to chew it. Impulsively, he reached forward to catch her chin, pulling her lip free with his thumb.

She turned to him with wide doe eyes, and he realized what he had done. Her embarrassment mingled more thickly in her scent as well as another that stunned him.

Mate. Priamos purred in the back of his head, and he shook himself again.

Shit.

Think.

Fuck.

"You'll aggravate the cut." It was a pitiful excuse. The spot that had split when Elijah had struck her several nights before had healed quickly with the salve and was nothing more than dry skin. But she nodded, pink dusting her cheeks as she turned her attention to her hands in her lap. Her smell intensified, and he had to curl his hands into fists to keep from touching her again. He really, really shouldn't try to tempt her smell to deepen.

Everything throbbed within him for a second.

Yes.

Nope.

She had asked a question.

Focus.

"To answer your question, yes. They're my pack. We benefit each other in many ways."

"How does one become a member of your pack?" She asked softly, her eyes still trained on her hands. Nikaius wanted to take one and tell her he would give her the stars if she asked. But Waric's voice cut in before he could. "There's a blood oath..." Nikaius' mouth fell open.

May the winter goddess Skia skin him alive.

Waric turned to Hawke with a broad grin when the top of Morrigan's ears turned pink.

Hawke grinned as well. "You do it naked." Morrigan's hand flew to her mouth, and she turned to face Aslin and Aquila.

Oh, fucking Fates.

"At the winter solstice..." Waric added.

Aslin shoved Waric off her lap, then moved to stand. "Shut up you idiots."

"Just because that is how you perverts do things, doesn't mean that applies to everyone." Aquila shook her head.

Morrigan's eyes jumped from person to person and Nikaius sighed, pinching the bridge of his nose, his headache returning.

It wasn't the only problem he was suddenly having, but if he ignored that in favor of the headache, maybe it would resolve itself. He shook his head, shoving up a mental wall to try to keep Priamos' primal desires from bleeding out into their joined space.

He would love nothing more than to give in, but with the others around, it would be a problem. Without knowing how Morrigan felt, it would be an even larger one.

Waric and Hawke guffawed at the door.

"That's enough." He didn't mean the words to bark out as they did, but he just wanted silence, and his tone guaranteed that. "It's been a long morning." He offered his hand to Morrigan. "I'll walk you back to your room, and you can rest before lunch." Her hand was small in his, but it felt so nice when she accepted. There always seemed to be a crackle of energy between them whenever their palms touched, but Morrigan either didn't notice or she just didn't show it when she did.

Chapter Seventeen

Morrigan

Corinth Manor

The trip from the study to Morrigan's room was only a few doors down but being by Nikaius' side for a short time was more than worth it. "I'm sorry that happened to you," she said, looking up at him as they walked.

"I don't want your pity, Morrigan. I stopped feeling sorry for myself years ago." He stopped them outside her door, but she wasn't ready to leave his presence just yet.

"That's not what I meant." As he reached for the handle of the door, she stepped into his path, impulsively reaching up to touch his cheek. He leaned his face into her hand, letting out a soft breath as his eyes closed. "I know what it feels like to not have control over yourself or things that happen to you." She wished she could share things with others, that she could give him calm and peace to combat the confusion and distress she felt from him. She wished she could let him know her intentions through her touch. His exhaustion lingered just under the surface, and she wanted nothing more than to take all the bad things away.

How could she care so deeply for someone she had just met?

"I feel terrible saying I'm glad. I'm not glad you went through that, but I'm glad you survived... We survived. It's nice to know someone understands, although I hate that it's you." Despite the small smile on his face, hurt stung in her chest. She pulled away quickly.

The sudden loss of contact made him look up at her in surprise. "Morrigan?"

"You hate that it's me?" She shouldn't be so upset by this, but the pain still came, a little zap of electricity to her heart. She dropped her hand and crossed her arms over her chest.

"No." His hands fluttered within her line of sight before he grasped her chin, lifting it to catch her eye. "I hate that you've had to go through something similar."

"M-Maybe I deserved it. My existence is enough to prove that." Morrigan tried to disengage from his grasp but when she moved, he followed, his thumb pressing gently against her bottom lip again, stroking over where the cut had been in the corner.

"I hardly believe that." His voice dipped into a whisper, and her back made contact with the wall. He leaned over her, resting his forearm on the wall above her head, and tipped her chin up so she could look into his eyes again. "I think the Fates destined you to great things, Morrigan. I can see it..." he leaned down more, his warm breath dancing across her lips as his words softened, his voice lowering. "I can almost taste it..."

This time, she didn't wait for him to make the first move. Even though everything about his body language screamed that he had control, Morrigan decided that she wanted it at that moment. She rose on her toes and fisted his shirt, dragging him down to meet her in the middle. Like the night earlier in the week, his lips on hers were a shock, like static electricity crackling between them, but it was a welcomed feeling. She had never felt so safe in the hands of a man before. The only other person she had ever cared for was simply a boy compared to Nikaius.

The hand on her chin grounded her, tethered her to him as he adjusted the kiss, and she was surprised when he didn't pull away. The way he kissed bled experience but the emotions that poured in with it; shock, amusement, pleasure, and joy, those told more than his words ever could.

She dared to reach up her hand, stroking it first along his jaw and then up so she could brush her thumb along his cheekbone. His groan of approval flooded her with courage, encouraging her actions. His hand dropped from her chin to her waist, and he pulled her closer, their chests flush against one another.

A laugh from down the hall caught her attention, and she froze. It sounded eerily like her sister, Amara, and she looked up at Nikaius with wide eyes. "What was that?"

"I... I don't know. The only people who are here are back there, in the study." Nikaius stepped in front of her as the disembodied giggle happened again. Chills raced down her spine as she clung to the shirt at Nikaius' back. "Stay here, go to your room, and lock the door."

"No. I'm coming with you." She moved to step around him, but his hand caught her across the stomach, and he frowned down at her.

"Stay behind me at least. I'm better equipped to take dark magic than you are." Her inadequacy laid out so plainly stung, but he had a point and she nodded.

Nikaius stepped cautiously, his footsteps soundless on the floor, but the rest of the hallway was empty. "Waric! Hawke!" Nikaius' voice was loud in the quiet hall and they waited. The two appeared shortly after in front of them, and Morrigan startled. She had thought they would have come from the study, not appearing there magically.

"Something is amiss. Search the grounds to see if we have a stranger among us." Hawke and Waric nodded as if it wasn't anything new.

"Come, I'll check your room." Morrigan watched Waric and Hawke disappear before nodding at Nikaius' words. A dull ache had started behind her eyes, and she was suddenly tired once more. Nikaius paused them at the door, his eyebrows dipping into a frown as he stepped inside. Curiosity ate at her, but she knew that if there was someone in her room or the chambers within, she would be of little help to him in a fight or anything magic related. As Nikaius had so blandly put it, Morrigan wasn't cut out to combat any type of dark magic that could be used because her gift was not of the same kind.

While she enjoyed being able to share some bit of empathy with those around her, she ultimately knew her power was useless. What good was a girl whose only talent was being able to tell how people felt? Sure, Elijah and Amara had teased her about it every time she had tried to tell them about her powers as a child. They would laugh and state that her supposed powers would be useful if only she could manipulate other's emotions to turn someone into a brainless warrior. Both of those ideas were repulsive, but at least then her powers would have some use.

She was startled when Nikaius' fingers caught her chin again. She was so deep in her thoughts, she hadn't noticed his approach. "Are you alright?" she asked suddenly, alarmed by the set of his eyebrows and the concern bleeding into her skin.

"No. Come with me." As he stepped out into the hall, Morrigan caught a glance of her room. Somehow, the magic on the balcony doors had been broken, allowing snow to enter her room. The way it looked scattered across the floor was serene, but the heeled footprints within them were not.

"What's happening?" Nikaius' grasp on her hand remained firm as he tugged her along behind him.

"I don't know." His emotions warred within him, although worry was the most predominant among them. "I don't know how someone broke the wards."

"What do you mean?"

"The magic that surrounds the balcony, those are pretty powerful wards, the elements can't get past them. You can still feel the chill in the air or the warmth of the sun, but things like rain and snow shouldn't be able to pass the doors of your room."

"Why my room though?"

"I'd like to know that as well. Has anyone from outside the Enclave been in your room recently?"

"I don't know. I'm not in there every hour of the day," Morrigan chewed her bottom lip as she allowed herself to be tugged along behind Nikaius. "The butler? There was a man who brought my trunk with my belongings this morning. He worked for Elijah. Do you think he did something? He was only there for a few moments. Aslin would know, wouldn't she? She came with him."

"Hmm. I'll have to ask her, but for now, you can use my room. I'll take the extra guest room for the time being until we can get a hold of a drafter to see what they think about the ward and if they can stabilize and repair it."

"A drafter?"

"They've got a particular spell set that focuses primarily on protection wards and the like." Morrigan jumped a bit when Hawke spoke behind them, his voice tense. "I couldn't find any sign of forced entry. Someone whose blood was tied to the wards can break them, but I don't know anyone here who could do such a thing."

"A-Am I tied to the wards?" Morrigan turned her wide eyes up to Nikaius who gave her a small smile.

"You are, why?"

"I thought I heard my sister's laugh."

"It's probable, but I know your sister, and she doesn't have that type of power." Waric frowned, crossing his arms over his chest. "The powers your family holds are not as capable as they believe, aside from Mae's. No offense."

"I know what I heard. We're twins, cut from the same cloth, when she's near, I somehow know." When Morrigan looked up, she realized how stupid she sounded. Embarrassment flooded through her, and she cleared her throat and looked away. "That makes no sense, sorry."

"I get it." Hawke's voice was hard like something was bothering him about the fact that they shared something in common. As he crossed his arms over his chest, the door to the study opened and Aquila stepped out, her hand outstretched to keep Aslin behind her as Nikaius had done to Morrigan moments earlier.

"What's going on?" Aquila's eyes bypassed everyone for Hawke, and Morrigan knew what he meant by understanding what she had said.

Growing up, she had heard that some twins were believed to be soulmates and had some forms of mind connections much like the ones that were rumored to happen when true mates became one. Amara and Morrigan never had that. As they all stood silently in the hall, it felt as if an entire conversation was happening between Hawke and Aquila with only the contact of their eyes.

"Someone's breached the wards." Aslin frowned as Morrigan explained, and her attention drew to Aquila as well.

"No one has been in or out since Elijah stayed. Our residence is private and even those that come in to help aren't just random people." Aslin looked as confused as Morrigan felt. It was reassuring that they both didn't understand it, but also a little jarring to realize that it seemed to be just Morrigan's room that had been affected.

"The man who brought my trunk earlier was a man from Be'Sala under my brother's employment."

"Yes, but I escorted him off the property myself," Hawke responded, his voice low but not in the argumentative tone he had used before. This one was softer, as if he was trying to reassure her. His behavior gave her a bit of whiplash, but she smiled, grateful to have the knowledge regardless.

"The house is clear so we should be cautious but continue." Waric's low voice drew her attention. He looked ragged and windblown. "There's a storm brewing, and it'll probably hit close to dark so we might want to prepare. It's pretty nasty from what correspondents say." Everyone nodded.

"I have to go back to court." Nikaius sighed as he ran his hand through his hair, dislodging it so that it stuck up slightly again. "Let's set you up in my room until we can have the wards fixed in yours, yeah?"

"I could just take the guest room, it's fine." Morrigan didn't want him to feel obligated to give up his room, and she was being sincere about being fine with the guest room. Her actual room still felt like one anyways.

"The guest room is next to the study, both rooms are built into the mountain, so they are mostly underground and have no natural light. There's no reason for you to be cooped up in an enclosed room." The fact that he knew she had enjoyed the sun in her room made her think that Aslin had told him how she had caught Morrigan standing quietly in the sunshine more than once over the last few days.

"Thank you." Her voice broke a little, but Nikaius' lips tipped to one side, and he gave a small nod before gesturing their group forward.

"Alright, we have more important things to do than stand in the hall." Waric chuckled as they headed back toward the study.

Nikaius' room was at the end of the hall, on the other side of the bathing chamber that they both shared access to. Of course, there access to the bathroom from the hall and now that she had thought about it, the fact that she had been set up in that guest suite instead of the other made her curious. Usually, the queen's suite was the only other room to share a bathroom with the master suite, or so she had been led to believe by the layout of every other house since she was a child.

She was thinking too much about it, right?

When he pushed open the door to his room, she paused in the doorway. Her brother's room had always been cluttered with whatever pastime he enjoyed, particularly things surrounding the history of magic, but Nikaius' room was simple and clean.

The furniture matched Morrigan's except in all dark wood as opposed to the light wood in her room. It was a complete contrast but almost complementary with the deep jewel-toned bedding and drapery. She realized the balcony of his room faced a different direction than hers, and she was drawn to it immediately, curious about what view she would find.

Drawing back the curtain, she gave a soft sigh. His room overlooked the courtyard. The morning had been bleak when she had woken up, reminding her of home, but the courtyard was a serene winter landscape that took her breath away as much the second time as it had the first.

"Morrigan?" Nikaius looked concerned when she looked over her shoulder at him. She had just walked by him to the balcony, so the concern was warranted.

"I forgot the magic extended to the courtyard," she told him shyly, pulling her hair over her shoulder to twist in her hands. "It's never snowed so pretty at home... back home... where I grew up, I mean."

"Well, I'm glad someone enjoys it as much as I do. We shall have to get you properly fitted for some decent warm clothes and then you can spend all day in it if you wish." The mention of clothes made her shudder at remembering how the morning had started. Nikaius must have caught her reaction because he continued. "Not today of course. I'll fetch your cloak and boots from your room." His eyes wandered over her, his eyes flashing that interesting light blue for an instant before he turned and left the room.

Morrigan breathed out slowly when he left, willing her nerves to calm. The start of the day had been crazy, and the headache still lingered behind her eyes, so laying down for a bit didn't sound too bad. She had only made it a few steps toward the bed when a noise from the bathroom startled her.

The door was ajar and opened easily when she touched it. That same eerie giggle from earlier echoed throughout the room and suddenly she was so chilled, she felt like she was naked in the snow.

"Nikaius?" The cold hurt her chest and made her cough deeply. Another giggle. It sounded just like Amara's laugh. The pressure behind her eyes worsened, and she turned to flee the room only to run directly into Nikaius' chest.

The growl from his throat was louder than any of the ones from earlier in the day, and his hand was rough as he yanked Morrigan around behind him, bringing her down into a crouch. Sounds mingled and echoed through the room.

Something was there.

Morrigan didn't have a name for it, but Nikaius and Priamos felt it, and she could too, a crackling in the air that made the hair on her skin raise. "Leave." She jumped at the loud bark of Priamos' voice as it echoed through the room.

Nikaius no longer stood in front of her. His posture was just as different as his voice, larger and more commanding. Morrigan thought he had been talking to whatever was in the room, but when his cool eyes turned on her, everything went cold, and her breath ceased in her chest.

"Morrigan, leave."

"What? No!" She reached for him, but suddenly something cold wrapped itself around her stomach and throat, stopping her scream from escaping. Terror flooded through her as she reached up to try to pull the ice away from her throat. She felt nothing from the places where her skin made contact with it. Did the thing even have skin?

Priamos' eyes were wide as he looked at Morrigan and whatever had a hold of her raised her, as if standing so high her feet couldn't touch the ground. She tried to struggle, tried to claw through the arm, but shards of ice were the only thing that stripped away when she tried.

The world warped as the vise around her throat squeezed harder, and she whimpered through what little breath she could manage. Kicking her feet did nothing but slide through the air.

Why wasn't he doing anything?

Chapter Eighteen

Nikaius and Morrigan

Corinth Manor

Nikaius had never seen an ice golem in real life, and he hadn't expected to see it when he turned to tell Morrigan to leave. When he had entered the bathroom after she cried out for him, he had sensed the magic, and tasted its wrongness on his tongue, but hadn't anticipated seeing *that*.

He had wanted to tell Morrigan to leave, but before either of them could do anything, she had been snatched up by the thing. He reached through the bond to seek out Waric's signature and pulled as hard as he could once he found it, but Waric didn't come.

The fact that this thing had somehow sealed off the room without his knowledge was astounding. Ice golems were large, animated ice creatures. Usually, they were chaotic and clumsy and easy to spot because of their snowy appearance; however, this one was uncharacteristically clear, and he then realized why they had missed it when they first entered. He could see completely through it and when he shifted, it became almost invisible. It looked as if Morrigan was being suspended by nothing.

He had so many questions, the biggest one being how this thing even existed. He didn't know of anyone who could create something so well-crafted and sneak it past the manor's wards.

A thought dawned on him then as he tried to figure out the best way to approach the situation. If it was so well crafted out of magic, the usual plan of attack wouldn't work.

Priamos grumbled from deep within and this time, Nikaius gladly stepped aside to let him take over.

Being aware while also not in control of one's body was weird, but at the same time, it was needed, especially in this situation.

He didn't like how long it took Priamos to work out a plan. Priamos was the statistician between the two of them. Their primal instincts should have blended, but the Fates had always had different plans for them. The ability to split had saved his ass sometimes, like now, but he was more concerned with the thing in front of them and how they were going to save Morrigan than anything else.

After a moment of assessment, something tickled in the back of his mind and Priamos faded away, allowing Nikaius awareness again. Waric hadn't picked up his call, but someone had realized they were missing.

"Morrigan, look at me. It's going to be fine. You're going to be fine, okay? Trust me." Something deep within him settled when she nodded. His senses had been particularly attuned to her before, but now he could almost hear how quickly her heart was beating in her chest.

Priamos grumbled in the back of his head and Nikaius nodded, moving to step to the side. The large creature followed them with his head. As crystalline as it was, he couldn't tell if there were any eyes in its head or not, but it shuffled along as he moved.

Morrigan whimpered as it shifted its hold on her, moving to swipe at Nikaius with one massive hand. Thankfully, he was faster than it was and could dodge out of the way. Ice and tile scattered as its massive claws made contact with the floor, and he had to throw up his hand to guard his face from the shards.

The motion left his side open enough that it could clip him as it swung back for another swipe. Whoever was guiding this thing wasn't much of a combatant. The only thing going for the golem was its size and strength. The fact that it had Morrigan didn't hurt.

"Come on!" He walked backward, trying to taunt it into dropping Morrigan. When it tried to swing again, this time with a projectile of ice, Nikaius was able to dodge and jump out of the way with enough time to strike it as well, but claws were no match for its ice. It swung a bolt of ice again, and Nikaius rolled out of the way, watching as it crashed through the back wall. Taking hold of another large shard, he mustered all of his strength to throw it.

Expecting it to just shatter against the thing, Nikaius was surprised when it jerked back, the pointed end of the icicle sticking out the side of its neck.

This didn't deter its advance much, but it gave Nikaius enough pause to use the now ice-covered floor to his advantage. Taking a running start, he slid beneath it, dragging his claws along its ankle as a tether to control just how far he went.

The creature let out a loud screech as it tried to turn and find Nikaius, but he clung to its leg to avoid being trampled. A warped, high-pitched giggle echoed through the room, and Morrigan screamed.

Everything within him pulsed painfully, and his heart stopped as she was flung through the air. Releasing the thing, Nikaius bolted as quickly as he could in hopes of catching her. He could withstand that fall, but he wasn't sure she would. On the dry ground, he was rather adept at speed and control, but with ice beneath his feet, his control lacked severely, and as he turned, he slid and Morrigan crashed into him. He hadn't been able to brace himself, and they both tumbled to the floor.

Her small body was so cold against his, the effect of her having been entrapped in ice for so many minutes. Priamos grumbled with displeasure at her state. Nikaius was unhappy with how easily Priamos, and his own body, reacted to being so close to her. She didn't seem to notice as she moved to sit up, her body trembling as her teeth chattered with the force of it. Sitting up, he wrapped his arms around her, impulsively pulling her closer before noticing that the golem's distraction had ceased, and it had focused on them again.

The giggle sounded again, and the creature swung out another round of icicles. Morrigan made a high-pitched startled sound as he rolled them so he could protect her from the shower of ice that rained down upon them when the ice hit the stone wall. She had been right; the giggle sounded a lot like one she gave when she had reached up to brush the hair from his eyes with a breathless "thanks."

"We have about fifteen seconds." Nikaius had been keeping track of each wave of ice and pulled them both up, trying to get an idea of what to do next.

The large shard of ice the golem had flung at the beginning had lodged far enough into the wall that cold wind blew in through the hole around it. A pull at his consciousness made Nikaius realize that the bond had snapped back into place somehow. Instead of heeding the call, he pulled back. Waric appeared in front of them, looking confused.

Another giggle sounded.

"Shit. Get down." Nikaius looked over his shoulder and swept Morrigan's feet out from under her, his arms banding around her waist and shoulders as he dropped them to the floor again, Waric following a second later.

"What the fuck is going on? Where were you? How the fuck did an ice golem get in?"

"*I don't fucking know.*" Priamos had enough of everything and shoved his way to the surface. "*We need to get her out of here.*" Another shower of ice sprayed over them and suddenly the temperature plunged even more.

"Ah fuck." Waric looked between Priamos and Morrigan. "We need Aslin." The creature clumsily swung again. Somehow, they had found their way into an alcove where the creature's swings couldn't get them, but they were still cornered.

As much as he hated to admit it, the extent of his power was no match to this. Realization dawned on him then. "You're going to hate this. I'm sorry." Clutching Morrigan to him, he grasped Waric's shoulder and pulled all the energy he could into his chest before willing them into the darkness and picturing the study.

It had been a long time since Nikaius had teleported with more than one person. So much so that dizziness hit him as they came through the wall into the study. Morrigan clung to him, shivers wracking her body as she sobbed softly against his chest.

"Shh. You're safe, we're safe." He reached up and pet her hair, stroking the damp strands from her face as he looked her over. She was pale, and her lips were a shade of purple blue that concerned him.

As he stepped toward the fireplace to warm them, Aslin burst into the study with a raised bat, ready to strike whatever she found. "Oh, my Fates! Where have you been?" Aslin rushed towards them, slamming herself into their sides as she wrapped her arms around Morrigan. "One minute you were right behind us and the next you were gone! It's been hours!"

Shock flooded through Nikaius, and he frowned at Morrigan, whose wide eyes had turned to him. "Hours?" Her voice trembled and broke. Nikaius moved to sit them down on the floor by the fire, running his hands up and down her arms.

"The entire town has been on lockdown while we've tried to find you."

"Aslin, what do you mean hours?"

"One moment you were following us and then you were gone."

"It was only a couple of minutes, Aslin, maybe fifteen at the most?" Morrigan's eyes never left Nikaius as she responded to their friend.

"No, it was noontime when you disappeared. It's close to midnight now." Waric shook his head before gesturing towards the door. "If you don't believe me —"

The door slammed open, and Aquila stormed in, swords drawn, and wings flared. She looked haggard and chaotic; brows furrowed as she took in the four people in the room. She was like an avenging guardian Valkyrie that had fought in the war years ago, and Nikaius was proud to have her as a friend. Priamos purred in agreement. Their pack was strong and capable of keeping themselves and their mates safe.

"My lord. What?" Her swords lowered.

"I don't know. It was only a few moments for us." Nikaius returned his attention to Aslin who frowned.

"Temporal shift?"

A loud sound startled all of them and ice shattered against the hall wall behind where Aquila stood. "We have a problem!" Hawke's voice was tense as he slid into view, blocking shards of ice with his sword.

"Right. Ladies, stay here." Waric pulled his sword from the ether and barreled out the door in time to deflect another round of ice.

Aslin nodded, but Morrigan clung to Nikaius as she watched the scene unfold outside the door. "This is my fault."

"No darling, this is the price of being a figurehead. Someone is always out to get you." Pressing a kiss on her forehead, he untangled her fingers from his shirt and stood, willing his own swords into existence before following his friends out into the hall.

Once Waric, Nikaius, and Hawke had left them to fight the now two ice golems in the hall, Aslin and Morrigan sat for a few moments mulling over what was happening.

"I have no idea how an ice golem got into here, that's some strong magic to break our wards and get it in." Aslin's mind seemed to be turning as she looked around the room.

"What type of magic would create that?" Morrigan knew very little about elemental powers, except her siblings who could manipulate ice. She had never seen them do something like that before though. Those in her family held only the most mundane amount of power, nothing that could create the ice golem.

"There are physical manifestations where people have to touch whatever they are manipulating. Visual magic requires you to look at something and manipulate it, and all that is needed for mental is thought and it occurs. My power is mostly mental manipulation. I can create portals, so I just think of the portal opening and where it appears."

Nikaius was confused when he stepped into the hall. The golem had somehow shrunk down and split in two. One was engaged in combat with Hawke, who was slowly chipping away at the weapon that was being wielded by the darker of the two creatures. The second attempted to charge Nikaius, but he was able to block it in time for Waric to ignite his sword with flint. Flames roared to life around his blade, and it easily melted through the arm of the creature.

"Nik." Having a bond with his friends made combat easier and helped him anticipate Waric's plan as he threw his sword to Nikaius who traded him as well. Dropping into a crouch, Nikaius watched as the ice melted away from his combat partner and then regenerated quickly.

"Waric..." The creature was able to draw back the water and refreeze. There was no way they were going to be able to defeat them this way, or on their own.

"I see." Morrigan's abilities would be physical because she has to touch someone to know how they felt, and her sister Mae has to touch people to heal them.
"So, we know this thing isn't being physically manipulated because no one else is here with us and they are not touching it, which leaves mental and visual." Aquila mused aloud.

Creature number two swung at Nikaius, and he tried to swing back, but creature number one slammed into his side. Pain seared through him when he fell into the wall, several ribs snapping in the process. "Fuck."

"My room has a view of the hall and bathroom from the balcony, what would happen if we blocked the balcony doors from view?" Morrigan shivered at the thought. Her hair was still dripping from the particles of ice that had clung to it while they were in the bathroom, but the thought that she had specifically been targeted chilled her even more.
"That's plausible. It's moved so maybe we could figure out which is being used." Aquila nodded, but the look Aslin gave her raised her spirits even more.
"We're not going to stay here, are we?" Aslin asked.
Morrigan smiled and shook her head, finally feeling useful. "Not when it's possible we can help. Can you get us to my room?" Aslin nodded and Morrigan reached for her at the same moment Aquila did.

Nikaius' pain flared, and everything throbbed for a second before Priamos took over. With his claws out, he flung them at the creature that had barreled into them and sunk his teeth into what would have been the throat if this had been some living entity. Ice tore away in chunks but it only seemed to entice the creature's actions further as it wheeled around before flinging them back into the wall. Usually, he and Priamos were better coordinated than this, but most of their opponents were things they had come across before.

He saw stars when his head hit the wall, and everything blacked out for a second as the frozen hand cinched itself around his throat.

Morrigan's head swam for a few moments, and she braced her hands on her knees trying to breathe through the surge of nausea that welled within her.

She hated magic.

Letting out a soft groan, she righted herself, the headache from before throbbing behind her eyes again. She wanted this to be over with so she could rest. It had already been a long day even without the supposed temporal shift that had thrown them off by several hours.

"Nik!" He could barely see Waric through the spots, but he couldn't make out what he was seeing. Had the creature doubled again? It appeared that way.

Aslin and Aquila had already begun moving furniture into position to block the doors, and Morrigan straightened to follow once she was sure her stomach would stay in place. They had covered the balcony, so she went to inspect the bathroom.

The large bit of ice that the creature had used to shatter the outside wall had melted away to allow the wind and rain to blow into the large space, but there was no trace of the golem or its creator. The thing had to have been watched well enough for it to be able to know how to exit through her room and into the hall.

It was frightening to know that someone had been able to manipulate their way into their home and held some malice towards them. What was its purpose?

Shaking her head, she closed the hall access door before heading back to shut the one to her room. "Bathroom is clear, there's no one there." Her trembling had subsided a bit once the door to the bathroom was closed, the chill lessening. She helped as best she could by making sure that every side of the balcony doors were covered before they gathered furs from her bed and headed back towards the hall. They would all need some warmth after this was over.

Entering the hall hadn't quite gone the way she had anticipated. The moment they stepped out of the room, ice came flying at them.

Aquila stepped in front of Morrigan and Aslin, throwing her wings out. Morrigan watched in amazement as the shards either reflected off the ebony feathers or melted upon contact.

"Hawke wasn't joking about not worrying about things impacting your wings," Morrigan murmured. Aquila chuckled before pulling a knife from her waist and turning to throw it at one of the creatures. The knife pierced the thing's head, and it shattered into a thousand shards. Without any contact, the second one shattered as well, and they were all drenched as ice exploded into water.

Nikaius' head throbbed as he struggled to breathe, and the sounds of the room faded before the ice shattered around them like a rock through a windowpane.

"Nikaius!" Morrigan was suddenly there, on her knees in front of him. She had regained some color but was still cold to the touch when she reached out to cup his chin in her hands. "It's fine. We figured it out." He only caught a hint of the grin she threw over her shoulder at the others before the world faded for a second.

Moving to sit up better, his vision cleared.

What had just happened? The entire hallway was soaked, as were the five other members of his household. Hawke and Waric supported some colorful marks and scratches, but the girls were just wet.

"What did you do?" His eyes wandered between Morrigan, Aslin, and Aquila. Everything hurt, but he couldn't put a damper on the pride that mingled in Morrigan's scent. He wanted to bask in it for as long as he could.

"Magic like that has to have some sort of connection, right? Aslin told me. Physical, visual, or mental." Aslin helped Waric stand as Morrigan offered a hand to help Nikaius up. He braced his hand on her shoulder to stand, giving her a nod at her shy smile. "I... I remembered what you said about the wards, and I thought that maybe... Maybe that's where the control was coming from for those..." She licked her lips and looked over her shoulder, "those things. The balcony has a view of the bathroom and hall when both doors are open." Her small hands encompassed one of his as she rubbed it, trying to bring some warmth back to him as he had done with her earlier.

"We blocked the balcony doors with the dresser. There are no windows in the hall, so I figured if…" She licked her trembling lips again. "If there wasn't any line of sight, then whoever was controlling it, maybe that would be the key to breaking the bond and making those things beatable."

"You're brilliant." In the short time since they had met, Morrigan never ceased to amaze him. His heart swelled at the smile she gave, and he couldn't fight Priamos when he decided to scoop Morrigan's face between their hands and kiss her. Nikaius wasn't exactly objecting to kissing her either, even though he knew they were taking a huge chance.

They couldn't have her, not really. She wasn't theirs to have and until she was free to make her own choice without feeling obligated to be whatever she had concluded in her head she should be; they couldn't have her.

Kissing her was warm and freeing, and being near her gave him a feeling he had never felt before. Everything within him and Priamos settled when she was near, and he knew the bond he, Priamos, and Waric suspected they held with her was one that that would never be broken for them. She didn't need to know that though. He forced himself and Priamos away and smiled when she gave a soft, pleased sigh.

"That was smart thinking." Hawke praised as he wiped the blood from his split bottom lip. It would heal with some salve, all their wounds would, except for the stabbing pain in Nikaius' torso. Because the healing salves only worked on external wounds his ribs would take a couple of hours to heal.

"Come on. Let's dry off and then I can tend to you." Morrigan's smile reached her eyes as she tugged his hand gently and led them back down the hall to his room.

Nothing blocked their path this time.

Despite being so cold, Nikaius' hand felt warm in Morrigan's, and she felt giddy with relief that she and Aslin had figured out how to take care of the things that had attacked them.

"Morrigan?" Nikaius' voice pulled her from her thoughts, and she gave him a small smile. Her hands were too cold to distinguish any feeling from where her hands were joined, but he squeezed it gently before bringing it to his lips. "You're amazing. I don't know if I've told you that yet. Blocking the line of sight was a brilliant move. I don't know why none of us thought about it before then."

Morrigan smiled shyly at her toes. "It was a collaborative effort. It felt weird to me that the wards were broken only in my room, and Aslin made the connection about magic types and how they manifested, and we just kind of stuck them together." Thankfully, that outcome was favorable. Morrigan wasn't sure what would have happened if it had been mental manipulation that brought those things to their door. "Do we have any idea why they were even here? You did mention something about being a person of higher power putting you at higher risk, is this something that happens often?"

Nikaius gave a distracted hum as he pushed open the door to his room slowly. Nothing seemed amiss and as he tugged her along to sit in front of the fire, she watched him curiously. His eyes scanned the room again. His shoulders dropped a bit as he took a slow, deep breath. He hadn't seemed to have heard Morrigan speak. "Nikaius?" She tugged his hand gently, but he stood beside her, head tilted as he closed his eyes and took a deep breath. He seemed to be struggling again, as he had been at Madame Eda's.

Gooseflesh had risen across his arms, and Morrigan tilted her head as she ran one hand up his bicep, trying to bring some warmth between them. "Priamos?"

His attention turned to her, pale blue eyes blinking slowly before his shoulders relaxed, and he gave a low soft grumble as he reached up to tuck a lock of wet hair behind Morrigan's hair.

Ah.

It was odd to experience what Waric and Nikaius had talked about, but she could see that now seemed to be one of those days when Priamos and Nikaius fluctuated. She didn't feel like now was the time to ask him questions. They both needed warmth and rest. "Let's gather some blankets and get warmed up, yeah?" His nod was short, and he tugged her towards the bed.

"Stay," he grumbled in that rich voice that sent a curl of calm through her. She nodded absently as his soft command settled over her. It wasn't an alpha command, but one she wanted to obey regardless, just to see what he would do.

Nikaius was kind and warm towards her, and she felt safe with him, but now that she was aware of Priamos' existence, she wanted to know which behaviors were his and which belonged to Nikaius, or if there was any difference at all.

He stepped away to dig in the closet across the room before returning quickly with a long tunic and extra fur draped over his arm. He offered the shirt with a gruff "change" before he began situating the furs on the bed.

She had never really been shy about her body when it came to being around people. The shyness had worn off long ago when that control had been taken from her, but it still felt odd to change with him in the room. Was it because she considered him a friend, and his opinion mattered to her, or because she was genuinely attracted to him?

"Morrigan, don't." His voice sounded strained, and Morrigan turned to him in surprise.

"Don't what?" Why was her voice so high?

He didn't look at her as she fixed the fur, adjusting minute details that only he could see. "I can smell what you're thinking."

He could smell what she was thinking. What was she thinking? She had just been thinking about being... Oh... OH! Self-consciousness flooded through her, and she turned away from him. "That's kind of rude!"

He made an amused sound, and his fingers curled in her hair as she watched him walk by. "Change." He nodded to the tunic in her hand before stepping out of the room.

The room felt colder with his presence gone, even though the temperature hadn't changed. she obeyed quickly, hanging her wet things over the chair nearest the fire before sliding the shirt he had offered over her head. It smelled like warm vanilla and earthy tobacco, a scent she knew from when her father had smoked pipes so long ago. Priamos had given her one of his own shirts to wear. She hadn't realized how large he was in comparison to her until then, the shirt only reaching just a bit above her knees.

Footsteps echoed in the hall, and she dove under the blankets and furs, suddenly embarrassed to have so much skin on display. She didn't want him to get the wrong impression. That might be a bit of a lie, but she didn't know if he would be in the right frame of mind for that. She'd have to ask in the morning if that was something to take into consideration in the future.

Stretching out under the heavy weight of the blankets and furs that warmed her a bit, exhaustion settled over her. She was so tired and ready to sleep off the headache that still lingered behind her eyes.

Chapter Nineteen

Morrigan

Corinth Manor

The door opening pulled Morrigan from sleep sometime later. She wasn't sure how long had passed, and she couldn't remember even falling asleep, but the fire had died down to embers that cast the room into a barely visible red glow. She blinked sleepily, watching Nikaius, or Priamos, she wasn't quite sure who was active at that moment, creeping into the room. He seemed to favor his side a bit as he sat on the edge of the bed. When he leaned down to take off his boots, he gave a soft groan. She had mentioned she was going to tend to him, but she wasn't sure how much time had passed. Surely his wounds should have healed by now.

"Are you alright?" She sat up a bit, and he seemed startled to see her there. He looked fine but moved slower than normal.

"I have some salve for your throat." His voice was gravelly, as if he had been talking for a long time. One boot thudded to the floor and Morrigan watched him wince as he went to reach for the other one. Sighing softly, she pushed the blankets aside, deciding that his pain was more important than her made-up modesty.

Wiggling out of the bed, she made her way around as the lights in the room flared slightly to offer better lighting and warmer floors. She had been told about the house's innate magic; it was what kept the temperatures perfect and the water just right. She still hadn't quite figured out how to work it. Looking him over, she sighed gently. Blood mottled his hair and the side of his face, but she wasn't sure of its source.

She cautiously entered the bathroom and retrieved a small basin and filled it with warm water. Collecting a cloth from the counter and returned to Nikaius' side. She watched him struggle with the boot a moment longer before she gave a soft chuckle. She set the water on the table and knelt in front of him.

"Morrigan."

She shushed him and easily worked the laces free. A tug of the heel and press of the toe and the boot met its mate at the foot of the bed. "I said I would tend to you. Your face is covered in blood" As he opened his mouth, probably to argue, she stood and dipped the cloth into the water. "I know you've probably healed already, but you don't want to bloody the bed." She knew her assumption that he was staying in the room with her was a stretch, but she wanted to tend to him anyways.

He grumbled softly but didn't protest as she dabbed at the drying blood. It took a few minutes, but once most of his face was clean, she determined she couldn't find a source. He must have healed as she assumed, and prodding along his hairline and head didn't seem to bother him.

"There, all done. You should be good as new soon." Wiping her fingers with the cloth, she turned to return it to the bowl, but Nikaius' hand caught her hip. She turned to him in surprise. "Are you okay?"

He shushed her gently as he rose and pulled the salve from the ether. She hadn't realized she had sustained any bruising until he spread the salve along her collarbone. The skin tingled wherever his fingers traced.

"Thank you." Her voice was soft as she whispered her gratitude. Part of her felt like she would break the calm spell around them if she spoke too loudly.

"No. Thank you." His lips pressing to hers made the rest of her thoughts fade.

Everything about him screamed desire and attraction when their skin met, but kissing him always seemed to short-circuit whatever senses she did have. It was a double-sided coin of relief from the constant influx of emotions she got when touching someone, but also left her feeling bereft of the ability to distinguish their feelings on separate planes.

One of his hands slid down her side and around her back, pulling her hips flush with his as the other found her hair and she gasped, pulling away for a moment to pull in a breath and meet his eyes. Ice and storm mixed in his eyes, but she was captivated by him and everything that he was.

"You're beautiful." The compulsion to stay connected to him was strong, so she lifted her hand to trace the lines of his face with her fingers. "Truly you are." He smiled against her fingers as she trailed them along his mouth and jaw but once he was free of her fingers, he kissed her again. They weren't the sloppy, over-eager kisses of a boy, but deeper, and claiming as if he was trying to steal her very soul with a brush of his tongue.

A chill ran down her spine as he shifted against her, and she could feel him hard against her hip. To have someone like him attracted to her was heady, and his desire tempted hers enough that she dared to let her hands wander elsewhere. His firm chest and shoulders felt as nice as they looked, and she knew the strength he carried in them with the way he had carried her previously. He was softer around the middle than she would have anticipated, but she could never fault anyone for that, and it only proved that his strength was out of necessity rather than any sort of vanity that held the attention of her brother and other males she had met. He gave a low rumble as her hands traced his sides, and she paused for a second to make sure she hadn't hurt him. When he didn't pull away she continued her exploration of his torso.

It was nice to know that he wasn't solely focused on appearance, and it gave her more hope that maybe he could be interested in someone like her. It felt right to want to be wanted by him, but it was a new concept as well. She hadn't really wanted anyone's attention since she was young.

"Morrigan." his voice had dropped an octave, his tone sultry as he reached up to brush wayward strands of hair from her face. "It is you who is beautiful, and we're lucky to be able to bear witness to that beauty."

Her cheeks heated, but she didn't dare look away from him, completely enraptured by the dance between the two colors in his eyes as his hands teased along the skin of her backside and hip, slowly drawing the shirt up as he went.

She knew where this was going and rose up to eagerly meet it, kissing him again as he tucked his hand back into the hair at the nape of her neck.

Him gently pulling her hair was guiding, not wrenching as many before had, and it sent a delicious throb through her as she nipped his bottom lip.

He growled. "You play a dangerous game firefly."

"I don't play games I don't intend to win."

Her mind shut down for a moment. *Uh, what? Excuse me? Where did that confidence come from all of a sudden? Fates strike me down.*

Nikaius' answering growl was the only warning she had before she stumbled backward into the wall. Feeling spread across her body from that one contact point and everything within her throbbed.

Was she feeling his arousal? Desire? It crept along her skin the way lust did, but not as prickles of ice. There was no pain in what she was getting from him, so her concern about his head faded into the background.

Her lips parted as he stepped closer. She could feel the heat of him against her chest, her back still pressed to the wall. His warm hand brushed her hair from her face, and she could feel him trace his nose along the curve of her neck, his warm breath on her skin making her tremble.

"You smell divine."

"L-like sunshine, I know." Her trembling ceased as she became hyperaware of what he was doing. The fingers in her hair trailed along the back of her neck before sliding up to cradle her head as he took another deep inhale. His other hand was suddenly on her as well, palm sliding across her back to curl long fingers around her hip.

He had touched her bare skin before when he had convinced her to bathe on her first day in his home, but this was different. It held deeper, more powerful connotations. "Gods, you smell like sunshine and earth." The way he spoke, his voice a low grumble, sent pleasure curling down her spine and straight to her core, the feeling only heightening when his hips drove hers back into the wall.

All questions flew from her mind as she cataloged every place where they touched. She tried not to drown in the sensations he was giving her, but there was so much going on between them that it all curled within her to become the opposite of the winter storm that seemed to wage behind his eyes. She was on fire. Everything hot and warm within her ached and begged her to move.

His teeth teasing the skin of her neck made her inhale sharply, making her head spin a bit at how his desire was so all-encompassing. Her desire rose to meet his with equal fervor. "Nikaius..." His name was a breathy sigh as she shifted, making him groan against the place between her shoulder and her neck.

Thoughts of wondering what it would be like for him to sink his teeth into the spot his tongue now trailed were fleeting, but Nikaius pulled away a bit as if he could sense it. He could smell what the thought did to her; he had said as much and that thought caused her to shudder.

"Tell me to stop, Morrigan." His lips started a slow trail of kisses along her shoulder. "If you don't tell me to stop, I don't know where this will go." His voice sounded pained, but nothing she felt was screaming pain, just heat... and chaos.

Another thrill ran through her as her mind tumbled over the sound of his voice.

Did she want him to stop?

No.

Not when she was curious about where this would go. Curious about how his hands would feel on her skin. How different would it be to be intimate with a changeling? With him? How different would it feel to be with someone she actually cared about and had feelings for? Everything tingled within her at the thought, and Nikaius' chest rumbled.

"W-What if I don't want you to stop?" Her whisper was hard, her voice hitching at the end as Nikaius' hand suddenly slid down the length of her leg. His fingers curled into the hem of the shirt she wore before his fingers slipped underneath and drew the linen higher, his palm spreading across her bare back. The growl that escaped him against her neck was a pleasing sound, almost a purr. The sound went straight to the aching pulse between her legs, and his fingers followed. A noise of protest escaped her lips as he pulled his hips away, but he shushed her with a kiss to her exposed collarbone, his free hand leaving her hair to trace down her other side.

His eyes flashed that enticing winter color, holding her captivated for a few moments until his hand found the tender skin on the inside of her thigh and squeezed. His grip was hard and would probably leave bruises, but at the same time, it sent a thrill through her that begged her hips to rock against him. "Oh, Fates." His hand moved then, soothing over the spots where his fingers had been before he continued.

Her thoughts hyper focused on him, tracking every movement of his hands before snaking her own into his hair. The strands were warm and dry, which meant it had been some time since they had left the hall, but how long was still to be determined.

As his right hand wandered lower, and his fingers dipped into her core, his left hand drew the shirt higher and palmed her breast. His bare hands on her skin felt like electricity crackling straight to her core, each dip of his fingers making her tense and gasp as the sensation and pleasure built in the spots he brushed within her. She felt almost overwhelmed with emotion; hers blurring with his in a way she couldn't comprehend.

Wave after wave of lust and desire curled around her like a welcome embrace as he pressed close again, his hands still moving. Her right hand found his left arm, gripping tightly as she rocked her hips greedily against his hand, her little gasps escaping with each press of his fingers.

Everything went silent when his teeth nipped the skin of her neck again. Her breath hitched and caught in her throat, and she tensed around him. His hand stilled, and he groaned low against her skin. Blood pounded in her ears and their ragged breaths were the only thing she could hear. His hands stroked every sensitive area he could find, making lightning zip through her veins as he dragged a nail across her nipple, and her knees trembled as his thumb caught her sensitive clit.

His teeth sank into her shoulder then, and everything tumbled down in an instant. Her nails dug into him as she clung to his back and shoulders. The entire world whited out for a moment, and she let out a giddy laugh. The barrier snapped and every thought and emotion flooded through her like white noise and blinding heat. Deafened to anything that wasn't his breath or the pounding of her heart, she wasn't sure if she even made a sound, as her breath rushed from her in heavy pants as her head met the wall.

His tongue soothed the stinging mark as she relaxed against him, his low grumble vibrating against her chest. Her entire body felt fevered, but she was no longer scared.

No longer scared of the unknown, or of whatever darkness seemed to lurk under Nikaius' skin or questioning the control Priamos held. She felt that they wouldn't hurt her, and somehow, she knew deep in her soul that she was right. That they were right for each other in an earth-shattering way.

She didn't register his hands moving until she was spun, breath forced from her lungs as they tumbled backward into the bed. His hands gathered hers and raised them above her head. She marveled at how large they were since he only needed one to hold both of hers in place.

His other hand, now free, repeated the path it had taken earlier, slowly sliding the shirt he had given her up and over her hips and chest. Knowing he could easily see her in the dim light thanks to his superior eyesight, she trembled at being held so bare before him.

"Please." She wanted to touch him, for him to touch her more, wanted more. She just wanted.

Wanting wasn't new for her, but getting what she wanted was, and his eager response to lean in and kiss her was something she didn't want to get used to.

He leaned on his forearm and captured her soul through another simple kiss. She knew kisses weren't meant to feel like this all the time, but in this instance, for whatever reason, it felt like there was a sudden connection between them that hadn't been there before.

The bite on her throat throbbed as his fingers trailed along her waist and hips. He didn't touch her where she ached again, but explored her with his fingers for a few moments, teasing gooseflesh to the surface of her skin.

"You're so beautiful. I wonder if you taste as wonderful as you smell." Morrigan gave a choked little laugh at his words. Hadn't he just tasted her by the bite on her skin?

"You already know that." She grinned, playfully lifting her chin a bit so he could see the mark he left.

Something about seeing that mark sobered him, and he pulled away, slipping his hand up to grasp her chin and tilt it so he could get a better look. His eyes flicked from the bite to her eyes and back. "Morrigan..."

Sitting up, Morrigan reached for him, curling her fingers in his hair. "Nikaius, it's fine. I'm not upset about it. In fact," she gave a feral grin, daringly shifting to her knees to tug him closer by the nape of his neck, seeking out a kiss that he willingly obliged, "I'm open for more."

"Morrigan." This time, her name was a soft groan under his breath. "You're going to be the death of me."

"Good." Giggling, she gently tugged his hair. "At least I'll be of some use."

"You're always useful to me, and not like that." Nikaius leveled her with a look that broadened her grin. How he could read her so easily was as funny as it was intriguing.

"Mhm." Untangling her hands from his hair, she let them wander down to tug carefully at the hem of his shirt. Nikaius gave a low groan as he pulled the shirt up and over in one smooth motion, and she realized why when he was bare.

What she had thought would be flawless skin was marred with small scars and mottled bruising coloring his side. With the quick healing that most changelings possessed, she hadn't thought he would carry scars.

"Your ribs.... That must hurt." She carefully stroked her fingers along the yellow and red mark, and he hummed gently.

His contentedness curled through her with an edge of nervousness. Was he nervous that she was touching him?

"It didn't really, not nearly as bad as this one." Shifting, he bared his unbruised side to her to show a long scar that cut along his side, his skin, interrupting the long span of unblemished skin. From a distance it would be hard to notice, but closer she could notice that it's a few shades lighter, lacking the golden undertones the rest of his body had. He gave a soft grumble when she traced it with her fingers goosebumps spreading out from where her fingers touched. The skin twitched under her hand, and she laughed, shifting away to tug up the shirt to show her the same side.

"I have the same scar." She turned a bit. "I fell off a horse last year. That's how Mae met Santiago De'Lyon. They're both healers. Mae did her best for someone mostly untrained. I ended up needing stitches though."

"Stitches?"

"Yeah… Like…" How did one explain something so mundane to someone who was high-born and lived a life full of magic and healing salves? "You know the sewing that Aslin does?"

"They embroidered your skin?" He leaned down to look at the scar with a puzzled expression. His touch made her skin tingle, and the stars on his forearm shimmered, but she laughed gently and tried to wiggle away.

"Be'Sala doesn't have much in the way of good healers most of the time. I was lucky that Santi had been visiting. He was an apprentice with a mortal surgeon at the time and knew basic healing strategies. With his help, Mae was able to heal most of it after a few minutes."

"Mmm. Mine was Bastian's claws."

"His claws?!"

"It wasn't the first or last time. I just fought him hard over this one."

"Stupid changeling genes."

A gruff laugh was the only warning she had before his hand slid down her back, and he pulled her close again. "You like my changeling genes."

"They certainly don't hurt. Good thing I like my men large and in charge."

"Large and in charge you say?" His voice dropped, and his grin grew dark.

"Yep." Something about that look made her feel like prey getting ready to be attacked by the predator.

Attack he did, leaning forward to capture her mouth again as he bent her to him.

Their chests pressed together as he rucked her shirt up further before pulling away to pull it off completely. He gave another growl before he easily grasped her by the back of her thighs and hoisted her up to hook them over his hips.

"Holy Fates."

He turned and sat on the bed, their hips meeting roughly. The contact of his pants to sensitive skin was a little jarring and uncomfortable, but his grin was devious. "I happen to think you'd be a great leader, Morrigan." The words seared a blush into her cheeks, and she realized he could see all of her. He gathered her hands in his, lacing their fingers together before he flopped backward, taking her with him so that she leaned over him, most of her weight supported on their joined hands.

"Lead."

Chapter Twenty

Morrigan

Corinth Manor

Morrigan didn't know how to lead something she had never led before, but she knew what she liked when someone else was in control. Part of her was certain she wasn't really in charge even though the illusion was there. The way she sat left her mostly spread out on top of him, and the urge to kiss him was the impulse she acted on first.

It didn't take more than a shift of her head to find his lips. The way she kissed him didn't seem to satisfy him enough, her tongue and teeth tentative against his bottom lip, because he wiggled a hand free from hers and grasped her chin, tipping it down just a bit so the kiss was more profound, his breath and tongue invading her mouth.

She enjoyed leisurely kissing him, but curiosity spurred her into nipping his bottom lip a bit harder. He growled low and deep in response, and chills shivered through her at the sound. His hand moved to the back of her hair again, and he gripped the strands before tugging gently. She bit harder, a little soft groan of her own escaping her as he scraped his nails along her nape.

The leisure had left in exchange for traded nips and shared soft laughter. She had never felt so at ease with someone before. Everything with him seemed to be new to her in some aspect, and she knew some part of her delayed taking what she wanted because she was insecure with the abilities she had been forced to learn to survive past encounters. Being with him was different. She wanted this. She wanted everything about this, but she still held some nervousness, even though she could feel every feeling he had as they tingled against her skin.

Her mother had been wrong about her greatest assets being the skills she had learned. At that moment, she knew that being able to feel what he felt, if she could distinguish it from herself, would be more useful.

As she shifted, his arousal spiked with hers. He was hard between his thighs and the fact that it hadn't diminished while they had chatted renewed the shot of pleasure along her spine.

The hand that had been in her hair trailed down her back before settling on her hip, grasping and rolling the skin before sliding up her waist. Even though she wasn't as thin as the fae women she had met, or the type her family prided on, something about the size of his hands made her feel small.

"Morrigan, you're thinking too much."

"You're thinking too much."

"Uh-huh." He reached up, tucking a lock of hair behind her ear before grasping her chin between his forefinger and thumb, the pad of which stroked along her bottom lip, his eyes following its motion. "What 'cha thinking about?"

"This feels weird." Honesty had yet to fail her when it came to him, but she was still worried he wouldn't react kindly to it.

"What does?" He moved and then grasped her fully around the waist as he sat up. Their positions changed minutely but Fates did it send shivers sparking through her. She gasped as she rolled into him, her worries forgotten as she rocked her hips forward again.

The desire to smack the grin off his face bloomed but at the same time, she didn't want anything to change.

"Morrigan..." His hands found her hips, and he pulled her close to him, chest to chest, and the tension melted from her as her hips met his stomach.

"I've never..." Oh Fates, why did that feel so good?

"Never?" He paused, and she mewled in protest as he disengaged with her. "You've never what, Morrigan?"

She rocked again, a giddy little laugh escaping as his fingers curled along her hip. "Controlled... Had control."

That stupid smirk returned as relief replaced the concern. "Almost stopped my heart there, firefly." His voice held a laugh as his hand smoothed down her throat. The tension he applied there for a moment blocked her airflow just enough that all she heard was the blood rushing in her ears. Redirecting the position of his hand, he forced her chin just a bit higher and seized her mouth with his.

The hand on her hip squeezed before his grasp turned broader, guiding her to shift again. Something about that position felt more open, even though they were closer now than they had been moments before. Morrigan couldn't quite explain it, but she liked it better.

"Control is just an illusion." Nikaius' voice rumbled through her, and she laughed gently.

"That's rich coming from you, *Atce'.*" Her words were a tease, she was curious how he would react to being called the Rekru'e word for alpha. Feeling him stiffen was the opposite of her intended reaction. Her worry that she had said something wrong was fleeting and dissolved in an instant when he growled low in his chest.

His hand seized her hair again so that his breath could play against her lips. "Dangerous game, little lady." His free hand jerked her hips again, and the air rushed through her with the force of the pleasure that coursed through her and forced a moan from her chest.

"We established I play the ones I'll win, *Atce'.*" Unsure what it was about that word, the Rekru'e word for a superior being or alpha, that got the reaction it did, but pure unbridled joy soared through her at the dark grin that spread across Nikaius' face.

Morrigan had always been the sort to want to fight authority, but from a young age, she learned to pick her battles, especially ones she knew she couldn't win. All of the possible outcomes that flashed through her head of her words and how the situation would go felt like a win in her book.

The tenderness in Nikaius' touch turned harder, pressing more into her skin as his lust twisted darkly through her. She was playing with fire, and she knew it. Having him under her skin like that made everything headier. She shifted as she felt her arousal slip from her. His wide pupils told her he could scent what she felt for him.

One smooth roll had her pinned beneath him, and he rocked into her, dark promises she could almost taste sparking under her skin.

"I don't doubt that at all, darling." His breath was hot on her throat as his mouth latched onto the mark he had left on her skin. Each draw of his tongue across it synced the throbbing of her body with the rock of his hips, and she felt it in every cell of her being. She was so close to reaching orgasm again that she gasped when he suddenly stood and walked away.

It shouldn't be attractive to watch a man pull his belt from the loops of his pants in one quick motion, but a thrill ran through her, and he grinned over his shoulder before entering the bathroom.

Despite her confusion, the moment of disconnect gave her clarity to devise a devious little plan of her own to make him work for it. He had asked her to lead, and she would lead.

Even if only for a moment.

"I love seeing that cunning mind of yours work." His belt thumped to the floor when he returned. As he looked her over as a fang caught his bottom lip.

"Fates alive." She gasped. Why was his fanged grin so enticing? Was it because of the mark on her neck?

Snatching up one of her feet, Nikaius pressed a kiss to the bone of her ankle with a low rumbling hum. He set her foot back down gently before resuming his work on his pants, undoing the buttons and sliding them down his hips with one hand.

Leaning over her again, he gave a low growl, one that she felt in the pit of her stomach, and she reached for him. His movements were fast, and her hand was pinned under his again as he bit her bottom lip. Gathering her wrist, he tugged her up to stand with him and stepped back with a wide grin as he kicked his pants away.

Part of her was torn between worshiping each space of new skin he bared to her, and the more devious part wanted to make him work for it just a little bit. Her eyes dropped to the vial he had pressed into her hand, curious.

Before she could ask what was in the vial Nikaius seemed to know what she was going to ask. "Contraception." He grinned down at her. "Also works for consent to prevent violations." She watched as he undid the cork of the vial with his teeth before downing its contents. When he tossed the glass away, it vanished, which elicited a giggle from her.

"I love magic." Undoing the cork on her vial, she grinned at him. She hadn't even thought of contraception. She'd never been in a situation where it was offered or considered. It hadn't occurred to her until that moment that she had somehow gotten lucky to not have had a child at that point with the attention that was forced upon her by others.

Did she want children? Absolutely, just not at that moment in time. The fact that Nikaius had considered that meant more to her than she knew how to express.

She stepped around him, and he frowned but let her go, watching her with those dark, tempestuous eyes. "Morrigan." That dangerous tone of his sank into her, but she didn't stop until she was several paces away, surprised he had let her go so far.

He barely held onto his anticipation and restraint, his hands opening and closing as he shook them out at his sides. She quickly downed the vial and tossed it aside before turning to sprint across the room.

His bedroom was larger than hers, but she only made it through the sitting area before his hands closed around her waist, and she was turned and pinned to the door. "Devious little minx." One hand found her throat while the other snagged her knee and hiked it up his hip, spreading her open for him against the wall.

Her breath hitched when he tightened his hand around her throat, forcing her chin up for a kiss before it fell away to trace down her chest and stomach to dip into her core. With two fingers, he teased just enough to send a thrill through her again before he removed them. She had expected, with the way they both shared heavy panted breaths, that he would have eagerly taken the first chance to bury himself completely within her, but the intrusion was slow. Each motion of his hips went deeper until he couldn't go any further.

She impatiently shifted her hips and they both groaned, her breath light in her chest, the air tingling as if she was falling. Maybe she was falling. The impact would hurt just the same, but she didn't want to think about that.

She wanted to think about him and how he made her feel. How his heat surrounded her and filled her and how every slide of their bodies together forced that feeling just a bit higher each time. The hand on her knee tightened, but he still didn't move as she rocked into him. "Good girl. That's how you get what you want." His voice sent a shudder through her. This was the first time someone cared about what she wanted.

It seemed it was a running theme with him, but in that moment, she didn't want to think about how she felt with him, but how he made her *feel*. Shifting her hips sank him deeper into her, but the small amount of motion she received wasn't enough.

"Use your words, princess." He knew what he was doing, antagonizing her the way he was. With a huff, Morrigan let a bit of annoyance flare and reached up to snag her fingers in his hair. A hard tug earned her a low growl as his head went back with the force of her pull. "Those aren't words." His grip was bruising as he whipped her hand from his hair and smacked it against the wall. "But I appreciate the fight. Stay." Ice and storm churned in his eyes and stole her breath as they locked on her. She knew what he was doing, but she was helpless to protest, not that she wanted to. She desperately wanted to see this through to the end.

Him pulling out of her was the only warning she had before his hands were grasping her backside, hauling her up. Her breath slammed from her as her back thudded against the door, and he secured her legs around his waist. One of his hands dipped between them, and he guided himself back into her.

"Oh, Fates."

The game he had been playing was up; gentle and slow completely forgotten. Had he reached the end of his rope like she had? Or had her repeated challenge to his authority spurred him on?

Her gasp was high and loud as his hips snapped against hers and suddenly, she was full of him. Her head thumped back against the door as a groan shuddered through her. Despite the command to stay, she reached for his hair again and twisted the locks around her fingers. Another tug earned another growl, and his teeth found the spot he had marked again.

She had anticipated his hand returning to snatch hers away again, but instead, his thumb brushed against sensitive nerves that had her tensing, a tremble rolling through her.

His pace slowed, and she could feel him grin against her neck. The sharp cut of his teeth on her skin sent fire through her veins, her fingers tensing in his hair as her body bowed against him. When he pulled away from her neck and started thrusting in earnest, he grinned like a feral dark thing before seeking her mouth in a kiss. Her blood was on his fangs, but it mingled with the taste of him and sent a thrill through her. The fact that she had forgotten he had fangs flicked to awareness one moment before it was gone. Her entire focus was on trying to match pace with him so she could drag him down into the depths of sin with her.

Every place where their skin touched felt as if it was on fire and the different emotions that sank into her made everything exponentially more divine. There were emotions she dared not to name, not because she couldn't, but because she had never felt them directed toward her. Each press of his body into hers pulled high sighs and groans from her, and she was sure there were going to be bruises on her inner thighs and hips from the assault of his hips and hands. There was no way that the rest of the house couldn't hear what was happening. But that wasn't something she wanted to worry about.

All of it muddled around her, but the feeling of rightness rooted entirely in him didn't settle. She chased the sensation in her chest, the feeling of belonging and contentment and desire, and used her nails on his shoulders as she tried to pull herself closer.

Something shifted then, and the press of his fingers on and around her clit changed just enough to throw her off the edge. Everything seemed to snap from her in that moment and the lights flickered as he pressed completely against her, muffling his groan against her neck.

"Fates, I felt that in my entire body." His laugh buzzed against her skin. They were trembling, but she wasn't sure who was the cause. A giddy little laugh escaped her as well before they were both sharing in the laughter. Something was calming about having that experience with him, as peace and belonging finally settled over the war that she had held within her for so long.

"Fates, you're beautiful." He stroked tangled locks of her hair from her face and grinned before giving her a sweet kiss that she happily sank into as he slid free from her and carefully settled her down onto her feet again.

"I've never—" The door lurched open, and she went with it, gasping as she almost fell. Nikaius' arms wrapped around her, banding across her shoulders and around her hips. The growl that came from him wasn't playful. It was a darker, more sinister sound.

"Morrigan?" Startled, her eyes opened, and she turned to find Waric staring at her in confusion. He looked mussed as if he had just woken from sleep, and his hand was outstretched as if he was about to summon his sword from the ether. "I... I heard you scream." He looked her over again before something in his eyes changed. "Morrigan..."

"What?" Looking away from Waric, she turned to focus on Nikaius again. His light gaze was locked on Waric, all traces of Nikaius gone. She had just been speaking to Nikaius, but something had pulled Priamos to the forefront. He had been lingering. Was this something that Priamos had wanted but Nikaius hadn't?

They had both taken the potion that worked for consent, so they had both wanted it at some point, right? Consent could have been revoked at any time but hadn't been.

"Whatever you're thinking Morrigan, don't." Waric's voice was firm, but Morrigan wasn't sure if he was warning her or scolding her.

"What's happening?" Morrigan asked looking from Priamos to Waric and back. Priamos' eyes flashed to hers before narrowing on Waric again.

"What's going on?" Aslin's sleepy voice preceded her into the hallway, and she blinked at the three of them gathered at Nikaius' bedroom door.

Priamos gave a low warning growl as Waric stepped forward. "Aslin."

Aslin reached for Morrigan as Priamos snarled, his hold sliding along sensitive flesh before Waric shoved him away from her. He only had a moment before the door slammed shut and something heavy thudded against it.

"What just happened?" Morrigan's confusion deepened as Aslin looked her over before dragging her into the room. Morrigan stared at the door in confusion.

"He's an idiot, and you're right there with him." Aslin offered her a blanket.

"What did I do?" Morrigan accepted the blanket, wrapping herself with a frown.

"Gave him what he wanted. Don't you know anything about playing the long game?" Her words were in jest, but still stung a bit, curling in her confusion. Her entire body still throbbed from her orgasm, and with it, her mind muddled. Her throat ached from his bite, but she could find no regret. She had wanted it as much as he had.

Shaking her head, Aslin tugged her across the hall to the bathroom.

The bite on her neck tingled, and she rubbed it, expecting blood to come away with it, but it was dry.

Chapter Twenty-One

Morrigan

CORINTH MANOR

It was a little odd to have someone watching her, but something about the entire situation was odd. Aslin hummed to herself as she collected clothing from Morrigan's room and a towel for her to dry with. Not feeling up to a full bath, Morrigan scrubbed the places that ached with warm water before settling down to think about everything that had happened.

She held no regrets, but how Aslin and Waric reacted raised some alarm. When Aslin returned, Morrigan accepted the clothing and dressed.

"Aslin, what's wrong? We both wanted what happened. I don't understand what everyone is upset about."

"No one is upset with you." Hawke sighed as he stepped into the bathroom. Morrigan was a little shocked that he hadn't even asked if the girls were decent before entering, but at that point in the night, Morrigan was ready to return to bed.

"It sure feels like someone is upset with me. Did I do something wrong?"

"No," Aslin sighed softly. "He's right, no one is upset with you. We're more upset with Nikaius for not being more cautious."

"More cautious about what?" Morrigan's patience was wearing thin, and she turned from the chair to frown at them both. "If someone could give me a direct answer, that would be great. It's been a long day and Fates forbid you could all stop beating around the bush about it. We had sex. Zero big deal. I'm probably not going to be the last girl he gets with, he's a lord. If you're worried about me being upset about it, I'm not. I wanted what happened. It was nice, and I would do it again, but if it doesn't happen again, that's fine. It's his choice." That was an absolute lie. It would hurt if he decided it was a one-time thing, but she also wanted to walk into this without expectations. Sex and love were two different things.

Anger bit into her skin as Hawke grabbed her chin harshly, and he tipped it to show the mark on her throat. "He was reckless. The implications for both of you are bad if this gets out. This makes you a target."

Morrigan scoffed and shoved away from Hawke. "It's a hickey. The healing salve you have will clear it right up. If not, I know other things that can heal or hide blemishes left on my skin by others. You forget this isn't the first time a man has left marks on my skin." Hawke's jaw set and it looked like he was grinding his teeth. "Fates forbid I enjoy being bruised by a man who knows how to make me feel good at the same time." Scoffing, she threw her washcloth at him before turning to leave the bathroom through the main door. She wanted nothing more than to return to Nikaius' room, but the low voices from his bedroom door as she passed made her think better of it.

Something was off, and she had only just now picked up on it. Once in the hall, she paused. She was supposed to be staying in Nikaius' room while he took the guest room, but that didn't seem to be an option at that moment, so instead, she entered the guest room and locked the door behind her.

With a heavy sigh, she flopped forward into the bed and buried her face into one of the pillows with a groan.

The door opened sometime later, and the bed shifted as she blinked sleep from her eyes. "Shh. It's just me." Nikaius' warm fingers stroked a path along her throat and down her shoulder. She shivered at the contact. "I owe you an apology."

Morrigan sat up so quickly that she almost collided with his chest when he wasn't quick enough to move away. His low chuckle was soothing but confusion still curled through her. "You don't owe me an apology. I thoroughly enjoyed myself."

"You... you didn't feel obligated?"

"The fact that you would even think that is insulting, Nikaius. I took that potion the same as you. If I felt obligated, it wouldn't have worked, would it?"

"Well... No but..."

"No. I wanted to. I've been attracted to you since the first night I met you. It happened a little sooner than I would have liked, but I have zero experience in actual normal relationships, so there are no real complaints from me."

"Sooner than you would have liked? What does that mean, Morrigan?"

"I... I don't know how to do this... Any of this." She gestured around vaguely. Drawing her knees up to her chest, she rested her cheek on them, watching him in the dim lighting that flared to life as he moved to settle better on the bed. "I know nothing about relationships, Nikaius. My sexuality has always been a bargaining chip for my mother. I'm a little insulted that you would think I'd be with you without a reason. Or that the reason wasn't genuine."

"I," she watched as he licked his lips, "I don't know how relationships work either. Not really." Moving to sit next to her, he gave her a little smile as he bent one of his knees up to rest his elbow on it. His hand slid into his hair as he rested his cheek on his bicep, almost mirroring how Morrigan was sitting. "I've certainly never done them the way my mother thinks I should either, so I guess we're on the same playing field."

"Why was everyone upset earlier?"

His fingers reached out to tuck a lock of hair behind her ear, and she felt his nervousness through the connection.

"Nikaius?"

"There are certain expectations that are placed on me that Waric can't fulfill, and I don't want you to feel obligated to be part of those expectations."

"What about Waric?"

"He's my mate and my right hand, but my parents are a whole other story." He rolled his eyes, and Morrigan giggled gently.

"I don't feel obligated to do anything. I've never felt one ounce of obligation outside of my first day here when I wasn't sure where I would fit in." The lights flared a bit brighter, and Nikaius sighed as he shifted and reached for her. Uncurling herself, she went to him easily. Being drawn to him felt so right, even when some confusion surrounding the entire situation lingered. His fingers traced over the mark on her throat, and he felt remorse. It wasn't regret that she felt his touch, but there was something sad about the emotion.

"I don't mind." She rested her hand gently on his and gave him another shy smile. "I have no problem wearing your mark while it lingers, Nikaius. I don't think we have anything to hide. We're both consenting adults, and we shouldn't have to worry about what others think just because I have a hickey on my neck."

"Right." He still seemed to be a bit unsettled, and Morrigan sighed softly.

"If you don't want this to happen again just say the word and it won't. One and done. That's fine." That didn't seem to settle him, but she was beginning to realize that nothing would. "It's been a long day. Let's just get some rest and face the repercussions in the future, yeah?"

"It's not that simple, Morrigan."

"Can't it be that simple? Just for tonight? It's been a long day, and we could both use the rest."

The soft sigh he gave signaled that she had won the argument this time, and she giggled as he flopped down onto the bed, wrapping an arm around her waist to drag her to him.

"I'll have to figure out how to make up for missing court."

"You could just host another day? I've not yet gotten to experience the market, not genuinely anyway. If we went together, maybe it would be easier to explain that Priamos took over when I was in trouble. I could carry the blame."

"I'm not going to stake the blame on you, Morrigan." His voice had dropped a bit, and she watched as he blinked sleepily at her, like a child fighting sleep.

"We'll come up with a solution tomorrow, Nikaius. Let's just sleep for now."

"Mhm." His eyes closed as he nodded, but he didn't make any move to pull away. Morrigan envied how easy it was for most people to fall asleep, but tonight she was just as exhausted as he seemed to be. His warmth and the weight of his arm across her chest were almost drugging as his fingers stroked slowly along the mark he had left on her neck.

Though she only knew a bit about changelings and their mating habits, she had heard stories about how mating marks worked and for tonight, she allowed herself to believe that what she had read was true and that there was a potential for them to be mates.

Oh, Fates.

Nikaius' warmth and weight against her should have added to the exhaustion of their activities and made sleep come easy, but it didn't. Despite her eagerness for everything that happened earlier in the night, anxiety bloomed heavy in the pit of her stomach and restlessness came with it. She had wanted what happened, but being with someone she actually cared about was new. He had treated her so kindly, and she had enjoyed herself. Why did she feel like she wanted to cry?

She carefully wiggled herself free from the bed and stood, looking around the guest room. If she was so happy, why did she feel like she needed to cry? There was no reason to panic. Waric's and Aslin's words muddled around in her head. Their concern warred with the enjoyment she had had earlier in the night. Was sleeping with him wrong? It didn't feel wrong.

She let herself out of the bedroom and had only made it a few steps before Waric stepped out of the hall in front of her. Oh Fates, she didn't need to have him see her break. She quickly turned, brushing away the sudden tears that welled in her eyes. She just needed to make it somewhere private before everything could break.

"Morrigan? Did you have another nightmare?" Waric's voice was soft, and she tensed as she heard him approach. There was nowhere to flee to and if she tried to go back to Nikaius, surely, she would wake him. Panic fluttered in her chest, forcing its way out of the thick tangle of emotions.

"No." Though she tried to keep her voice steady, it broke at the end and Waric sighed, the only warning she had before his hand curled around her upper arm and turned her. The concerned look in his eyes was what broke her. Her soft sob was loud in the quiet hall. So many emotions burned through her in the well of things she had been collecting over the past few days.

"Are you hurt?" Waric's arms wrapped around her as she shook her head. His fingers found the spot on the back of her neck that Nikaius had used to calm her, but it only made her sob harder. She didn't know why she was crying, not really. Just that everything had flooded up all at once.

"Just big emotions with nowhere to go. That's alright." Waric squeezed her tighter, and she rested her cheek against his chest, letting the tears flow free. Everything was so overwhelming, but she couldn't make sense of the chaos that was in her head and heart. "Getting it out is the best thing to do. I'll be here until you're done." Waric swayed them as his fingers stroked through her hair.

She did just that. Curling her fingers into his shirt, she pressed her face into his chest and let herself break.

Confusion was at the forefront; everything was so new, and she didn't know if she had the capacity to keep up. With that confusion came affection for people she barely knew. Though she had only been with them a few short days, they had been undeniably kind to her in a way that she didn't think she deserved. She was grateful for everything that Nikaius and his pack had done for her, but she was afraid to express that gratitude out of fear of it being used against her.

The past few days had shattered one expectation after another, and her eagerness to experience everything had overshadowed her need to sit back and process things. She wanted to be good for them in the best way she could, but she had also been neglecting her own needs in fear of being seen as too selfish. Nikaius' attraction to her seemed to be the catalyst to everything. He hadn't approached her directly. She had been the one to make the first move in the hallway before the attack and afterward. She had given so much of herself that she hadn't stopped to think of the toll it would take on her.

She had begun to treat herself as her mother and Elijah had treated her without realizing it.

Another warm hand found Morrigan's back, and it renewed the tears. She had woken Nikaius. Shame curled through her as she pressed closer to Waric, surely, they would see how weak she was and cast her out now. What good was a girl who couldn't control her emotions?

"It's okay," Nikaius' words were soft and warm as he pressed closer to her, encasing her between him and Waric and rested his cheek against her head. "A lot has happened, just get it out."

His words mirrored Waric's and while it was soothing, it also encouraged the knot in her chest to continue unraveling, the shards splintering and breaking apart as they painfully pulled themselves from her chest.

She didn't remember moving, but when the tears finally stopped, and everything ached a little less because she was numb, she realized she was curled between Nikaius and Waric in Nikaius' bed. Tiredness creeped in then, and she struggled to find any embarrassment. Only calm and contentment stroked her skin as she finally found sleep.

Chapter Twenty-Two

Nikaius

Kunmei Plaza

Nikaius woke up with Morrigan sprawled across him like a small child. She was resting on her side, her cheek against his shoulder and her leg thrown across his hips. She was so warm and smelled so lovely that he didn't particularly care that his scalp stung from where her fingers were coiled so tightly into his hair. Her weight was warm, grounding, and it settled Priamos. He lingered, purring softly in the background, but Nikaius wanted to enjoy the moment for himself because he didn't know how long it would last.

He hoped she would be okay after the burst of emotions she had in the night. He knew so much of their world was new to her, as were their behaviors and forwardness, and it seemed they had overwhelmed her a little bit. Waric had assured him that it wasn't anything like that and that sometimes even non-changelings had a hard time processing emotions in a reasonable timespan or in a logical way.

Priamos had latched onto the notion that she was their mate. She very well could be, Nikaius wouldn't be opposed, but he had convinced himself that she deserved to live freely instead of going from one cage to another. Being the wife and mate of a lord was no easy feat, especially one who shared a mate bond with another, and his head with a feral wolf.

Even though he doubted she wanted to be with him, Priamos and he wanted to give her every experience she could ever want, hoping that maybe once she had her fill, she would be content to stay.

He knew that would never be because his time frame for fulfilling his parents' wishes was soon approaching. Until then, he would give her what he could.

"You're thinking too loud over there." Nikaius startled at Waric's voice, and he shifted slightly to find his mate sitting in the chair by the fireplace, setting up a tray of breakfast foods.

"I didn't hear you come back." His voice must have roused Morrigan who hummed gently as he spoke.

"Is it time to get up?" Her voice was soft and sweet even though it was laced with sleepiness.

"You're welcome to rest more." Waric's voice lowered a bit, his smile turning soft. There was something about Morrigan that had settled over both of them. Waric and Nikaius had been mated since they were teenagers and had learned how to utilize their bond efficiently when needed. Their relationship was perceived as odd by outsiders because two alphas mating was rare, but they had concluded that it felt like something was missing. It wasn't from lack of provision, just a phantom feeling that they weren't complete despite their attraction and love for one another.

They had met a few people who had attracted their attention, but ultimately the person they found either pitted them against each other in some strange mind game or didn't understand the dynamic they held and wanted it to change.

A change wasn't needed, not in either of their opinions, but Morrigan seemed to fit well between them.

"I'm awake now," Morrigan murmured but made no effort to move. Nikaius wrapped his arms around her and squeezed gently. "What's on the agenda for today?" She asked.

Nikaius shivered as her fingers untangled from his hair and slowly stroked up and down his neck.

"We have to return to court today. It should only take part of the morning, so we should be able to join you for lunch if you'd like."

Morrigan shifted back to look up at him with a shy smile before turning it to Waric. "I'd like that."

Nikaius' cheeks heated a bit. He felt like a shy teenager again. "We could show you how the courtyard works afterward?" Why did he feel so silly about this? They had rather fantastic sex, you would think attempting to ask a pretty girl out on a date would be less terrifying than that.

Huh? Nikaius blinked, shaking himself a bit to gain freedom from the sudden awkwardness he felt as Waric cut in with an explanation. "It changes depending on what the first person to enter needs." Waric lazily picked up a forkful of eggs and shoveled them into his mouth. "We've been swimming after the winter solstice before."

"Really?" Morrigan sat up so quickly that Nikaius' fingers tangled in the ends of her hair as he tried to move away. Gasping, she fell backward onto the bed again and blinked up at him in surprise. "It didn't work when I tried it, so I would love to see it do something other than snow."

"Yes, really." Nikaius sat up and carefully picked through her hair, unweaving the locks from between his fingers.

"My favorite is warm summer rains," Waric smiled as he stood to offer his hand to Morrigan, leading her to settle at the table. "Sometimes you need to escape, and that courtyard is a blessing from the Fates."

"I never learned how to swim," Morrigan admitted, pushing her hair from her face and scooping it up to drape over one shoulder so she could play with the ends as Waric dished her a helping of everything on the plate.

"Well, we can teach you if you want." Waric's voice was soft, and his smile spread slowly across his face.

Waric was the lover of the group, and that was why he and Aslin got along so well. They both enjoyed teaching new things and giving others new experiences because they didn't have those opportunities growing up. They both watched Morrigan take a few bites of the food provided.

I think she's alright.

I know, but it still makes me worry.

She's fine now. I promise. Big emotions get away from us sometimes.

Aslin had been groomed to be a lord's wife from a young age, and Waric had been tapped to be his uncle's heir. Neither ended up on their predetermined paths and Nikaius was grateful for it. They were his closest friends, and he wouldn't be where he was without them.

"I'm not sure," Morrigan admitted, licking her bottom lip as her eyes danced between him and Nikaius curiously.

Nikaius made his way over to the table and settled on the other side of her, watching as Waric reached out to twist a lock of her hair around his finger. "How about we just start with court, and then work our way up to the more adventurous stuff?"

Priamos gave a pleased grumble, which made Morrigan giggle. "That sounds alright to me. I hope I won't be too big of a distraction."

"Never," Waric gave a teasing tug of her hair, and stood, offering her a hand. "Let's see what Aslin can find you to wear while Nikaius and I dress."

"Maybe we could go back to the shop too. I really could use something other than the dresses I have."

"As you wish." Pressing a kiss to Morrigan's hand, Waric grinned and shooed her from the room.

The walk to Mountain's Edge was longer than what it would take to teleport, but with Morrigan's lack of experience, Nikaius had decided that walking would be better. There had been a lot of forced exposure to magic, and he was worried about how much she could take before she developed some sort of illness.

Considering they didn't know how exposed to magic Morrigan had been, he felt that being safe was better than risking her health by throwing too much at her at once.

He watched her as she interacted with Waric and Aslin, pleased to see that whatever nervousness she seemed to have been holding was lessened by her time in their company. He was glad that last night hadn't affected her as much as it seemed to affect him.

Maybe she's just good at hiding it. Waric raised an eyebrow at Nikaius but kept the majority of his focus on Morrigan who was frowning at whatever Aslin was trying to get her to eat.

Be that as it may, it's still something that needs to be talked about at some point.

Does it? Waric asked. *It seemed like the two of you had a great night. But if it was terrible, you know where to find me. Wink, Wink.*

Did you actually say 'wink wink' at me?

Well, actually turning to wink at you would be weird, don't you think?

Weird for who?

Well, I mean we haven't had the chance to have a conversation with her about the finer things in our lives so I think there's a possibility that we might need to wait. One event at a time, yeah?

Nikaius tuned into the conversation Aslin was having with a wide-eyed Morrigan. In Aslin's hand was the leg of a cooked pheasant.

"You said it smelled good."

"That was before I knew what it was."

"I don't see the problem." Aslin plucked a piece of meat from the bone and offered it to Morrigan, who frowned and stepped away.

"I... I can't eat that... How can you eat that? It's like eating Aquila's cousin."

Aslin paused with the piece of meat halfway to her mouth. "What?"

Waric stepped between the two, looking back and forth before turning his eyes to Nikaius, who shrugged and laughed. "I've got nothing."

As he let out a slow breath through his nose, Waric settled his hands on Morrigan's shoulders, dipping his height just a bit to catch her eyes. "Morrigan, sweetheart. No." Their entire party was at a loss for words. Obviously, her education was lacking in more than just the magical aspect.

"I'm confused." Morrigan's soft sigh broke the dull buzz of confusion from Nikaius' mind, and he smiled, reaching out to catch her hand and tucking it into his elbow.

"Changelings aren't related to animals. The Fates blessed certain families with the ability to change, but no animals were graced with that blessing. Eating pheasant, quail, and chicken isn't like eating changelings."

"We're too gamey." Hawke teased. Morrigan jumped at his sudden approach behind them and swung around to frown up at him. With a broad grin, Hawke snatched a piece of meat from Aslin and hummed as he ate it. "Hm... That's actually pretty good."

Waric shook his head and tugged Morrigan away from Nikaius to lead her further down the street. "Really though, what Nikaius said is true, changelings are different, no relation. I promise we're closer to fae than animals."

"Not that you're a Primal changeling or anything" Nikaius teased, elbowing his mate with a laugh.

"Primal changeling?"

"Yeah. Those who change into animals are considered Primal changelings. I'm not one of them." Waric grinned and stepped back, looking over his shoulder before closing his eyes.

The change started slowly, first with his hair darkening and growing longer, then his skin color deepened, and his height spiked just a bit. Before them suddenly stood Aquila.

Morrigan gasped in surprise and reached out to gently touch Waric's face. He playfully nipped at her fingers before changing back.

"Can you do their voices too?"

"Mmm. The biggest downside is the same as a Primal: if I stay in one form for too long, I'll start to lose myself."

"Like what happened when you shifted and hurt your brother?" Morrigan turned astute eyes to Nikaius, who nodded.

"Yeah, kind of like that. The older you get, the longer it takes to lose yourself, but it can still happen."

"I heard that's what happened to the head of Barnam," Waric added.

Morrigan frowned. "The bear territories? They've been gone for over a decade, haven't they? My father died protecting Cadoc Kaan. There are no more Kaans." Nikaius shared a look with Waric, but both remained silent.

"Cadoc Kaan?" Hawke caught up to them and slowed his pace to match theirs. "I haven't heard that name in years."

"Really? My mother told me he and my father died fighting threats from the East, but some of her stories are kind of exaggerated. I just know he went to visit his friend, and they were never seen again."

Hawke frowned at Waric who caught Nikaius' eyes for a moment. The time frame between Morrigan's father's death and the last time they had seen Cadoc Kaan didn't add up to what they knew. Nikaius had personally seen Cadoc at his appointment when he was eighteen. Seven years after her father's death. Correspondence had only ended shortly after then.

The silence lingered for several minutes before Aslin reappeared, hands clean and a smile on her face. "Why do we all look so glum?" Linking arms with Morrigan, she smiled. "Madame Eda asked after you. She said she had some things ready whenever you wanted to pick them up. We also have events we're going to that we'll need something more formal for."

"You could go do that and then we'll meet for lunch," Nikaius suggested.

Morrigan frowned but nodded, giving him a shy smile. "I'll try not to freak out this time."

"Don't make promises you can't keep." Waric teased, giving Morrigan's hair a playful tug. She swatted him away before allowing herself to be led by Aslin to Aquila who waited closer to Madame Eda's shop.

Nikaius sighed as he watched her go before turning his attention to Hawke. "Any word?"

Hawke nodded, adjusting his scarf. "Imriel Gorlassar has agreed that he will meet with us after Solstice and extended everyone an invitation. You know how the cold affects the Velamo. I wouldn't want to be out in these temperatures either if I were them. Most of my kind don't do well either."

"We're just lucky you're made of sturdier stuff." Waric teased, thumping Hawke on the shoulder.

"Mm. I suppose." Hawk smiled before he resumed his daily report. "We've let people know that there'll be another session held today. Most understand the situation and don't fault you for that."

"That's good, I'm glad."

"Silas has word from Santi regarding those putting in requests for attendance at the Solstice Selection Night in the Pridelands. So far, he has several families wanting to present their heirs for engagement, but he has received letters from a few others regarding missing people. The numbers keep climbing, but they can't tell us where they're going. Our scouts are still combing every area they can to see if there's more than just one camp."

Nikaius sighed. This was becoming a larger problem than what they had initially conceived. "Have we had any success with gaining access to it?"

"We haven't." Hawke frowned, letting his hand rest on the hilt of his sword as a group of men passed by. Something was up that Nikaius didn't have knowledge of. Typically, Hawke was more relaxed even though he was always on alert, but something had gotten to him recently.

"What about a word from the Valkyrie? I know Aeshira mentioned that more and more Valkyrie have been going missing. Do we think Aeron's gathering forces to act against her?" Waric's question drew Nikaius' attention back to him.

Figuring out what was wrong with Hawke would come later. Now was not the time for trying to unravel things within their group. The larger picture needed to be in focus today. "I don't know. I know he's upset that he's not going to be the head of the tribe, but no one ever promised him that. It's not like with Bastian."

Their group fell silent as they walked.

Nikaius sighed. He and his brother had never gotten along, but when their father decided to give Nikaius the Corinth Manors and Kunmei Court, Bastian resisted. He had been raised his entire life believing that he would be the sole owner of the courts, simply because Nikaius hadn't presented at twelve like the others. Nikaius understood his brother's resentment. Being groomed for something and then having that taken away would upset anyone, and Nikaius wasn't sure he would have ever presented. If Bastian hadn't taken delight in torturing Nikaius and forcing his change, they may have never found out his designation. Bastian could have still been the holder of both courts and Nikaius would have nothing. Bastian's need to always be in control and the highest point of attention had brought on his downfall.

Letting out a low sigh, he rolled his shoulders and nodded. "If Aeron's planning to make a move against Aeshira, he'll have to go through us first. The Valkyrie, De'Lyons, and the Velamo are our allies, and I intend to offer whatever assistance we can if they need it. I know they would do the same for us. Let's get to court and see what the rest of our world is up to." Hawke and Waric nodded, winking out of existence before Nikaius took a slow breath and looked over his shoulder.

Morrigan would be safe with Aslin and Aquila.

Taking another low breath, he cleared his mind and willed the world to change around him. The tingle of magic spread from the top of his head to his toes and back. He took a step forward and warmth replaced the cold and the buzz of the market softened and silenced into dull murmurs from the hall.

Rolling his shoulders, Nikaius lifted his chin and stalked into court.

Most days that court was held was just for updates on things going on in his court.

"The boundary bridges have been repaired but the dam could use a good revising. I've sent requests to the other courts for drafters." One of Kunmei's gold clad guards reported.

Nikaius nodded. The rain and snowfall for the area had been unseasonably high, and Nikaius knew that they needed to petition Bastian to do his part but having everything lined up prior to the request would guarantee its success. "I'll reach out to the De'Lyons to see if they've got any to spare as well. I know the fires have been rough this year for them." The guard nodded as Nikaius quickly wrote the summons and handed it off to the guard.

One of the farmers from the higher land was next: "There have been more and more large game being found dead near the territory lines. They're mostly fresh and still usable, but the rate is becoming more and more alarming."

"I'll offer ten gold per person, per day, for anyone who would like to take up the task of boundary men. We are only as safe as our weakest border. Waric, if you would take names and put out word to others to see if they would be interested?"

"I can do that." Waric held up his hand, pulling a book from the ether and stepping towards one of the tables to the left of them. "I'll take names and availability here."

A woman Nikaius hadn't seen in years was the next in line and surprise lit through him. He grinned as he stood from where he sat behind one of the tables and stepped around to hug the woman with delight. "Sable, it has been years."

"It has Bec, it has." Calling him the Rekru'e for pup wasn't a jab at Nikaius, but a term of affection Sable issued to those she cared for. No one knew how old Sable was, just that she didn't look any older than when she had been his tutor growing up.

"You look well." Nikaius sat again.

"I am well. I've come to ask a favor though." Sable gave him a smile.

"Very well, I am here, after all, to offer help to all who ask for it. I didn't realize you were a member of my court."

"I'm not, that's the thing." She stepped closer, resting her hands on the table so she could lean in, lowering her voice so only he could hear. "I'm currently in Barnam, running the children's home."

"You are?" This news was new and Nikaius filed it away to bring up to Waric when there was time. They hadn't been aware that a children's home had been created. That wasn't a good sign.

"Aye, their men are still disappearing at an alarming rate. But I didn't come for that. I was hoping you could spare some gold to re-roof the children's home."

"What of the lord overseeing your home?"

"We haven't seen him for many years, all of our requests go through, but are never answered." This matched things they already knew. Cadoc Kaan had been the head of the bear tribes in Barnam for many years.

Letting out a low breath, Nikaius sighed. "It's against the laws for me to interfere." He looked away, eyes searching the room, trying to come up with an idea of how he could get around those rules.

"I belong to all courts, my lord."

"Mmm. This is true."

"And I did tutor you for free."

"Did you now?" Nikaius grinned up at her, thankful for the way her mind worked. "Well, I must remedy that at once. Create a bill and bring it to the bank and your bill shall be honored, madame. After all, a life debt is not one I wish to incur any interest on."

Sable laughed, reaching out to pat his cheek before stepping aside for the next person.

Court didn't take nearly as long as he thought it would, but he knew his response to Santi De'Lyon would need immediate attention. With a heavy sigh, Nikaius knew he wouldn't be able to meet the others for lunch and sent Waric in his stead.

Chapter Twenty-Three

Morrigan

*Kunmei Plaza -
Corinth Manor*

The excursion to Madame Eda's was a lot less chaotic the second time. They had walked for one, and Morrigan's measurements had been mostly completed the last time they were there, despite Morrigan's meltdown. Madame Eda seemed to have completely forgotten all about the incident that had only happened the day before. So much had happened in just a day that it felt like it had been longer.

"You have a lovely figure; we should highlight that." Morrigan blushed at the comment. Her figure was not often positively commented on, so the newfound attention she was receiving jarred her a bit, but she enjoyed it all the same. It was nice to feel appreciated and seen.

"I'm thinking of a low neckline, accentuating the chest, and that lovely mark on your neck, and a long skirt. You could wear heels to add height, and you'd be the belle of the ball." Morrigan couldn't picture what she was talking about, but she didn't have to wonder for long. Moments later, her assistant was bringing in a dress that Morrigan eagerly pulled over her head. Now that she knew what was happening, she allowed herself to feel some form of joy at being able to experience something she had never gotten to before.

The dress was daring, and she clapped her hand over her chest as they adjusted the back so that it sat snug against her skin. "I'll surely fall out of this if I move." The black jeweled bodice was lovely, but the neckline plunged nearly to her navel where the skirt started. The top layer of the skirt was black mesh, but the underskirt was a deep red that faded to black when she moved. She looked like smoke and flame, and she loved it.

"I love it, but how does one dance in things like this without falling free?"

"With magic of course." Eda laughed and pulled something from one of the baskets offered to her by one of her helpers. "Most of my gowns fit perfectly once spelled correctly, but if it makes you feel better, I'm sure Aslin has some of this. It's a double-sided tape. One side sticks to your skin and the other sticks to the garment, holding it in place." That did make Morrigan feel better, but as the shop girl adjusted the straps and back of the dress, she wasn't sure she would need it.

"I love it."

"Fantastic, you're a basic size, which is perfect because that means you could pick any dress from within our store and not need it drastically tailored." Not need it tailored? Morrigan's mother had refused to get her anything new because she had stated that all her clothes would need to be specially made because of her size and the placement of her curves.

"Changeling women tend to favor weight." Aslin's voice was soft and Morrigan frowned, turning to face her friend, surprised that Aslin had known where her mind wandered.

"Fae pride thinness but here we accept bodies as they are. One cannot bear healthy children if you are malnourished, especially not primal children who tend to be larger. I'm sure your mate is pleased that you are healthy. His appreciation is evident."

"Huh?" Morrigan looked from Aslin to Madame Eda and back in confusion. Did she assume Nikaius was her mate?

"We need to be fitted for Solstice and Nikaius' birthday too. I think this green would look lovely on her, what do you think, Madame Eda?"

"Oh, very lovely. Yes." Suddenly, Morrigan was in her undergarments again. She watched as the slip she was wearing changed before her eyes to better suit the dress that Aslin was bringing over. She twisted a bit with a giggle.

"I love magic."

Aslin laughed as she gathered the skirt of the dress to help her pull it over Morrigan's head.

Three more dresses followed, each as lovely and perfect as the last. After formal dresses came more mundane everyday wear. They all seemed to trend towards fancier, everything in the store did, so Morrigan kept her concern to herself about the wear and tear.

Aslin seemed to favor pants over dresses, but Morrigan wasn't quite sure how she felt about them. She had only ever owned one pair of pants and those were for chores. Her mother had very loud concerns regarding how wearing fitted clothing would show off too much of Morrigan's shape, but Madame Eda insisted she try a pair, just for a day, and Morrigan agreed.

One day wouldn't hurt, right?

As they stepped out of the shop, tension rose within her. Would people stare? What would everyone else think of her in pants? Sure, Aslin looked amazing in them, but having so much of her shape on display was very distracting, and she was glad for the need for her cloak.

"Nikaius is still holding court. He said we could meet him over there or go without him." Waric approached, his grin bright. "Morrigan, you look lovely." Her cheeks heated as he looked her over.

Aslin shoved him by the shoulder. "Stop that! You're going to make her change her mind."

"What? I can't compliment my lovely lady when I see her?" He pulled away from Aslin and snatched up Morrigan's hand, bowing with a cheshire grin. "Surely if I don't make my thoughts known, every other male within a mile will think she's available for courting and fall over themselves to gain her attention. Why shouldn't I be the first?"

"Don't laugh, Morrigan. You'll only encourage him." She hadn't realized she was even smiling until Hawke said something, and she quickly slapped her free hand over her mouth to fight the giggles that were threatening to escape.

She didn't succeed. The laugh that escaped was loud and not very lady-like, but her gathered company didn't seem to mind as they joined along. Was this what having friends was supposed to feel like? It felt comfortable and happy.

The last time she felt genuinely happy was a blank in her mind, but she could get used to feeling so warm and whole. Being with Nikaius had opened something within her that allowed her to breathe a bit deeper and feel a bit clearer. It was something worth protecting.

To Morrigan's disappointment, Nikaius did not join them. Something pressing had called Waric and Hawke back to him before they had even started their lunch.

Experiencing the marketplace was just as overwhelming as being in Atce' Plaza on Selection Night. Most of the people spoke Common, but everything was written in Rekru'e. It was disorienting and a bit embarrassing to have to rely on Aslin to lead her through the market and read everything to her.

Aslin reassured her that there were plenty of books written in Common for those who needed them, that moment of being uncertain made Morrigan realize that learning the predominant language was important. If she wanted to stay a member of Nikaius' court, she wanted to feel as if she fit in.

The evening led her to follow Aslin as she held a class for children. Where Morrigan grew up, everything was private tutors and nannies, but here it seemed that children of all ages attended classes together.

"It eases the strain between classes here," Aslin explained. "In most areas, only the rich can afford to educate their children, but here we offer it for free so everyone can learn. We have several parents who attend some evenings as well. Just because you have gifts doesn't mean reading isn't a necessary skill." Morrigan couldn't have agreed more and was thrilled when Aslin suggested that she start attending as well so that she could help the younger children learn Common while she learned as well.

Morrigan had always prided herself on being a quick learner; however, it was refreshing to be welcomed to learn with the younger children as they learned their letters and reading.

Initially, she had felt a little foolish at Aslin's suggestion, but those in Aslin's classroom who could read and write Rekru'e were eager to help her and others when on their breaks.

She and Aslin returned home just before supper time. The whole house smelled savory like Atce' Plaza had, and Morrigan's stomach grumbled, earning a giggle from Aslin. Morrigan wondered who was cooking, since she and Aslin had been out for the entire day. "Welcome back!" Aquila peeked her head out of the kitchen with a grin, waving at them before dipping back into the kitchen. As they made their way to her, Morrigan noticed that the door to the study at the end of the hall was open. Morrigan could see Waric and Nikaius talking to Hawke, whose attention was focused solely on the brown envelope in his hand.

Nikaius and Waric looked concerned, and that concern sparked through Morrigan as well. Had something happened to Hawke? He had been distant since the beginning of her stay, but she still cared what happened to him. None of them seemed to hear Morrigan approach. The three of them were deep in conversation that Morrigan only caught pieces of.

"You can tell her. Nothing bad will happen."

"You can't just keep avoiding her, it's impractical, and what if Mae asks about her?"

Her sister's name sparked Morrigan's interest. "Mae?" All three men's heads snapped up to watch her approach, Waric clapping Hawke on the shoulder as Hawke clutched the letter to his chest.

"What's going on?" Morrigan asked softly, glancing between Hawke, Waric, and Nikaius curiously.

"Do you want us to stay?" Nikaius asked softly, but Hawke shook his head. Nodding, Nikaius stepped away, patting Hawke's shoulder. As he passed, he pressed a kiss to the top of Morrigan's head, and she couldn't help the pleased giggle of surprise that bubbled from her. Being near him still made her a little nervous, but remembering the night they had and the new knowledge that he wasn't actively avoiding her eased that. Waric gave her a grin as he passed, giving her hand a gentle squeeze as he went. She picked up a bit of nervousness from his touch, but pride and worry were there as well.

"Are you alright?" Her concern for Hawke grew when he flinched as the door closed.

"Everything is fine. I just..." He looked up at her, his brows furrowed as he looked her over. "I know you. From before you met us in Atce' Plaza. I don't think you remember, but I was one of the guards at the winter solstice party last year that the Ayrdens' hosted and your sister's wedding." Morrigan frowned as she tried to recall. Mae's wedding to Santiago De'Lyon was a large affair because she was marrying a high lord, a male who oversaw a large territory.

"But I thought you belonged to Kunmei?"

"I don't belong to any court."

"How's that?"

"It's possible because four of the primary court heads are Rekru'e. Each one of them needs to have an unbiased Velamo or Kyilzar as their second for most diplomatic things. So I'm a neutral party."

"Okay, that makes sense. I'm glad you're so trusted that that honor was bestowed upon you." Morrigan was a little confused about what this had to do with her and her sister, but something like that wasn't an easily made decision and was worth some praise.

His smile was shy as he looked at the envelope in his hands. "Thank you. It's been an experience, for sure." His eyes met hers, and she couldn't help but return his smile. Something about him seemed so relaxed and happy. "Your sister asked me to watch out for you. On Solstice. You weren't there. I know why now, but I did try. I made several deliveries to your home and was there when Mae and Santi collected her things."

Morrigan tried to think back but couldn't recall ever meeting him before. Whenever Mae was around, she was always fixated on her and Santi, and if he had arrived alone, she probably wasn't paying attention, other duties were first in her mind. The guilt burned the back of her throat, and she stepped forward, reaching out to touch his arm gently. "I don't remember ever seeing you. I'm sorry. I usually kept to myself at home. It was easier."

Hawke reached up and took her hand. "I know. I'm not admonishing you for not noticing. I just wanted you to know that I did try. I didn't protect you like I was supposed to, but I did check in as frequently as I could. I..." She felt his worry cool their connection, and she searched his eyes for the cause.

"I'm the reason you were brought to Atce' Plaza." He paused. Surprise lit through her again as she searched his eyes to try to determine if he was telling the truth.

"How? Why?" She didn't pull away from him. His confusion matched her own, and she wanted to know more about the sudden revelation.

"It was Santi's idea really. You know how you and your sister knew him as Bax?" Morrigan nodded remembering the chaos that had happened when Santi had given them an incorrect name when they first met him. "He used that to his advantage. He wrote correspondences to Elijah under the guise that he was Bastian. He never questioned it because I was the one bringing the letters back and forth." Morrigan was speechless. Santi was deceiving her brother? Before she could ask, Hawke continued. "There was a plan in place. I was to meet you at the gate with Elijah and deliver you into the hands of Luca De'Lyon who was to bring you home to Santi and Mae."

Embarrassment flooded through their bond, and Hawke pulled his hand away to run his hand over his hair with a soft sigh. "Your sister wasn't completely in the loop, but she would talk about you all the time. She adores you so much. She told me everything." He looked over her shoulder before locking eyes with her again. "She told me about your powers and how kind you were despite your upbringing and the hand Fate dealt you, and I sort of..." His eyes dropped away from hers, and he looked as if he was grinding his teeth, something she had seen Nikaius do when he was trying to choose his words carefully. Morrigan worried something bad had happened to him when he was with Mae and Santi.

"You sort of what? If you overstepped, I'm sure I could talk to Mae, and we can explain it. I learned all my kindness from her and surely—" His hand on her chin caught her attention, and she blinked up at him in surprise.

"Morrigan," his eyes were bright, like molten amber, as his gaze searched hers. "I had hoped they would... letmecourtyou." His words were so soft and said in such a rush that Morrigan couldn't make sense of them.

"You what?" Her bottom lip trembled as curiosity burned in her chest. The moment felt so shy but also profound. His emotions were a mess against her skin, warring between embarrassment and resolve and a little bit of hope thrown in.

"I was going to ask to court you." Oh. *OH!* Heat flooded her face at the realization of what his words meant. He had liked her before he had even met her. That... That was new. She couldn't fight the giggle that erupted from her, but when Hawke tried to pull away, she caught his hand and kept him close to her.

Her heart soared. Knowing someone had wanted her after knowing everything she had gone through made her feel so much lighter. Someone besides her sister believed in her. "Okay."

Hawke either didn't understand her meaning or had just ignored it in his need to get the rest out. "But then Luca backed out of the deal and disappeared before I could get to you, and I panicked. I couldn't let you go back to them. I didn't know what would happen to you if you didn't leave with me from Atce' Plaza. I panicked and went to Waric because I knew they would have done something." The warring emotions felt abrasive under her skin, but she didn't pull away. Not when he seemed like he really needed to get them out. Pulling his hand from her face, she held it between both of hers and let him continue. She again wished she could take emotions from others, even just for a few moments, to soothe whatever chaos was going on in Hawke's head.

"I'm sorry for the way I behaved that night after we met. When I saw Nikaius with you and the way he behaved, I realized that there was something between you that I couldn't have."

"You were jealous?"

"Maybe a little." He gave a shy, boyish grin that made her heart flutter. There was the man who had conversed with her about paintings. "It doesn't excuse my behavior though."

"I think it does a little bit. At least it makes sense now. You think you failed me and my sister by the plan not going through. That wasn't your fault, Hawke." She took a breath, stepping closer to him. It was strange to be making the first move. But he needed reassurance, and she wanted to give it. "The plan changed, and you did what you had to, to ensure at least part of it went how you wanted to happen. You could have just given up, but you didn't. Have you talked to Mae and Santi recently? I'm sure they would say the same thing."

"I haven't. I've been too embarrassed. And when Nikaius and Waric noticed, they kind of pried it out of me."

"Did you tell them everything?"

"I did."

"And what did they think?"

"They said I should tell you and let you make a decision."

Morrigan laughed. It was weird to be given the power to make decisions, but she knew what one she wanted to make.

"I'm a little confused about where I stand with Nikaius, but if he doesn't have an objection to it, then I don't either. I'd be more worried about his reaction than anything else." She was still unsure, nervous that she was being put through some test, but it also felt nice to have his attention.

She looked at him again as she waited for her words to sink in. Until that moment, Morrigan hadn't realized he wasn't wearing his wings.

In front of her was an unguarded man.

A slow grin spread across Hawke's face, and he stood a bit straighter. "Yeah?"

"Yes, Hawke." The grin that spread across his face was brilliant and gave her little warning before he swept her up into a tight hug. She gleefully wrapped her arms around his neck and let him swing her around once with a laugh of her own.

Choosing herself was so freeing, and she felt like she could finally breathe for the first time in forever. Things were different here, and she didn't want to waste another minute worrying about the past, when it appeared she finally had a hold on her future.

Chapter Twenty-Four

Morrigan

Corinth Manor

Waric and Nikaius grinned when Morrigan and Hawke entered the room. It made her feel a little self-conscious to know that they knew the conversation that had been happening, but the two just looked pleased. "Just in time for dinner." Waric's grin was infectious as he pulled Morrigan's chair out for her. "There's a wedding down the hill tonight we were talking about attending. Would you like to come?"

Morrigan looked between the three men curiously. Nikaius and Waric knew how Hawke felt about her, and they knew she had been with Nikaius previously, but no one seemed upset with the other. The ease with which they existed was nice.

"I would love that! Though I don't think I have anything to wear to a wedding."

"What you have on is fine." Waric and Hawke responded together. The attention made Morrigan blush, and she fought a smile as she settled into her spot between Aslin and Waric to pick at her dinner.

"I'd like to go then, yes." She gave a little nod, pleasure curling through her at the thought of seeing how Kunmei weddings differed from others she had attended or served.

Dinner was a simple meal of roasted vegetables, pasta, and meat, which had again been set aside for Morrigan to try without being pressured into eating it. She was pleased to know that they thought of her even when cooking and quietly thanked them as plates were passed around.

With supper being light, it was finished quickly and Morrigan happily helped Aslin clear the table and wash dishes.

"Whatever you and Hawke talked about seems to have eased him a bit." Aslin was astute in her observation, but her wording made Morrigan wonder why Nikaius and Waric hadn't said anything to Aslin about it. Surely, secrets weren't kept in a group so tight knit. Morrigan mulled over her words for a bit before nodding. She needed to start trusting people if they were to become the friends Morrigan wanted them to be.

"He's the reason I was in Atce' Plaza. He asked to court me." Morrigan explained the rest of the details to Aslin as they washed and dried dishes.

Aslin's silence as she thought was unnerving, but Morrigan relaxed when she spoke. "That's why Nikaius and Waric were so giddy earlier. They're so weird."

"That's what confuses me. I slept with Nikaius, and Waric's been overly friendly as well. Who do I hold the most obligation to? It's wrong of me to be interested in being courted by Hawke when I'm attracted to Nikaius too, isn't it?"

"Oh, not at all. You're all consenting adults. No one has a claim over you just as you don't have a claim over them. If they had an issue with it, surely, something would have been said before now."

"You're sure?"

"Absolutely. Being with more than one partner here isn't uncommon. Some people prefer monogamy, but most don't. I know Nikaius is mostly a solitary man, but Waric's been in many people's beds. I'm not sure about Hawke's stance on it, but he wouldn't have said anything if he wasn't willing to try." Aslin's happiness was genuine as she grasped

Morrigan's arm and tugged her out of the kitchen. "Just relax and have some fun. That's all that needs to happen."

Morrigan nodded. Aslin's thoughts made sense. Taking a deep breath, she let the decision settle over her. She wasn't committed to one person, so she could see how things went with them at her own pace. Yet another thing she would have to learn. But this time, she felt more prepared and with more realistic expectations.

Once they were adorned in their cloaks again, Aslin and Morrigan met the others at the door, grateful that they hadn't insisted on teleporting again.

The sun was setting over the large wall that outlined the border of Kunmei, the town having already been cast into darkness was lit by the same lights that were in Atce' Plaza.

"What are those lights?" She asked, adjusting her cloak before accepting Waric's offered hand.

"Just bits of magic."

"Bits of magic?"

"Yeah, drafters can pull them from the ether to make them shine upon the world. It's a special skill some have."

"They're lovely."

"They are." Hawke caught up to match his stride with hers, grinning at the two of them. "Wait until you see the wedding."

Excitement buzzed through her, seeming to match what she felt through contact with Waric as they made their way down to the plaza.

Stepping through the gate at nighttime was so different than during the day. Morrigan had caught a glimpse of it as they left the schoolhouse, but she hadn't imagined it to be anything like the event spread out in front of her.

All the houses and businesses bracketing the main square were covered in a rainbow of different colored flowers, each building holding its own hue, their doors wide open as if inviting anyone who wanted in. Fire pits were spaced every so often in each cardinal direction and people gathered around them while watching those dancing around the fountain. Morrigan couldn't tell where the music was playing from but she knew the song; she had heard played at different events her mother held.

Everyone around them seemed so happy with a couple dressed in bright yellow seeming to be the center of attention.

"Nikaius!" Someone across the way called his name and Morrigan watched him turn, a grin spreading across his face as he waved to the one who called his name. Recognition sparked, and Morrigan turned to Waric excitedly. The blond who had drawn Nikaius' attention was one of Santi's brothers.

"That's Silas! Can we go see him?" Waric looked from Nikaius to Hawke and back to Morrigan with a frown.

"They have things to discuss, but later. I promise." The kiss that Waric pressed to Morrigan's hand didn't dull the sting of dismissal, but before she could mention it, Hawke's hand slid into hers.

"Could I be so bold as to request a dance, milady?" His grin was inviting and the joy that spread through their touch made Waric's distraction ease.

"Absolutely!" Though she had somewhat learned to dance prior to her marking, being asked to dance by someone who actually wanted her to was thrilling.

Hawke's hand was warm in hers, and he felt like excitement and adoration as they swayed to the beat of the song that had just begun. He didn't seem to know the steps and was unable to lead them in what the others were doing but he seemed to be enjoying himself with a soft grin permanently affixed to his face as they swayed. She wanted nothing more than to live in that moment for as long as she could.

Nothing could take away from that moment, and Morrigan let genuine happiness and peace sink into her.

The next morning, Morrigan tagged along with Aslin again. Court business had called everyone else away, and Morrigan was more than happy to help Aslin with the children. The evening before, Aslin had suggested posting a flier and sending out letters to parents offering lessons outside of the children's school day so as not to disrupt the lessons already in progress.

To their surprise, several parents agreed. While the majority of the population was able to speak the Common language, most didn't know how to read or write it. Along with some children, parents and siblings signed up, which made Morrigan's heart swell.

The fears Morrigan had held previously of being seen as an outsider within the court were slowly being soothed by just how eager the people of Kunmei interacted with her.

The initial lesson was held two nights after the first responses came in. She hadn't anticipated it happening so quickly, but with Aslin's reassurance, Morrigan agreed to head the lesson.

Walking into the building was a shock when she saw it housed a large group of about seventeen.

Most of the people gathered were ones she had met before. Whether it be people at the wedding, parents of the children she met with Aslin, or even the shopkeeper's helper, Adia, everyone greeted her enthusiastically.

Morrigan had never had so much attention on her before, but with every handshake and every greeting, she only received excitement and curiosity mingled with a bit of nervousness.

The lesson started smoothly, with everyone talking quietly among themselves while she worked on carefully writing the Common alphabet on the chalkboard.

A young man named Keyon with a basic knowledge of Common language offered to add the Rekru'e alphabet above her Common. She eagerly agreed, happy to have someone to help if she got something wrong.

"My little sister can never stop talking about you on the days when you help. I'm glad to note that she wasn't exaggerating about your beauty." Keyon's voice was soft as he leaned over Morrigan to write the equivalent of the letter she had just written.

Was... Was he flirting with her? "I'm glad to meet your approval then." Morrigan's response surprised her, and she laughed at how ridiculous it sounded. Was she crazy?

"Mmm. Lovely and smart are grounds for approval around here." He loomed over her as she paused in her writing to lick her lips. He was flirting with her, but did she like it? No, she decided, she didn't. He wasn't nearly as tall as Hawke, or warm as Nikaius, and he didn't smile quite like Waric did.

Swallowing in an attempt to relieve her dry throat, she whispered, "I appreciate the compliment." As she finished her letters at the same time as him, he carefully took the chalk from her hand and set it aside before reaching up to touch her cheek.

Morrigan jerked back instinctually, and Keyon laughed as he steadied her. "You have chalk in your hair."

"Oh." He was so close, Morrigan could only smell his faint ashy scent. He was one of the blacksmiths that worked in town. It wasn't a bad smell, just not as soothing as others.

Her mind flashed to Nikaius and how he always seemed to smell like vanilla and tobacco, or Waric's cinnamon and cedar. Even the smell of leather was better than the arid scent of things that were burned.

"Keyon?" They hadn't heard the door open, but Morrigan's thoughts halted when she heard Nikaius' voice.

"My lord?" Keyon sounded surprised, his eyebrows raising before Morrigan whipped around to stare at the lord who darkened the door of the schoolhouse as if she had summoned him purely by thought.

"Nikaius?" Her surprise must have been evident on her face because the corner of Nikaius' lips tilted up before he turned to address the room.

"Evening everyone. I heard that lessons in Common were to be held here, and I figured I'd join."

"Don't you already know Common?" A young girl named Abbigale asked, her brown eyes wide as she looked from Nikaius to Morrigan and back.

"It was something I never quite grasped as a child, and I figured it would be worth another shot to try to learn. After all, no matter how old we are, we should never stop learning. Right, my lady?" The way he addressed Morrigan made her heart flutter, and she nodded. She stepped forward, Keyon forgotten, and reached for a notebook and pencil.

"I quite agree. I think your first lesson, *sir*, should be how to enter a classroom quietly when you are late for the start of the lesson." Her raised eyebrows brought a smile to his face, but Nikaius gracefully bowed and accepted the supplies.

"My apologies, everyone please carry on." Once Nikaius had found himself a seat in the back of the class, Morrigan returned to the board where Keyon still waited.

After reviewing the letters on the board, Morrigan nodded and thanked Keyon. Despite his apparent disappointment, she chose to ignore it, as she was acutely aware of the watchful eyes around her.

"As you can see by the wonderful work that Keyon did, Common and Rekru'e have the same number of letters and a few of them overlap.

Most of this is just learning the different styles of each letter." Morrigan gestured to the board momentarily, letting her eyes wander off the letters again. It was a bit overwhelming to have so much focus on her, but she knew that Aslin would step in if she became too overwhelmed.

"Several students know that I'm currently learning Rekru'e. Most of us here can speak both languages, which is wonderful because we can all help each other learn. This is a safe space for us to learn and so if I mess up, I expect you to kindly correct me as I will kindly correct you. You are all also welcome to help each other." When she looked around, it surprised Morrigan just how attentive everyone was. She had never had so many people eager to learn something she knew.

She began the lesson by reading the Common letters aloud before letting everyone have a moment to copy them down.

"Let's start with names. Names and proper nouns aren't things that drastically change between languages. So I'll start with my name. In Common it's simply 'M-o-r-r-i-g-a-n.'" She carefully wrote her name on the board before pausing to look at the Rekru'e alphabet. It took her a few moments to translate it into Rekru'e, with most of the letters having sharp edges as opposed to the curves and curls of Common. "The biggest difference between Common and Rekru'e in writing is that Rekru'e doesn't use double letters. Which is why my name has a dash here. So, if you have a dash in your name, in Common you would couple that letter. Abbigale's name in Common would be A-B-B-I-G-A-L-E because she has the dash between the B and I in her name when written in Rekru'e." Abbigale smiled at her mother who nodded.

Turning her attention back to the group as a whole, she nodded. "I would like for everyone to practice writing your name in Common, and I will come around to help those who need it."

Pencils started working as she turned toward the board, intent on working on some commonly known names such as Kunmei, Kunmei Enclave, Atce' Plaza, and Be'Sala.

"You flipped the middle consonants in Kunmei." Nikaius' voice was soft in her ear, and her heart flipped as he reached forward to correct the accents she had written. "See how the Common N has one space, and the M has two? They both start the same, but the accent creates the extra dip. So instead of Kumnei, the god of deception, you have Kunmei, our home."

"How do you know I wasn't purposely writing Kumnei instead of Kunmei?" Morrigan asked in jest. He was so close; she could feel his laugh rumble against her shoulder.

"Because," he reached up, brushing her hair off her neck before walking his fingers up from his mark to her chin, his amusement sinking into her skin, "you wrote it correctly in Common." Jerking her head away, she frowned as she looked over the words again. He was correct.

"You're right, of course. Thank you." Turning back to him, she gave him a smile that made him pause. His eyes searched her face, and she wondered he was thinking, but before she could ask, someone cleared their throat behind her.

"Excuse me, miss, I'm having a bit of trouble."

"I'll leave you be," Nikaius stated softly, pressing a kiss to the top of her head before stepping away. With a soft hum, Morrigan nodded after him before accepting the notebook of the man who needed help.

Chapter Twenty-Five

Morrigan

Corinth Manor

After that night, Morrigan split her lessons into two lessons for eight people per week. The smaller group size helped her better accommodate the number of people who were interested in learning and furthering her knowledge as well. Since the two languages were very similar, hiccups were few and far between. Morrigan found that she was picking up both reading and speaking Rekru'e quickly with only a few moments of confusion along the way.

One such event happened when Morrigan found a note in the book she was reading. It had become customary for everyone to sit quietly for a while before dinner and do their activities, Waric and Nikaius were usually replying to some sort of correspondence or another, Aslin sewed, and Morrigan read. That night in particular, she had found a note in place of the bookmark she usually kept in her book. A blush heated her cheeks, the penmanship was sweeping and neat. Standing, she went to Waric, then set the book and note down for him. "Ie amar Ae? What does amar mean, Waric?" She asked, lifting her eyes from the bookmark to him.

"Hmm?" Waric picked up the note and looking it over before handing it back, a low grin spreading across his face.

"I adore you."

His words were soft, but Morrigan wasn't sure if he was speaking to her or reading the note. Her heart fluttered regardless. As her eyes searched his, the grin grew, and she heard him flip the note over. He looked at it, breaking whatever spell had her heart beating heavily in her chest, and she looked as well.

'I adore you' was written in messy trembling Common. The longer she looked at it, the more realization sunk in. The angled script on the front, written in perfect Rekru'e was slanted to the right. The author was right-handed and didn't write Common nearly as well as Rekru'e.

Nikaius?

No. He was left-handed.

She had never seen Hawke write.

She looked at Waric again. His grin remained and so did the scattered fluttering in her chest. He adored her? What about Nikaius? Was this some sort of power play? Was he trying to pit her against Nikaius?

"Waric?"

"You're thinking too hard, princess."

"I don't understand."

He stood then, and she stepped back, startled by the sudden motion, clutching her book to her chest. "What part don't you understand?"

"A-any of it?" she hadn't meant it to be a question, but her voice quavered as he parried her step back with another of his own.

"Anything specific?" Her back hit the bookshelf with her next step, and he still prowled forward, one eyebrow arching as he tilted his head at her. There were so many similarities between Waric's and Nikaius' behaviors, it was as if they both shared some part of the other. Physically, Waric didn't look nearly as intimidating as Nikaius.

To be completely honest, Hawke had them both beat on size. But the look Waric wore was nearly identical to the one that Nikaius had held when he bracketed her against the wall outside her room the last time they had been together.

Just as Waric was doing then. His fingers touched feather-soft along the curve of her jaw, encouraging her to lift it. This could be some test.

But would it be so bad to kiss him?

"I asked you a question, pet." His hand carding in her hair felt so nice, and the way his thumb traced right along the gland under her jaw was soothing. She felt like she would melt if he kept it up for longer than a few moments. There was no real boundary in her relationships with anyone, was there? No explicit line had been drawn in the sand. If she was going to burn everything to the ground, it might as well be with the person who held so many similarities to the other.

"No..."

"No?" He was impossibly close now, his nose brushing under her ear before his teeth teased the lobe.

"Oh, fates." Warm spices invaded her senses as he dipped his head, tongue lapping at the mark that Nikaius' teeth had left, and the world fell away. Electricity sizzled in her veins as everything within her throbbed. The book tumbled to the floor as she fisted her hand into his hair, afraid her knees would give out as the other braced back against a shelf on the wall behind her. She could feel his grin against her skin.

"I wonder if I can get you to make the same noises he did." His voice was a low rumble, but his hand in her hair, guiding her mouth to his, silenced her before she could respond.

His teeth were vicious against her bottom lip, fangs easily scraping against the soft inside to draw blood to the surface. His low hum of appreciation rumbled through them both before he pulled her away from the bookshelf.

Her eyes flew open as she gasped, catching herself on his forearms as his hands sank under her skirt to brush against bare skin. His fingers bit into her skin as he grasped her hips, then thighs, his mouth returning to the mark on her neck before he hauled her up by her thighs. She knew where this was going, but the distance wasn't what she had anticipated, and she let out a startled noise as her back hit the wall with a thud as he settled her atop the bookshelf she had been leaning against. His shoulders wedged under her bent knees, and he wedged himself closer, spreading her legs wider as he pressed her hips back against the wall.

He wasted no time and barely allowed her a breath before he was shoving her undergarments aside and slid his tongue low and slow, up to trace along her clit. The sudden temperature change made her shudder, and the quick flick of his tongue elicited a loud gasp from her. Thoughts scattered from her mind with the draw of his lips pulling sensitive skin into his mouth, and she bowed into him when fangs nipped the inside of her thigh, her fingers digging and twisting into his hair with a breathy laugh.

She had nothing to compare this experience to. She never had a man been where Waric was, and she couldn't imagine anyone else ever living up to this. His mouth returned to her clit, and Fates, she could die that moment and still be the happiest woman alive. The pace he set was quick, and she trembled as he groaned against her. Her breath caught as he teased a finger along her slickness before easily dipping it into her core. She dug her fingers deeper into his hair, unsure whether to pull him closer or push him away. Neither motion made much sense until he pulled her hips towards him a bit more, his tongue replacing his finger. He devoured her with astonishing enthusiasm.

The library was silent except for the sounds they made. Everything else was a dull roar in her head as her pleasure ratcheted higher. The wet sounds of his mouth were obscene, but the groans and hums against her skin only lit the fire higher, making her head hit the wall as she bowed closer, seeking him out when he pulled away to catch his breath.

"Gods you're beautiful."

Morrigan tensed. That was not Waric's voice.

Startled, she sat up more properly onto the bookshelf, chest heaving as she locked eyes with the twisting blues belonging to Nikaius and Priamos. Oh gods. Her heart fluttered quickly in her chest as she took him in. Both men's eyes were trained on her before Nikaius' hand around Waric's throat slid up, cinching tighter and tipping his head back as his other hand traveled lower. Waric moved to reach up but the low warning grumble from Nikaius made him pause, his breath hitching as the lower hand slipped into his pants and grabbed. By the sound Waric made, it hadn't been a light grab and Morrigan gasped.

Priamos was going to hurt him.

"Wait. Nik don't." She pitched forward, forgetting she was seated on the top of the shelf, and let out a screech as she slipped from it. One of them made it to her before she hit the ground, and she stumbled as she was righted by the hands on her elbows and at her waist. When her feet touched down on the floor, the edge of her almost orgasm pulsed through her, and her knees buckled, but she didn't get far.

Being wedged between two lean bodies made it nearly impossible to move.

"Are you okay?" Nikaius' chest rumbled under her hands.

Thoughts swirled through her mind as her body still buzzed.

Okay was the last thing she was.

This had been stupid.

It had been a trap.

She had supremely fucked up.

"Morrigan?" Waric pulled the hair away from her bare shoulder and ran his knuckles up along her throat. "What's going on in your head, princess?"

"Don't call me that." She tried to move, trying to elbow Waric away from her, but Nikaius had a firm grasp on her forearms, making the motion impossible. Nikaius' low chuckle made her more desperate to escape, but trying to pull her arms out of Nikaius' grasp was impossible as well.

Tears welled in her eyes as Nikaius caught her chin. "Morrigan?"

She needed to get away.

They were playing a game with her.

Had they been playing with her the whole time?

She couldn't breathe.

She needed to get away.

She needed to make a plan before they decided to send her back to her mother.

She couldn't go back.

She wouldn't go back.

Chapter Twenty-Six

Nikaius

Corinth Manor

She was panicking. Nikaius could hear her heart racing and feel where his hands were wrapped around her forearms. Her eyes were shut tight, and she kept murmuring to herself.

"I won't go back. Please don't send me back." Her voice was a soft whimper that broke Nikaius' heart a bit.

"Go back where?" She jumped when Waric asked, and Nikaius shushed her gently.

"Morrigan look. Open your eyes and look at me." He slid his hands up her arms before sinking his fingers into her hair, pressing his forehead to hers. "I'm sorry. I didn't mean to upset you."

Morrigan pulled back, blinking up at him through the tears. "Why are you sorry? I'm the one who failed whatever this was." Her bottom lip trembled, and she hiccupped on a sob. "I'll do whatever I have to do to fix this. Please don't send me back." Her warm fingers curled around his wrists as she sniffled. He was so confused about her reaction. "Send me to my sister if you have to send me away but please don't make me go back."

Nikaius' eyes caught hers, and he pulled Priamos closer, letting him settle into their voice. "Breathe."

The deep breath she took seemed to do nothing to soothe the welling panic.

"You're fine. You're safe. You're not going anywhere. Take another breath for me." She took another slow breath, and he smiled, glad she was hearing him just enough to listen to him. He didn't like using alpha commands unless they were warranted.

"I think some wires got crossed somewhere." Waric's voice was soft as he ran his hands up and down Morrigan's arms, eyes meeting with Nikaius' over her shoulder.

"I think they did." Nikaius agreed; his hands shifting to cradle Morrigan's face, his thumbs brushing the tears from her cheeks as she hiccupped another sob. "Take another breath for me, and we'll explain."

She took another breath, this one deeper, before giving a small nod.

"Here, come sit." Waric slid his hands down her shoulder to tug her hand free from Nikaius' wrist. Curling his fingers in between hers, he lifted her hand and pressed a gentle kiss to her knuckles before tugging her away.

Morrigan gave a small nod and allowed him to lead her over to the couch. Nikaius could still hear the way her heart fluttered, but she willingly followed Waric to the loveseat. Nikaius dropped himself onto the ottoman across from them with a heavy sigh.

"I'm sorry. It never occurred that it would have to be explained. Most people sort of just realize it." He sighed and ruffled his hair with his hand. "Where to start?" He looked to Waric for guidance.

"From the beginning I guess." Waric shrugged.

Very helpful Waric.

Laughter echoed through his head. *You asked, I answered.*

Asshole.

Love you too buddy.

Morrigan's eyes bounced between them as if she was following their conversation, but Nikaius knew that the notion was impossible unless she accepted that she was their mate and the bond snapped into place.

Letting out a slow breath, Nikaius nodded. "Right well. Rites of passage are shitty, let me tell you that." He looked at Morrigan. She knew that. She had been branded. "I mean, I know you understand going through the Culling and all. Ours was the participating in the branding." Even the word made him cringe and Morrigan frowned, leaning into Waric slightly as if seeking comfort from the memory. "We were almost sixteen, and my father insisted that winter's Culling be something we were part of before he would consider me mature enough to take on some court tasks. It was to test my strength and composure or something like that, I don't fucking know anymore."

"Nik had to hold a girl while they marked her. It nearly destroyed him." The memory was something that they would remember for the rest of their lives. The thirteen-year-old girl had clung to him, begging him and the Fates to let her go. "It was not easy by any means. We had to hold the ones who failed the tests while they were being branded. There was this girl. She was so small and pale. You could tell she was terrified, the only one of her family to be marked. Her freckles stood out so starkly against her skin." He took in Morrigan's appearance and could almost see that little girl reflected in her. Wide jade eyes and ruddy tear-stained face.

I keep telling you it's her. Waric's voice flickered through Nikaius' mind again.

I don't want it to be. She deserves so much better. They both do.
You're an idiot.

Nikaius swallowed, licking his lips as he continued. "Our bond was forged that day. We had to hold her while she was branded. Waric knelt by my side, shoulder to shoulder as she screamed into the other one. The stars on our wrists? They're our mark. His is on the opposite wrist, the ones that were touching." Nikaius absently rubbed his chest where the lingering pain of having done something so horrendous lingered. He had lost a piece of his soul that day but had gotten another. Waric took the other, showing Morrigan how the marks lined up.

Morrigan's eyes locked with Nikaius, and she looked like she was thinking, not looking at him but through him.

Waric continued the story. "His father was furious. Same gender mates are fairly common, but it's frowned upon amongst the higher-ranking families. The need for heirs and all that stupidity." He waved his hand dismissively. "He sent us off to different training camps, but we couldn't stay separated. When Nik gained rights to this court at eighteen, he dragged me back, and I've been here ever since." His grin was infectious and Nikaius felt himself smile as well. He wouldn't have survived anything if it hadn't been for Waric. He had been his rock, preventing Priamos from taking control and ripping everyone to shreds just to save the girl who smelled like sunshine.

Maybe Waric was right. But Nikaius knew he didn't deserve someone like Morrigan, especially if she was that girl. They had ruined her life.

They waited for her to speak, to say anything, but Morrigan just nodded, licking her bottom lip as she looked at her hands and picked at the cuticle of her thumb.

The silence was only broken a few minutes later by Aslin peeking her head in to announce that dinner was ready.

Chapter Twenty-Seven

Morrigan

Corinth Manor

For the most part, Morrigan had blanked out the trauma of being branded. Of all the things about it she did know was that Bastian Ayrden had been the one to brand her. Mae had gone on a wild tangent about it when she found out she was to be courted by him some years later. That was how Morrigan also got her scar. Mae had tried to save them both from falling into the hands of the Ayrden family.

Would Mae be upset if she knew where Morrigan was? That she was halfway to falling for Bastian's younger brother and his mate. Being courted by their guard. Acid churned in her stomach at the thought. Would Mae be disappointed in her? Of all people, Mae would know best what it's like living with changelings, so perhaps she wouldn't pass judgment on the situation Morrigan found herself in.

Mae had always been an outlier in the thoughts and expectations her family held. She didn't hold as many of their mother's thoughts as Morrigan had expected, but they hadn't ever had time to really discuss what had changed so drastically from when she had wed Santi and when Amara had wed Bastian just over six months later.

Surely, Mae would be happy that Morrigan was happy and safe.

Letting out a soft sigh, she mulled over all the new information that she had received. Had she been the girl that they had held when she was branded? Someone had. Nikaius was the man who plagued her dreams for years to afterwards, but she could never place who he was. The thought was dizzying. But he was mated so what did it matter if he was the one? There were no such things at triads. Three people couldn't be mated together, that was unheard of. Plus, what of her relationship with Hawke?

"I need a few minutes if that's okay." She realized Nikaius had offered his hand to her, and she blinked up at him before giving what she hoped was a reassuring smile.

"Yeah. Sure. Take your time. I know it's a lot to process." Nikaius gave a jerky nod that hinted at him not being as sure as he sounded. Waric stroked his fingers through her hair before he stood as well to follow Nikaius from the room.

When the door closed, Morrigan stood and paced the room, twisting her hair into a braid as she went. Could they have been the ones? What would that mean for her?

They were mates. Waric and Nikaius were mated, which meant regardless of what physical relationships Morrigan had with them, there was no tangible way for her to be with either of them in the long term.

But they had become her friends, and she didn't want to immediately leave them just because she was confused. Sighing softly, Morrigan went to collect some stationery and a pen.

Something drew her eye to the letter addressed to Nikaius beneath it.

While her lessons had improved her understanding of Rekru'e, she still wasn't the best at translating it to Common. Most words that jumped out at her were basic words; however, one sentence jumped out at her, and it almost seemed to be a threat.

You will be aeonie when you turn twenty-three as is customary. What did "aeonie" mean?

Frowning, she collected the stationery and her book and exited the room. Something about the tone of the letter seemed very forceful, like someone was telling him he had to do something against his will. But what? Was it a threat that they would kill him before he turned twenty-three? Panic welled in her chest as her mind turned over the possibilities.

She stumbled into Waric without realizing it, and he frowned as he held her at arm's length. "Are you alright?" Should she mention the letter to Waric? She didn't know how upset they would be knowing she had come across a letter that wasn't meant for her.

Shaking her head, she sighed and bit her lip before deciding to ask. "What does aeonie mean?" Waric narrowed his eyes as he looked over her shoulder with a frown.

"Did someone ask that of you? Or ask if you would?"

"What? No! I overheard the staff talking about it and was curious, but they were busy, and I didn't want to ask them and seem stupid, you know?" Waric's expression softened, and he stepped aside to let her walk ahead of him as he thought.

"It, like most things, depends on the context of what you are asking. It loosely means becoming attached, such as dating or marrying." Morrigan's stomach plummeted. Nikaius was to marry before he was twenty-three. That was a short time from then, within the year. "Some people use it as an innuendo for sex and others have even worse words they use."

What were they planning? Was this why she was here? They seemed to get along well enough, and obviously, Nikaius' father didn't see him marrying Waric. Maybe she should offer? Now that she knew the things she knew, even if they weren't destined to be mates, they still shared something, right? Being forced into marriage seemed like the worst way to start one. She could understand where the stress would lie if it was a custom that had been upheld for generations. Maybe she should ask Nikaius before she assumed too much.

Her first chance came when she sat across from Nikaius for dinner, but the thought of the unknown and the possible answers he could give twisted knots into her stomach.

Not being able to get to know him and Waric seemed like just as bad of a thing. Something drew them together in a way she couldn't explain, and she didn't want whatever they had to prematurely end.

She didn't eat much and returned to her room to mull over everything that had happened that day as well as write a letter to her sister.

Sleep didn't come easy for her that night.

"No, Please!"
The voice rang out as bruising fingers dropped Morrigan to her knees. She had failed.

She had watched her sister, Amara, go before her, envious of the ease with which she pulled the coldness to her and made little rabbits from the ice. They had danced happily around the snow, skipping between the gathered lords. Amara's powers were the same powers her older brother and their mother had.

Her hands were too cold, and she couldn't feel anything when they asked her to prove what she could do. She couldn't even feel their skin under her hands when they told her to try.

"Please no, she can't use her magic while being this cold. Warm her up and give her another chance!" Mae's voice was hoarse as she shouted. She had been yelling for what felt like hours, adding to the chill in Morrigan's heart. Mae was the only one who treated her kindly, and Morrigan had failed her. She didn't care about her mother or her other siblings, just making Mae proud.

The ice was cold and hurt as it dug into Morrigan's bare knees and shins. Her hair was so saturated with water that it clung to her in chunks of blood red against the starkness of her skin.

She hadn't known they would be out in the elements when they were tested or maybe she could have been better prepared.

Maybe?

Mae continued screaming, but Morrigan couldn't make sense of what else she said as she trembled. It was so cold, and every breath burned as it went in and scalded as she breathed out. Her lips were sore from the constant worry of her teeth on the flesh and the dryness from the cold.

She had failed.

"It will be over in a second." A boy with dark hair knelt before her on the snow. "It's going to suck, but it only takes a second, if that, and it will

be over." His voice was low and soft. He sounded like a man but was still gangly with youth. This was the first kindness she had been given since this whole ordeal had started. Did he care? Why?

Who was he? A young Nikaius.

Why was he there?

"Just keep your eyes on me, and we'll both be done, okay?" Her eyes met his, a shade of stormy blue that almost matched the darkening sky above them, and a bit of calm settled within her. He felt safe, his breaths low and slow, and she nodded.

Another boy stood over them, this one close in age to the first. He had a bright wide smile that was reassuring, even if it was fake. "Hey there, princess."

Waric.

Morrigan let out a little giggle despite the scalding tears and the way her bottom lip quivered. She was terrified, but they didn't seem cruel like the others.

Maybe they were right, and she would be okay. The second male took her hands and set them on their shoulders, connecting her to both of them. Their hands were so large, the heels of their palms touched where they braced her. Their heat surrounded her chilled skin, and it was almost soothing, as if she could feel the calm radiating from them. It wasn't a situation that warranted calm, so she was sure she was just making up things in her head to soothe herself.

Their posture shifted once, and they looked at each other before looking over her shoulder.

There wasn't any warning before pain exploded across her shoulder and the back of her neck. The sting of fire and magic etching deep into her skin followed as she tried to jerk away, but the two males held her, their shoulders trembling under the weight of her nails digging into their skin as she screamed. One of the males growled.

When the magic pulled away, the entire world went with it.

Morrigan gasped awake as she hit the cold stone floor and everything within her trembled as she tried to move but couldn't muster up the strength. While her mind was awake once more, her body still felt like it was locked into the memory of her failure. She hadn't dreamed about that night in years. Not since right after it had happened.

Her skin burned from where Nikaius had held her, and her knees felt bruised from the snow. When her fingers curled, she felt snow below her palms but knew she was in her room in Kunmei. Every breath felt like fire as it twisted through her, and nothing made sense as she closed her eyes and pressed her forehead to the floor.

The gut wrenching sobs that pulled from her were untamable, and she couldn't even move to cover her face when her door slammed open, and footsteps approached. "Morrigan?" Hands scorched her body as she was heaved from the floor, and she cried out at the pain.

"Fuck you're freezing." The voice was gruff with sleep but did nothing to soothe the tears that fell and the breaths that caught. She had failed her sister. She had failed everyone she cared about. She couldn't work the magic of the house or be a good mate to Nikaius and Waric. There was no plausible outcome to Hawke courting her because she had failed.

The brand on her skin made her worthless, and there was nothing she could do about it. There was nothing anyone could do to reverse the damage that was done.

The world shifted, and Morrigan's head throbbed as warmth engulfed her. The fur felt rough on her skin, scratching at the places where the handprints burned, but she had no energy to pull away, no will to fight the hand that stroked through her hair and the voice that rumbled under her cheek.

"It's okay, Mor. It's alright, you're safe now. I've got you." The words were the same ones Mae spoke to her when she came to after her marking, but this voice was lower, and the person smelled like leather and wind. "I've got you." They shifted again, and she gasped as she became weightless, and her head spun again.

Finally, her body started to respond to her, and she curled the fur closer despite the oversensitivity of her skin. The room they entered was warmer than hers, and she shivered at the contrast before she was settled onto the bed.

The light from the fireplace stung her eyes before it was blocked out by the person who sat on the bed, swiping away the tears as they fell. "I've got you." Blinking away the tears, she finally saw the world as it was, Hawke leaning over her with a look of concern.

"Hawke?"

"Hey princess. Welcome back." The fluttering of his wings overhead caught her attention, and she sighed as she watched them shift in the firelight. There hadn't been time for Aquila to keep up her promise of letting Morrigan touch her wings, and she probably should have asked before reaching for them, but the wing dipped down within her reach, and Hawke hummed as her fingers traced the corded muscle of the tertials that lay over his shoulder blade.

"They're softer than I thought." Her voice sounded broken, and her throat felt raw as she spoke, but Hawke smiled regardless.

"They are. Are you alright?"

"I..." She fought back the tears that clogged her throat as she pulled her hand away. "No. I don't know. It felt so real."

Hawke hummed as he looked her over. His gaze was warm, his eyes bright as they had been the night at Atce' Plaza, but as she tucked the fur around her chest better out of shyness, his expression changed, and he reached out to catch her elbow with a frown.

"I don't think the wards were updated as well as we thought." Concern rolled up her arm, and she gasped as the stinging pain from before returned. Looking down, she frowned.

It seemed not everything from her dream had been fake. Across her bicep was a dark red handprint, as if someone had reached out and burned their palm into her skin. Panic welled within her, tightening her chest and turning her stomach as she scrambled away from Hawke.

Someone had been in the room with her.

Someone had touched her in her sleep, burned their mark into her skin.

Oh Fates. What would have happened if Hawke hadn't arrived?

"Morrigan."

Was this payback for not doing as her family had wanted?

Was this Elijah or Amara playing games with her?

"Morrigan!"

The door slammed open, and Morrigan screamed. As she flinched back against the headboard, Hawke stood quickly, his wings flaring wide as if he was trying to block Morrigan from view.

"Waric?"

"There's someone in the house." Waric's voice was deep and gravelly from sleep. "I can't find Morrigan."

"I don't think they're here anymore." Stepping aside, Hawke let his wings drop. Morrigan trembled as her eyes met Waric's. He had stormed in, swords drawn with a wild look in his eyes. His hair was windswept, and he only wore black sleep pants, his breaths heaving as he looked around the room in confusion.

Now that Morrigan was regaining feeling to her body, she noticed that static buzzed through the air as if they were stepping through a portal. "The air feels wrong." It was the same feeling she had when she and Nikaius were in the bathroom when they had been attacked.

"I know." Waric's hands dropped, and his swords vanished as he stepped closer. His eyes looked her over, snagging on the mark seared into her arm. "Morrigan, are you okay?" Morrigan gave a quick shake of her head, hand fluttering over the mark as if she wanted to hide it but also afraid to touch it.

"Someone was in my room." Her voice broke at the admission as panic welled within her again. "They touched me." Why was this worse than any other time she had been touched without her consent? Was it because she had settled into some feeling of safety in Corinth Manor? Or because she knew that it wasn't someone in their home. Someone had deliberately broken in just to get to her. Oh Fates. Tears burned her throat again, and she couldn't stand the look that Waric gave her and buried her face into her knees as a sob broke through.

Someone shuffled closer and Hawke asked Waric, "Where's Nikaius?"

"Patrolling the house, I think." Waric didn't sound too confident.

Hawke let out a low breath, and the bed dipped beside Morrigan as she tried to fight more sobs. She wasn't sure how much more energy she had and crying would only deplete that. Crying wasn't what was needed at that moment. She needed to be on alert if something happened again.

"Morrigan, I... Can I touch you?" The fact that Hawke asked caused another sob to rip through her. How could these people be so kind to her? Seeking comfort in others was something new, but in that moment, that was all Morrigan wanted. She needed to feel cared for and that was what Hawke was offering. Nodding, she uncurled herself and surged up into Hawke's waiting arms.

"I've got her if you want to go find Nikaius. We'll stay right here." Hawke's voice buzzed against her cheek, and she snuggled closer. He was warm and safe, and she knew that even if her mind was still on high alert. The comfort he provided was enough to keep the panic at bay.

When Waric left and the door clicked shut behind him, Hawke pressed a kiss to the top of her head. "I've got you. I won't let go until you're ready, okay? You're welcome here as long as you need, but we need to treat that mark. We might be able to get it cleared up."

"Do you have to leave?" The thought of being alone right then made her stomach churn as if she might be sick by the very thought.

"No. I can pull things just like everyone else." She watched him reach out and pull the healing salve from the ether.

A little giggle escaped; she didn't miss the humor of the situation. "I'm surprised we have any of that left. I've been using it consistently."

Hawke chuckled gently as he opened it. "I like that."

"Like that I keep having to use it?"

"No." His smile spread to a full grin, and he swiped some of the salve along the mark. It burned a bit, but Morrigan was distracted by how close he was. "I like the way you said *we*. It makes everything feel more real. Like you're settling in and are accepting your place here. With us."

The lightness of his words and the hope he spread across her skin with every swipe of his fingers made her smile. "With us, or with you?"

Closing the container, he willed it away before adjusting them so he could cuddle her to his chest again, vanishing his wings so they could stretch out on the bed. "Why not both?" The kiss he pressed to her mouth was a sweet one, full of adoration and awe. Happiness welled within her, and she kissed him back. It wasn't a seeking or burning kiss like with Nikaius or Waric but just something simple and sweet.

Thinking about Nikaius made her sigh, and she pulled away to search his eyes before closing her own. "I found out that Nikaius is supposed to marry when he turns twenty-three."

Hawke didn't tense as she had expected him to, instead, he reached up and stroked a lock of hair away from her face. "That's a standard custom, yes."

Taking a slow breath through her nose, she shifted onto her back and licked her chapped lips. Nervousness crept up, and she swallowed it down, squeezing her eyes shut. "I was thinking of offering to marry him."

Expecting anger or upset or something acidic to burn from Hawke's touch, she was surprised as his emotions remained the same. "Okay, why?"

"You're not upset?"

"I want to hear your reasons why before I make a judgement."

"Which is why you're paired with all the Rekru'e leaders."

"Exactly." He twisted a lock of her hair around his finger. The peace he gave off was reassuring, and it was nice to have someone who willingly offered comfort when she didn't feel she could ask for it.

"They, Waric and Nikaius, told me about the Culling, and I think I might be the girl they marked." She took a breath. She knew she should pause to let Hawke process and respond, but anxiety made her want to get it all out before she got his reaction. "It makes sense, and if I'm their mate, it's a logical decision to make. But even if that wasn't the case, I think Nikaius and I get along well enough, we all do, and I can't imagine marrying someone he doesn't know would be great for him. Most people wouldn't understand Priamos either."

"Those are all logical reasons, but what do you want?" He gave her hair a playful tug, and she giggled and swatted his hand.

"I want to be able to get to know everyone and for him to be happy. If he marries someone else, we don't know where they'll stand on Waric, much less me and you and everyone else."

"I think it's a reasonable conversation to have. Regardless of the outcome, I'd still like a chance."

"Of course! This isn't me choosing someone over the others, but a…" She could see where it seemed like a conclusion and searched for the right word to express what she actually meant. She didn't want anything to change, she just wanted everyone safe and happy.

"A failsafe?"

Relief flooded through her at his suggestion, happy to know he understood where her thoughts were. "Yeah, something like that. It guarantees that nothing has to change."

"Having multiple partners isn't really frowned upon here either, but you're right, there's no telling who Nikaius' father, Nikola, would choose. He's always been against Nikaius and Waric being together regardless of their marks."

"Yeah." A yawn broke free, and Morrigan covered her face in an attempt to hide it. Hawke shifted and settled on his side next to her.

"Alright little dove, I think it's time we try to sleep again." She wasn't sure she could, but when he pulled her to him, she curled against his chest, settling into the warmth he provided. His arm wrapped around her waist, his palm spreading securely between her shoulder blades as he tucked the other one under his pillow. "Rest. You're safe here." His wings appeared and one tucked in close along her back as well. It was as if they were snuggled in a cocoon of warmth. "The feathers are an extension of myself. Any change of temperature or air currents will wake me, and I'm not going anywhere."

That was reassuring. The extra layer of protection definitely made her feel better and once she was comfortable, sleep found her quickly.

Chapter Twenty-Eight

Nikaius

Corinth Manor

Nikaius stumbled over his own feet as he searched for Waric. When his friend hadn't shown up after fifteen minutes in their hiding place, he began to worry that he had gotten caught. Waric's father wasn't a kind man, and Nikaius tried his best to prevent Waric from getting into trouble, even if it meant throwing himself in the line of fire.

"Hey! Ouch, Stop that!" Nikaius heard Waric's voice and changed the direction he was going in order to search for his friend.

"Bastian, stop, or I'll tell your mom."

"Awe little baby's gonna go cry to mummy. Boo-hoo." As he slid around the corner to find Bastian holding Waric on the ground, kneeling on his friend's back with one of his arms wedged up high, his anger grew.

"Bastian, leave him alone! He hasn't done anything to you!"

Bastian laughed as he watched Nikaius approach. "His existence is an abomination. He shouldn't even be here. He's nothing but a half-breed." In his distraction, Waric was able to roll away from Bastian.

"It's better to be a half-breed than a bully!" The boys that had gathered with Bastian were ones Nikaius barely knew but had recently become friends with Bastian. Not that he was worthy of having friends.

"Poor little Niky not knowing how to hold his tongue around those that are better than him." Nikaius flinched as Bastian suddenly appeared in front of him. Recently, his brother had gained a few of the more prominent alpha traits, such as quick movements and alpha commands.

Nikaius had been on the receiving end of those commands, but mostly only in private. He wouldn't dare gain their mother's ire in public.

"I said leave him alone!" Nikaius shoved at his brother, but the other male didn't move far. Before Nikaius could move, Bastian's hand was around his throat, pinning him to the wall.

"I said no." Though he turned his attention away from Nikaius, there was nothing he could do to fight against the hold around his throat. "Who wants to see if I can make him shift? Ten gold says I can."

"You're not supposed to do that, Bastian."

"Yeah, it's against the rules."

"Who's going to tell on me if I do?"

Everyone remained silent.

"That's what I thought." Turning his grin on Nikaius, Bastian cinched his hand tighter around Nikaius' throat. Locking eyes with him, Nikaius trembled. "Shift." Bastian's voice had gotten lower, dropping a few octaves that sent a thrill of fear through him. This was dangerous.

"I can't. you know that!"

"That's because you're pathetic and weak. Shift." This command was deeper. "You're a useless second son who has nothing going for him."

Panic flooded through Nikaius as he struggled against his brother's hold. There was no way he could save himself. What would happen to Waric if he died? "You're unworthy and unlovable. Everyone would be happier if you died. Shift!" Anger so deep and powerful pulled itself from within Nikaius' chest. It hurt so badly, it brought tears to his eyes, and he felt like he couldn't breathe. Nothing of the world made sense to him and suddenly everything was too bright, and his mouth tasted like blood.

The screams that followed were loud. Nikaius couldn't see anything. It felt as if his entire being had been ripped in half and one entire side of his body was in excruciating pain. But it changed, never settling on one side or the other, just ever-changing shards of ice bowing his back and breaking everything down one small cut after another.

His breath was his own but wasn't, and his thoughts were his own, but they weren't. Why was he so hungry? Why did everything hurt? Everything smelled so strong, the scent of blood and fear? How could he smell fear? How did he know it was fear? Before he could think too much more, everything came to a screeching halt and dissolved into darkness.

Nikaius sat up with a gasp, trying to shove away the shards of ice that pricked his skin. Everything hurt, and he felt as if he was on fire.

You're unworthy.

He knew it was Bastian talking. His brother had somehow gotten into his head again. Taking a slow breath, he untangled himself from the bed and rolled out his shoulders. Morrigan had seemed to have fun with Hawke the night before, and he was glad she was happy. But a bit of jealousy burned his throat at the thought. She wasn't his to claim but part of him still worried that she would choose him over them. Because Hawke was whole. One with his animal, not some scarred half-beast.

The night was quiet when he entered the kitchen, glad that no one seemed to be awake.

You're pathetic and weak.

Nikaius sighed, rolling out his shoulders and fighting the low grumble of Priamos wanting control. He knew he could only hold off the primal for so much longer before he took control by force, but Nikaius had so many things he needed to figure out.

You've only got friends because they pity you.

Would Waric really have stayed if they hadn't been marked?

He knew this line of thought wouldn't do him any good, and he shook himself as he tried to work the nightmare from his system.

His thoughts always turned kind of errant and depressive so close to the drop but with fighting it as long as he has, Nikaius knew he was only buying himself a small amount of time before everything snapped. He needed to be sure that everyone was safe before that happened.

Everything within him ached in a way that felt as if he was covered in a large blanket that weighed him down. Not wanting to bother the others with the chaos in his mind, Nikaius decided that a late-night run would be better. Running always cleared his head, no matter if he was in his mortal form or that of Priamos' beast. He knew the likelihood of it actually clearing so close to the drop would be nearly impossible, but he still wanted to try, fearing that he would snap at someone just because Priamos lingered so close under his skin.

Priamos was becoming more and more unstable.

The run didn't help. In fact, it made Priamos more on edge and did nothing to stop the well of thoughts that flooded through his mind. He knew most of it was because of the moon, but it still unsettled him that it happened to be when the newest member of their household needed attention and protection more than anyone else.

The sun had started to rise when Nikaius made it back home.

"Where have you been?" Waric met him at the gate to the house looking weather beaten and wild. Alarm bells rang in Nikaius' head at Waric's tone.

"What happened?"

"Morrigan was attacked. Where were you?"

"The memories crept in again, and I went for a run."

"That's really shitty timing."

"Tell me about it. Is she okay?" Nikaius tried to step past Waric, but his mate's hand on his shoulder made him pause.

"She's fine. She's with Hawke, but despite the drafters fixing her wards, someone was able to get in and leave their mark on her."

Priamos snarled, and Nikaius shoved past Waric. They would find whoever marked her and destroy them.

"Hey, no. Wait." Waric stepped in front of him, pressing his hands to his shoulders and dipping down so their eyes met. "She's with Hawke and probably back to sleep. We need you to be clear-headed if we're going to figure out what happened and how to fix this."

"No. I failed her. I was supposed to be here to protect her."

"Nikaius, she has all of us to protect her. It's not just one person's job, and with you being so close to the edge, I don't know how capable you are of protecting yourself let alone anyone else." Waric's words stung, but Nikaius knew that Waric was right. The closer to the full moon it got, the more Nikaius needed to rely on Waric. This now meant taking care of Morrigan as well.

Letting out a resigned huff, Nikaius nodded. "You're right. Priamos doesn't like it, but you're right. Let's get breakfast going and then we'll see what the day brings."

"That's a good idea." Curling his hand along the back of Nikaius' neck, Waric pressed their foreheads together. "We've got you, and we've got her. It'll be fine. I know it."

Nikaius wasn't so sure, but he chose to trust his mate and nodded, following him back into the house.

Chapter Twenty-Nine

Nikaius and Morrigan

Corinth Manor
- Kunmei Park

It took longer than Nikaius had expected to finally see Morrigan again. She slept through breakfast and though he was on alert for her the rest of the morning, court things drew him away for the afternoon. When he returned late afternoon, he finally caught her bright and springy scent before he entered the study. He tried to make his steps slow and leisurely as if he wasn't seconds from finding Waric and begging to be put out of his misery. He wanted to curl up beside her and beg for her forgiveness, but he was worried it would be too much.

"Well, if it isn't Morrigan, always with a book in her hand." Nikaius chortled as he entered the study. He hoped he was being natural despite all the warning bells going off in his head that he was overplaying everything. The doubt of his abilities still rang loud in his head, and he could hear Bastian laughing in the back of his mind.

Leaning over, he plucked the book from her hands and grinned as he turned a page in interest, hoping he would catch her reading something dirty that he could tease her about. He understood none of what was on the page and the realization tightened his stomach in anxiety. He didn't really have anything in common with her.

"As if you could fathom the words upon those pages, Nikaius. Why? What need would you have for reading when you have a lordship on your side?" Her words were a tease that she hoped would ease some of the tension between them. She stood quickly and moved around the couch to retrieve her book. "Hand it over." She held out her hand, but he danced away, laughing again as he turned back to her page and read.

The book in his hand was an old scientific journal written in Common that had belonged to her father. Nikaius tilted his head as he browsed the page. "Do you understand this?" His brows furrowed as he lowered his hands to look from her to the book and back.

"Yes, why? Don't you?" Morrigan stomped over to him, snapped the book shut in his hands, and used it to smack him on the arm.

"I don't."

Morrigan paused mid-swing. "Really?"

"Seriously. I'm not very good at reading Common, and I never did well with math or many sciences. Do you understand any of that?" When she nodded, Nikaius grinned. "Please enlighten me while we walk. I'm sure Waric would love to know he has a fellow lover of science in our home." Something seemed off with her, but Nikaius couldn't put his finger on what.

You're unworthy, and she likes your mate more than you. Shaking the thought from his head, Nikaius heard someone approach and turned his attention to the door.

Before she could say anything about the sudden shift in the air between them, Aslin peeked her head into the room. "Did I hear something about a walk?" Morrigan lowered the book at Aslin's raised eyebrow.

"Yes. I was asking Morrigan if she could enlighten me on the theories presented in her book. I'm not afraid to admit when I don't understand something that I've read. I wouldn't be taking lessons in Common if that weren't the case." *You're just stupid and can't comprehend the basics of science.* Bastian's voice in his head made Nikaius roll his shoulders in an attempt to make the thoughts subside. Now was not the time for rash behavior or thoughts. Everything was fine.

Aslin laughed but nodded, her eyes flickering between the two. Aslin had brought breakfast to Morrigan and Hawke, and they had updated her on what had happened during the night. Morrigan was surprised that neither she nor Aquila had heard anything, but when she asked about it, Aslin just blushed and stammered that they were heavy sleepers. "Well, it just so happens that the children and I were heading to the park for science lessons today. They love the meadows and streams there." Morrigan's stomach plummeted. How could she have forgotten that today was one of the days she spent helping Aslin with the local school children?

It was so different to have a say in how her time was spent that she kept forgetting things she had agreed to do. The lack of routine was a bit disorienting, but Aslin always managed to pop in with a kind reminder when Morrigan forgot.

"I would love to join you and the children, Aslin. I shall fetch my coat." Nikaius dipped into a playful bow, earning a giggle from both of the women before excusing himself to collect his outerwear.

When Aslin looked at Morrigan, and a nervous flutter settled in her stomach. Morrigan had no objections to spending time with Nikaius, but how long should she wait before saying something about what she had read? Even if she didn't make her offer, telling him what she read would assuage some of the guilt that had settled in her stomach.

Aslin looked from Morrigan, to the door, and back with a raised eyebrow. Morrigan couldn't help but feel silently chastised as Aslin tilted her head. As if she could hear Morrigan's thoughts. "Morrigan?" Her voice was one she used on children when she knew they were up to something they shouldn't be. "Do I want to know why there's suddenly a weird air between the two of you?"

Morrigan shook her head, laughing as she stepped closer. "I haven't the foggiest idea what you're talking about."

With a final look and a disbelieving hum, Aslin shook her head and linked her arm with Morrigan's so they could gather their things before collecting the children.

The air was brisk when they reached the schoolhouse, and the children eagerly greeted them when they entered. This particular school session was for children aged four to twelve. Around the age of puberty, powers tended to present themselves for fae children and they would be sent to where their talents would best be nurtured and tamed for safe use.

Typically, children who held no powers were marked like Morrigan was and sent to the Farm. Morrigan wasn't sure what Nikaius' stance was on that, but she felt like maybe he would be opposed to such a notion.

She also wasn't quite sure what the standard was for the changeling children. Several of them seemed to have some aspects of their animals already, including wings. Playful growls emitted from a pair of boys who were tumbling around in one of the corners.

Many were excited to see Nikaius, and he seemed rather excited himself. He knew everyone by name but seemed particularly fond of the ones who possessed changeling traits.

When he picked up a small red-headed girl, Alya, and threw her in the air, Morrigan gasped, daring forward to reach out to catch her if needed. Nikaius chucked, and Alya giggled loudly.

Her wings, a beautiful tawny and rose hue, fluttered before expanding completely, catching the air on her downfall just enough for her to hang mid-air for a few moments before tumbling back into Nikaius' arms.

"Your wings have gotten stronger!" Nikaius' voice conveyed that was proud of the advances that Alya was making, and Priamos purred happily as he cuddled her close. She sniffled a bit as she buried her face into his chest, and he patted her back gently. "You just have to keep practicing. Remember last time I came to visit, and you couldn't even open them at that height?" Guilt welled within Nikaius as he swayed the small girl in his arms. Alya had imprinted on him when she was a babe and with the chaos of Morrigan's arrival and court happenings, he hadn't had time to visit her. Imprints were bonds foraged between infants and caregivers within the first few days of life. If an infant didn't imprint, their survival rate was typically low.

Nikaius and Alya's imprint had been an accident, one born of visiting Hawke and Aquila's home for solstice in order to attend their elder sister's funeral. He had held Alya for all of a minute before he felt the imprint settle over him. He wasn't ready to have complete custody of a child, having been in his position for less than a year, but with Alya's father gone, the decision had been made that she would come back to Kunmei with him and Aquila while Hawke settled other affairs. They had found a Kyilzar family who had one other child. An agreement had been reached, and she had settled well with frequent visits from Nikaius.

Two weeks wasn't that long of a span of time, but with Alya snuggled in his arms, he realized part of his ongoing agitation could be attributed to their bond. It had been the first time they had been separated for so long.

You've failed to keep Morrigan safe in your own home, how can you protect a little girl you gave to someone else instead of raising her on your own? Bastian's voice chided again. Taking a deep breath, Nikaius shook him from his mind again. Would there be no end?

As Nikaius talked to Alya, his face softened in a way that Morrigan had only seen a few moments of in private. He looked as if he finally stopped grinding his teeth; his shoulders relaxing as he kept Alya tucked against his chest with one hand and the other slipped up to stroke her hair gently away from her face. She continued to sniffle but didn't cry, and Morrigan knew he was calming her.

His eyes locked with hers and the feeling of being caught made her heart hiccup in her chest as he gave a little smile. Morrigan returned it, aware of the heat that tickled her face, but she couldn't look away from the image he portrayed.

So many things rushed into the forefront of her brain at that moment. Some she couldn't name but others she could but refused to because she knew she would be embarrassing herself if she did. This included the one where he held a different redheaded child, one with soft blue eyes or vivid green, not the lovely caramel Alya had.

"My momma says there's going to be a wedding soon." One of the older children, a nine-year-old boy named Rylan chirped, and the image in Morrigan's mind shattered, her attention drawn away when she realized they had been caught...

What had they been caught doing?

"What?" Her question wasn't a question, but more of a realization that in the moments they were connected, her mind had gone blissfully blank.

"They're getting married?" Eleven-year-old Abbigale asked, her eyes bright as she looked from Nikaius to Morrigan and back. Morrigan remembered then that Abby could vaguely read minds. It was more of an impression than actually reading the thoughts. Morrigan wondered what Abby had sensed to conclude that she and Nikaius were going to get married, and she blushed more.

"No." Her voice sounded weak, and she cleared her throat with a shake of the head. "No. No one is getting married."

"Oh..." The children's faces fell.

"Why not?" Little Alya's voice rose above the rest, her little face so hopeful. It made Morrigan's heart hurt because she vaguely held the same hope that maybe, somehow, they would feel the same way about each other, and she would be able to prevent him from having to do whatever he needed to satisfy the demands that seemed to have been placed on him.

"Lord Ayrden hasn't proposed yet." Summoning bravery from somewhere deep within herself, she looked at Nikaius again. His eyebrows rose, and his lips parted as if he wanted to say something, but Aslin chimed in first.

"That's quite enough of that. We're going to the park today, remember?" Aslin stood, looking between the two with an amused expression, her hands on her hips and eyebrows raised. Distracted, the children cheered and rushed to gather their coats and cloaks. Alya eagerly wiggled herself around in Nikaius' arms before jumping, clipping him in the jaw with her wings as she fluttered herself to the ground and took off after her friends.

The stunned look Nikaius wore as he held the side of his face pulled a laugh from Morrigan that she quickly covered with her hands. His laugh followed before the children returned, eagerly pushing and tugging each other towards the door.

Once everyone was out in the brisk morning air, the smaller children rushed to follow Aslin as others chased each other in a game of tag. Morrigan reached for the basket of books that were regularly used for lessons, but Nikaius snatched it free from her fingers before offering his free arm to her.

"Please Morrigan, explain the workings of your book to me." He gestured to the book Morrigan still held and smiled, holding them back a bit so that the last of the children were more than a few steps ahead.

"I would have thought you had learned such things in fancy schools growing up." Morrigan paused for a second to collect a stone from the ground before tucking her hand into his elbow again.

"I wasn't a difficult child, but I did have a difficult upbringing. They anticipated my brother. He's everything that should come from our parents' breeding." Even though she couldn't feel exactly what Nikaius was feeling because their skin did not touch, the sound of his voice pinged sadness through Morrigan. "Second sons are rare. Somewhere along the line, I also ended up with a different animal. It makes a bit of sense since my mother is the last descendant of the La'mir Pack and my father is an Ayrden, a distant cousin of the De'Lyon pride. Typically, the genetics follow the male line, but the wolf still managed to sneak in somewhere."

It's because you're the weakest link. The Fates took pity on you and that's the only reason you are where you are. You're pathetic.

Nikaius fell silent as they walked, his gloved thumb brushing along the back of Morrigan's hand. The longer Bastian's voice lingered in his head, the harder it became for Nikaius to breathe through it and remember why he was wrong.

Nikaius' silence strengthened Morrigan's resolve to ask him about the letter, but Nikaius' warm hand covering hers, his thumb stroking her knuckles, slowly drew her from those thoughts. "I already knew this. It doesn't explain your education."

"Ah." Morrigan realized how close she had drawn herself when she felt Nikaius' ribs expand and contract against her elbow when he spoke again. "It was harder for me to learn control than most." His blue eyes met Morrigan's, and he tapped his temple with a playful grin. "He's a bit unruly at times."

The fact that Nikaius' wolf was a separate entity reminded her of the trauma he had suffered, but she decided that it wasn't the right time to let the anger and sadness she felt for him in. He was genuinely interested in what Morrigan had to say. "So you weren't difficult, but you had a difficult time. That makes sense now. If you really would like to learn, how can I say no?" The smile he gave her melted her heart before she returned it tentatively. Looking ahead, she made a note of Aslin, who had settled herself on a bench, reading a book to some children as others ran and played.

Pulling away from him, Morrigan opened the book to the first chapter, mainly for the diagrams, not so much the words. "This book is about the mortal Newton's Laws. The first one is about motion. A thing, like a rock," she gestured to the rocks at their feet, "will not move unless another force acts upon it." She moved the rock with her toe and looked up at him with a smile. He surprised her by paying rapt attention to what she was saying. Never had someone paid mind to something she had found fascinating.

"The second portion of the law is that a thing in motion will stay in motion unless another force happens upon it and changes its velocity." Holding up the rock she had retrieved earlier, Morrigan threw it as far as she could. "If gravity were to not weigh the rock down, it could go forever unless something stopped it."

Like your head against the wall where I could have killed you but didn't.

"Like cricket?" Nikaius' brows furrowed as he tried to come up with a comparable idea and ignored the faint words in the back of his head. Priamos grumbled.

"Yes!" Excitement flooded through her. "Yes, just like cricket! The ball would continue for however long unless something, the wickets in most cases, stops the ball."

"What about the bat?" Nikaius' question made Morrigan's smile broaden. She was enjoying how engaged he was.

"That would be Newton's third law of force."

"Force?"

"Yes. Everything has force and objects use force against one another. Like when the ball hits the bat. For some, their force isn't enough, and the ball has more, so it flings the bat backward and smacks your shoulder. Some forces equal out and that's when the ball hits the bat but falls to the ground."

"Okay?" His brow furrowed, and Morrigan's skin heated at how deeply she seemed to hold his attention.

"And finally, when you swing the bat, I imagine in most cases you send the ball away in a different direction than the one it came from." Nikaius nodded, licking his lips as his eyes danced between hers. She didn't feel the words leaving her at that point, more interested in watching him watch her. "That shows that your force is greater than the ball's force, so not only is the third law applied but the first as well because in every one of those instances you are impacting the inertia..."

She'll never look at you with such excitement. That's saved for Waric and Hawke. You can't keep one person happy; she needs two others to be content. What a waste of space.

Without thinking, Nikaius surged forward, hand clasping her jaw as he leaned forward and kissed her. Bastian's voice died away. His words weren't true. None of them were. The nightmare was fucking with his head, that's all it was.

Morrigan's hand spasmed and the book fell as her back hit the tree she hadn't realized was behind her. With her free hand, she reached up, curling her fingers in his hair as she shifted just a bit, taking a gasp of air before returning the kiss with equal fervor.

Gone were the thoughts of inertia and science and gone were the muddled thoughts about how she felt thinking he was going to marry someone else. All she felt from him was wonder, and she smiled as her eagerness rose to meet it.

Aslin's voice pulled them apart and Morrigan gasped, clinging to the shirt at his back as their heads snapped toward where her voice had been heard.

Oh Fates. He had just kissed her to get his brother out of his head. He really was as terrible as Bastian said. The Fates knew he wasn't worth her time. "I... Sorry... I... Well. Yes... I'm sorry. I shouldn't have done that." He picked up the book and returned it to her hand before turning to leave.

Frowning, Morrigan caught his wrist and summoned all the courage she had. "Nikaius... Nik." He turned to face her, letting out a slow breath.

"Morrigan," her name was painful to get out. He just wanted to flee, to sort out his own mind and figure out what he was going to do. He was such a mess.

"I... I know about the letter." Her confession tumbled from her lips in a single breath.

"What?"

"You could marry me. I know you said your father doesn't support you and Waric even though you're mated, but we could..." She cleared her throat and stepped forward using her hold on his wrist to pull herself closer to him. "Marry me." Her hands shook. Her entire body shook as he stared at her as if he had never seen her before. "We-We're friends, right?" Why were there tears in her eyes? Why did her voice break like that? "Surely marrying someone you actually like would be better than marrying a stranger."

"I... I can't do that." He pulled free from her grasp and rested both hands on her shoulders. "We can't do that, Morrigan. We can't."

"Why not?" She didn't understand. She didn't understand anything at that moment. Why did her chest hurt so bad over something she already knew?

"Don't... Don't do that." His voice cracked as a soft sob bubbled from Morrigan's chest. "Don't do that Morrigan..." Oh Fates, Waric and Hawke were going to be so mad at him. While he knew her thoughts were ones of kindness, he didn't deserve it.

"You don't deserve to be unhappy because your father is a jerk, Nikaius!"

"Neither do you, darling. I'll figure it out on my own. I always do." He pressed a gentle kiss to Morrigan's forehead and fled. Priamos roared loud in his head, the beast struggling for control Nikaius didn't want to relent.

Chapter Thirty

Morrigan

Kunmei Park

Morrigan sat for a while, nestled under a willow, and listened to the snowfall. She hadn't known it was going to snow. Sure, the day had started dreary and cold, but she didn't know enough about the weather patterns there well enough to be able to predict them. She had only been in Kunmei for a short time.

A short time.

The branches of the willow swayed softly, slightly disrupting the flow of the brook behind her. It was soothing where she was, and she didn't feel like leaving. She didn't want to.

Who would show their face after spectacularly embarrassing themselves like she had?

No one, that's who.

What had she been thinking? Who offers to marry someone they just met? An idiot.

An idiot who had developed a delusion that she could be the third in a mated pair.

A lovesick idiot who jumps at the first person who shows her affection. Three people? That was a lot to ask of someone.

At least he had been kind about it.

Not that it didn't hurt any less.

She had been there only a few days, and she was offering herself up to one of the first people who made her feel seen and heard and had treated her like she was a person, not a burden. They all had, and each expression of intent had made her happier than she could ever believe she could be. But Nikaius' denial still hurt somehow.

She wished Mae was with her. She would know what to say, what to do to make her feel better, or at least less bad. She would sit her down and tell her that "It's okay to feel this way" and "Genuine kindness is a gift.. Morrigan would believe her of course, but believing herself was another story.

Despite being able to tell people's feelings by touch, she realized her version of how the world worked was skewed. Had the harsh treatment of her family made her overly accepting and so desperate for connection that she had jumped without looking?

Probably, but she had engaged in a few relationships in the past. This was new, but she wasn't sure how true her perception rang.

Footsteps crunched in the snow, and Morrigan covered her mouth with her hand to stifle the sob that had threatened to break through. She was wiping the tears from her face when the branches of the willow parted and Waric stepped in.

"Morrigan!" His relief was evident in the way his shoulders relaxed and a smile spread across his face. "I've been looking for you everywhere. Nikaius—" Morrigan dropped her eyes from his face, "said he had left you by the willow as if he did— Are you okay?"

Nodding, Morrigan pressed her hands to her eyes. "I'm fine. Just stupid." She hadn't noticed he was carrying anything until warm fur was draped over her.

"I doubt that. You can do all sorts of things like knit and outwit Hawke, and you're good at getting Nik to take himself less seriously."

Her hiccup at Nikaius' name must have given her away because Waric sighed.

"What happened?"

"As if you don't know," Morrigan scoffed.

"I don't actually." Slipping down the trunk of the tree, he settled next to Morrigan on the cold ground.

"Right, you're mated, as if you don't share everything. That's how it works. That's how men work. Lead someone on, reject them, and then brag to your friends about it afterward."

"Who hurt you?" Waric's voice was low. Concern laced up Morrigan's arm as he slipped his warm hand over hers and squeezed.

Did he mean in general or presently?

Morrigan let out a sarcastic laugh. "Do you want a list?" She couldn't stand his concern or the look in his eyes, so she jerked away and clamored to her feet to stalk away.

She didn't get far.

Before she could stomp her way out from under the tree, Waric's hand snagged her elbow. He tugged her so harshly that she stumbled and thudded against his chest.

He was taller than her by a couple of inches and was able to rest his chin on the top of her head as he wrapped his arms tightly around her.

"It's okay."

"It's not okay." Her voice broke at her protest, and she struggled a bit, trying to pull away.

He didn't need to be there.

He didn't need to be warm and confusing.

He didn't need to see her break down over her stupid acts and his mate.

"It's okay, you're allowed to be upset about things you can't control. Whatever is bothering you is bugging Nikaius too. He shut me out and sent me here." Morrigan let out a pitiful shuddered breath and Waric squeezed her closer, swaying them side to side. "He didn't tell me what happened but told me to come find you. What happened?"

"It's stupid."

"I hardly think that something that has upset you is stupid. You're allowed to feel how you feel. Zero judgment."

"I..." How did she explain it? She was happy her face was tucked against his shoulder as he stroked her hair. While Nikaius was wild, and she felt as if she was always wired and alive with him, Waric was calm and soothing. Settling. "Remember when I asked you about that word, aeonie? I... I saw a letter addressed to Nikaius. He has to marry before he turns twenty-three, right?"

Waric stiffened against her before he resumed petting her hair. "I didn't know that. I knew it was a tradition, but I didn't think they would hold Nikaius to it."

Morrigan nodded. "I talked it over with Hawke, and I might have told him I would marry him."

"And like an idiot, he said something like 'I'll figure it out' in that stupidly reassuring way that he does and then sauntered off like a moron?"

Morrigan giggled at the voice he used and leaned back to look at him. "He does that often?"

"Only when he's doubting his worth. He'll come around. I promise." Waric smoothed Morrigan's hair down before cupping her face in his hands. "Come, we have more important things to do than cry over the stupid man we love."

Morrigan didn't have time to react to the kiss he placed firmly on her mouth, but after a breath, she nodded and followed. It was still a little confusing to have the attention of multiple men, but she didn't think much more about it as he tugged her through the snow by her elbow. Reacting with emotions was not the solution that anyone needed, and it was something she would need to work on.

Just like in the courtyard, Morrigan was left breathless at the scene around them. The snow had fallen heavier than she thought; the world blanketed entirely in white while thick fat fluffs of snow drifted from the sky. "Oh, mortal physics!" Waric waved her book in front of her before tucking it into one of the saddlebags of his horse.

Morrigan approached the large russet horse and reached out to pet his side. A hard gust of wind stirred the snow and twisted her hair and skirt around her. Picking hair from her mouth, she frowned. She would have knots in her hair later. "Isn't it cold for him?"

"Nah, Rowan doesn't mind the snow. He likes to prance around in it when we turn him loose."

"I'd like to see that!" Morrigan laughed at the image. She stroked her hand down Rowan's side again, humming to herself. He gave off so much heat it made her a bit sleepy.

"It doesn't hurt that magic is a thing, right? His saddle and the barn are both warmed, so he has somewhere to go when the chill gets to be too much. Speaking of which…" Cold slushy ice scattered across the side of Morrigan's face, and she let out a loud startled screech.

"Waric Cavanaugh!" Wiping her face free of ice, she scooped up her ball of snow and packed it. Her aim was right, and she pegged him in the back of the head as he turned to run. "Hah!"

It didn't take long for Waric to reload and throw another ball at Morrigan, but she dodged behind Rowan with a laugh. "Now what are you going to do?" She was too short to peek her head over Rowan's back to see what Waric was planning, but a second later, his strong arms were snagging her around the waist and swinging her around. They both tumbled to the ground, and Morrigan gasped as she landed with a thud on Waric's chest.

"Oh my goodness! Are you okay?" Morrigan moved to sit up, but Waric laughed, securing his arms around her shoulders and waist so she wouldn't move too far.

"I'm fine. Do you feel any better now?"

"A little." She knew they should move and get up out of the snow, but Waric was calming the chaotic thoughts in her head. "I think I might go visit my sister. I don't think I can face Nikaius again after embarrassing myself like that."

Waric hummed and sat them up, stroking his hand through Morrigan's wet hair. "I promise you this isn't your problem. It's his problem."

"So you keep saying." Morrigan sighed.

"I promise you that it is." He pushed Morrigan off him gently and stood, offering her his hand before pulling her to her feet and brushing snow from both of them.

Morrigan mulled over all the information she had been told over the last few days. Everything in her life had happened so fast since the night in Atce' Plaza and despite the embarrassment that still lingered, she was grateful they had been there when she was. When they reached the barn, Morrigan smiled at her surroundings. Everything was so different in

Kunmei, but the barns were the same. "Did you know who I was when we were at the plaza?"

"No, we had just gotten word from Santiago De'Lyon that there would be trafficking, and he needed us to be there." Removing the saddle from Rowan, Waric gathered brushes and offered one to Morrigan while stroking his other along the horse's side.

Morrigan accepted the other brush and started stroking it along Rowan's wiry coat. The motion was soothing despite the way Waric's words made her stomach knot. "I think Priamos knew before either of us did. Nikaius kept saying the world felt off, and he could smell sunshine."

"He's told me a few times that I smell like sunshine."

"You do. But I wasn't sure at first, but it feels like we have this weird tether to you. I've only felt this way once, and that was when Nik and I were separated after our marking. It was this weird feeling that something was missing. A phantom limb of sorts. I didn't want to overwhelm you. Nikaius is close to a drop, so his control over Priamos is severely lacking as of late. And Priamos is convinced you're his other mate, so he's been more excitable."

"But changelings can't mate with the fae."

"Santi and your sister Mae are mated."

"They're Fated mates, that's different. They bear a mark from The Fates. I don't bear any marks except the brand."

"You have to accept the bond. We were young and open to the possibility that anyone could be our mate because we were raised that way." His words paused for a few moments and the only sound was their brushes sliding along Rowan's hair until he found the right words. "You were raised to believe that the fae don't have mates the same way. You were never open to the mark, so you haven't gotten one. It's like a mental block but only you can unblock it."

Morrigan stood, mulling over everything that Waric had just told her. She could be a changeling's mate without it being a true mating like Mae and Santi?

"What's the difference between the marks that you and Nikaius have and those that Mae and Santi have?"

"That... Uh..." It seemed like he wasn't expecting that question. "Fated Mates are marked by the Fates. Their bond knows no limits and can span across different lifetimes. Fated mates are always destined to be together, even if it's not in this lifetime. What Nikaius and I have is different because it's more of an emotional bond that's secured through high emotions. We're meant to be together too. We were just blessed in a different order than true mates."

"There's more than one type of mark?"

"There's two from what I've learned. Marks from the beginning and from the middle. The gold marks around Santi's and Mae's wrists symbolize they were meant to be together from the beginning of their creation. These are ones that have to be confirmed. What Nikaius and I have is a blessing from the middle. We weren't initially thought to be together, but the Fates changed their minds and realized we worked together well enough to be together now and until the end."

"Does the End have a mark?"

"Not that I'm aware of. We'll be meeting with members of the Valkyrie at the New Moon Council. I'm sure one of them would love to explain the workings of Fate better than I could." Waric smiled, and Morrigan nodded, she would love to meet a Valkyrie.

They were the closest people to the Fates aside from those who had been blessed with the sight. Imriel Gorlassar was one such person that Morrigan knew of because Mae had been his tutor when he noticed the mark she shared with Santi.

Waric took the brush from Morrigan and smiled. "Let's go up to the house and get warm. I'm sure you've got a lot to think about. If you genuinely want to leave, I'm sure we could work something out."

Waric seemed content with the idea that they were mates, but Nikaius was fighting it. As they ventured back to the house, Morrigan sighed as she thought it over.

"Why does Nikaius have a problem with us being mates?"

"It's not so much that he doesn't think he deserves us specifically, but that he doesn't think he deserves anything good because he's a little broken inside."

"Ah. And nothing we say can change his mind?"

"I'm afraid not. He's kind of bullheaded sometimes. He has to work through it on his own." They stepped into the house, and Waric turned to wrap her up in his arms again, pressing a gentle kiss to her forehead. He felt calm and resolved, which left no room for doubt about where he stood. Morrigan relaxed into the embrace, curling her fingers into his shirt before letting out a soft sigh.

"I'll get changed and maybe we can talk to him over dinner?"

"Mmm. Maybe." He didn't seem convinced, but Morrigan decided that was a problem for a later time as the cold wetness of her clothes settled on her skin and made her shiver. Thinking while she was warm was probably a good idea.

Chapter Thirty-One

Nikaius

Corinth Manor

It had been an hour since Nikaius had walked away from Morrigan. What had she been thinking about offering something like that? She didn't know what she was getting herself into, but whose fault was that when he refused to even broach the subject himself? He refused to believe that there was even a chance that they could have what he and Waric had. It was so rare, and he didn't want to get her hopes up, especially not when they had only known her for a short time.

What good would it do to bring it up for it to not be true?

He stared at the letter he had been writing. It was to Santiago De'Lyon. Since Morrigan had come into their lives, the monthly poker night had yet to happen because part of Nikaius had been worried about Morrigan being overwhelmed by seeing Santi. The other, more selfish part of him, didn't want her to get the idea of leaving them to go back to her sister.

She'd be better off there.

He knew that Mae and Santi would take care of her. They always had from what he had heard before their marriage. He knew that Mae had tried to fight to get custody of Morrigan but something about that hadn't gone the way they wanted.

This would never go the way he wanted either. Sure, Waric and Priamos had decided that it would be worth it. But Nikaius still wasn't sure.

There were so many other people that she would be well suited for.

"What the hell did you do?" The door to the study slammed open, sending a ripple of air that scattered papers from the desk where Nikaius sat. Waric was livid. Nikaius could smell the anger on him and see the evidence on his face. If their bond had been open, it probably would have consumed him long before.

"What do you mean?" Nikaius knew exactly what he meant. He knew what he meant because he hadn't stopped thinking about it since he had walked away from Morrigan.

"What did you do?"

"You need to be more specifi—" Nikaius' words cut off as Waric fisted his hands into the collar of his shirt and pulled him from the chair. He was unsteady and stumbled, but Waric's hands didn't relent. He wasn't that much shorter than Nikaius, but even with the height difference, Nikaius was still wary of his temper.

As teenagers, they fought regularly. Between Nikaius' volatility in learning to control Priamos and Waric's difficulty regulating his own shifting, things were broken often, including their bodies, but they had come out on the other side as good friends.

Priamos was too close to the edge, and Nikaius had reached the point where he couldn't shrug him off easily. It had been getting worse the last few days and the nightmare had fucked with his head so badly he couldn't tell his own voice from Bastian's any longer.

He knew what it meant, but he had ignored the warning signs in the hope that he would get more time to spend with Morrigan. More time to learn about her and enjoy her presence before she turned and ran at the sight of what she was getting into.

It was terrifying to think that they could be something unique, beautiful and rare, but that terror controlled everything. It wasn't the first time they had thought someone fit well with them, Aslin had been one of those people, but it hadn't gone the way they had intended. She wasn't the one they were looking for.

But as it became more and more certain that it was possible that Morrigan could be her, the panic threaded deeper and deeper. His control on Priamos was slipping by the hour, drop dragging him further from the surface. But if he let go, what would he find when he returned? It would be better if she wasn't there when he returned. It would be safer for everyone.

It could just be him and Waric again. Waric was his mate, and nothing could take that from them.

"You need to let Priamos out. He's fucking with your head. It's become pretty fucking clear that she is who we were looking for." Waric shook him, their mark tingling through Nikaius' shirt.

Morrigan felt different.

Every moment they were around her was another moment that Priamos would become more convinced she belonged with them.

All she would have to do is accept the bonds and they would appear. If she accepted them now, it would be like breathing.

"She's confused, and she's thinking about leaving." Waric gave Nikaius a pained look. None of them wanted her far. Not until they were sure she would remain safe. Too much had happened in such a short amount of time. Her safety seemed to always hang in the balance.

"Maybe she should leave." Nikaius finally moved, shrugging Waric off. He ran his hand through his hair as he paced away from Waric. "She might be safer. Send Hawke with her."

Waric followed. "No, she wouldn't. She belongs here with us. She tried to tell you that by offering to marry you."

Nikaius turned on Waric, Priamos letting out a snarl to hide the hurt. She only felt bad for them. That was why she offered. "Then you can have her. Because I can't. We both know why I can't."

Waric sighed. "She's not like everyone else." He reached for Nikaius again, curling his hand around the back of Nikaius' neck and the other roping him in by the hip so they stood close, foreheads touching. "I know it feels like everyone else has run when they've met Priamos. But let me tell you: that woman out there who just cried her heart out to me knows the difference between the two of you and doesn't understand why you don't want her. She's not everyone else. She wants to be here, but now she's hurting because of your stupidity."

Nikaius pulled away.

Waric's words hurt.

Priamos grumbled softly as Nikaius ran his hand over their shared mark again. "I'm not used to this. I don't know how to do this. I'm—"

"If you say too much, I'm going to hit you."

"I am though. Everyone who has tried gave up because I was too much. Too overwhelming, too eager, too chaotic."

"Nikaius, listen to me. I know we bonded when we were young, but I could have rejected that as we grew, but I'm still here, aren't I? I'm absolutely in love with you, flaws and all, and you know that just as everyone else does. I'm not going anywhere. Hawke and Aquila have been here even though they aren't bonded to you. Aslin is here. If Morrigan didn't want to be here, she wouldn't have offered. I'm sure she would have asked to see her sister long before now. There's a reason you told Mae she couldn't see her. It's because you want her to want to stay just as much as I do and as much as Hawke does. You just have to get your head out of your ass. Let Priamos run and everything will be fine."

Logically, Nikaius knew that Waric was right.

With his head such a mess, though, he wasn't sure what his change would look like and if anyone would get hurt in the process. Everything was so unstable and felt so wrong.

"It feels different with her. It's different. I can't force her into a life of obligation. I can't make her be stuck with me for the rest of her life. What if she decides later that she regrets the decision, or resents me for it? She's happy with you and Hawke." The air Nikaius was breathing was cold and didn't make it far into his chest.

"So, the dynamic will have to change a bit. It's not something we can't work through."

"You're wrong." The words didn't feel like they came from Nikaius' mouth.

The world warped.

Oh no.

"Nik?"

Fuck. The world wavered again and the only sound in Nikaius' head was the rushing of his blood.

Waric sounded muffled as Nikaius tried to breathe, but he couldn't make the air move. Priamos' power surged through him. That wasn't good. He had overexerted his power over the primal.

The pain started low in the back of his head before turning into a snarling tornado of pain.

His breaths wouldn't come.

Anger and rage burned through him, lighting every nerve ending on fire. It had been so long since he had fought the change and Priamos was taking over by force.

You can't do this. You don't deserve her. You don't deserve any of this. Bastian's voice was a snickering, dark thing in his head.

Not good enough. Pain rippled through his chest.

Pathetic, Nikaius' head pounded. He watched his hands move, but he couldn't feel them.

Oh, Fates.

You'd be better off in a cage.

Priamos reared to life, snarling and spitting and fighting for dominance.

His claws caught something, but Nikaius couldn't see.

The world went dark.

Priamos hated this.

He hated Nikaius.

He hated everything.

Nikaius had made both their mates cry, and he hated it.

She wanted to leave, and it was his fault.

They were never good enough.

The world stilled as Priamos snarled.

He was protecting them both.

Nikaius knew what Priamos was doing, but he hated himself even more.

He should be stronger than this.

Cold hands on Priamos' muzzle froze the world.

"Nikaius?" ***I'm so tired of being here.***

"Priamos?"

Priamos purred, their chest rumbling with it. They could feel it again. Good.

The fingers in his fur were trembling. They shouldn't be doing that.

Concern.

The air smelled like concern.

"Priamos, shh, it's okay." Something within the turbulence in their chest settled.

"It's okay." Nikaius felt like he was underwater when Priamos was in control, but he could hear her voice. It wasn't okay, but with her around, it felt a bit better.

"Shhh." Someone was sobbing. Was it her? Nikaius couldn't reach her, not with Priamos in the way. He grumbled and suddenly Nikaius could breathe again. It was quick and panted breaths, but it worked. The world flashed cold.

Nikaius was still dizzy, and his vision was blurred.

Everything hurt.

"You're okay." Her voice was soft as her cold palms pressed to his chest and neck. It was grounding, even as he fought against the exhaustion that tried to take him away again.

His voice broke as he reached blindly. "Please stay."

Chapter Thirty-Two

Priamos

Priamos' tail thumped as he slowly came to. The human was silent, but he knew he sat quietly at his mates' feet. Dozing with them nearby made him feel light and content. Being away from Earth was lonely, but now that Sun was around as well, it was even nicer. He felt whole.

She stood, and he fumbled up, tripping over his paws to follow. She was new, and he needed to be sure she was safe, but he paused before he crossed the threshold to the door, looking back over his shoulder at Earth. Having them separated felt wrong.

Shoo, you silly beast. Earth's voice slid into Priamos' mind, and he grumbled but willingly followed Sun from the room, padding behind her into the kitchen.

She searched for something, and he settled by the table to watch her with a happy rumble. Priamos rolled his shoulders and huffed gently when he watched her dip her fingers into a jar of something that smelled sweet. Stalking around the table, he watched her before leaning up to lick the sticky syrup from the rest of her hand. "Hey!" Her voice was soft. Priamos liked her voice, but he didn't like it when she pressed his nose away and wiped her hand on her shirt.

Messy Mate.

He snuffled at the shirt and licked it, but she shoved him away again. "Priamos, leave it."

He sat back on his haunches, tilting his head. She's the first one, aside from the pack that has called him by his name.

We've talked about you. The human was awake. With a huff and shaking himself, he shoved the man back down in favor of keeping his attention on Sun.

He watched her eat, listening to her hum to herself. No one else came into the room, which was nice. He just wanted to spend time with her. She smiled at him, and he happily thumped his tail on the floor.

After she finished eating, Sun put the food away and left the room. Priamos followed, but he wasn't quick enough to slip into the next room before she shut the door.

Despite Priamos' whining, the door didn't open.

Earth passed by sometime later, and Priamos decided to follow him outside.

Yes. Outside was where he needed to be.

The world bloomed with colors and sound, and Priamos eagerly nudged Earth's knee.

"Hold on. I have to stretch you, chaotic beast."

Fine.

Priamos stretched as well. It had been too long since he had been in control. Too long since he had taken this form and run. Strong corded muscles pulled and rolled as he stretched and yawned.

"Ready pup?" Earth had a mouth on him. Priamos would have to remind him of his place once the human form came back. For now, they would race, and he would win.

Earth took off without warning, and Priamos gleefully darted after him.

There was something so freeing about running. About letting everything fall away and being just himself in nature. He would have to drag Sun out for a run one of these days. She seemed like she'd be the sort to enjoy it. Maybe Earth could teach her how to ride the big hooves so they could go as fast as he could. That would be fun.

Time passed differently when running. Time passed differently as a wolf too. He had left home some time ago, but the moon was still high, and he was still in his territory. He could still smell himself and pack and those who were under the man's care. He knew every scent by now and nothing was off in his territory. Everything was as it had been.

Something cracked nearby. Sleeping birds scattered and Priamos paused. There shouldn't be anything out there. He was close to his border's edge. North enough that if he were to crest the height of the mountain path, he could easily slide into the Pridelands. Maybe he should. The Lyons were nice. Friends. The alpha was pack as well.

The sound came again.

This was wrong. The wind changed and with it came an unknown smell. It was wild but familiar.

He turned, assessing, before he carefully started picking his way through the brush, heading in the direction the other animals were fleeing. Small rodents paid him no mind as they scurried away just feet from him. Someone was trespassing.

A movement to his left made him turn, and he watched as a puma prowled into the clearing where he stood. This was not familiar. His scent was mixed with powers he recognized but couldn't place.

The two animals circled each other in the clearing before the puma pounced. They rolled and thrashed, teeth clashing with bone and digging through flesh. Blood painted the snow like a painter flicking red paint across a blank canvas, but neither relented. The puma went for Priamos' shoulder, and Priamos tore a chunk from its flank. Claws sunk into Priamos' side as he went for the other creature's paw. They tumbled through the brush. Priamos threw the other against a tree before it tried to take off across the snow. He finally got the upper hand several feet from the cliff's edge, which would lead to them plummeting into Pridelands. Pinning the wildcat by its throat, he growled low and dark in his chest, willing the other to submit. Alpha powers didn't seem to work though as the creature still fought. He tightened his teeth, preparing to rip it from the body. This was his territory, and no one would get anywhere near his mates or his pack.

The puma whined and keened as it squirmed and kicked, attempting to get free.

A loud sound echoed through the area and sharp, vicious pain tore through Priamos' side, and he rolled away, tumbling off the edge of the cliff and down the grassy embankment. Everything hurt suddenly, and he stumbled as he tried to stand.

He turned, seeking out the attackers again, trying to cover his flank, but they were gone. Their scents faded with the wind.

Huffing, he limped towards the underbrush and found a place to settle, hidden within one of the large, nearly dead trees he remembered from running with the Lyon.

Whatever had hit him was impeding his healing, and he wasn't sure how long it would last.

His head hurt, and his vision was fading.

Hopefully, he had breached their wards.

Afterword

Thank you so much for starting this journey of chaos with me! If you enjoyed this book please, please, please leave me a review on Amazon and Goodreads!

To keep up to date on where I am in writing the rest of the Empathy Series, other writing projects, and more chaos and nonsense please follow me on Facebook and Instagram as Siri Pielski, and Tiktok @authorsiripielski

https://linktr.ee/authorsiripielski

Also follow my friends on tiktok and join us almost every friday night at 8pm EST for "Why Would You Write That?": our weekly indie author live that features indie authors of all genres!

Acknowledgements

First and probably most importantly: my book bestie Ashley. Our friendship started with me abruptly asking "Is that an ACOTAR tattoo?" mid-conversation with another co-worker. Then there was me begging you to read FBAA. Then ATOD and KBB to meeting freaking Scarlett St. Clair with me (OMG That Happened!) Thank you for being so-so-so-tolerant and amazing and screaming with me about these two idiots, whether that be over Teams at work (when we're supposed to be working, oops) or on Messenger, Tiktok, Instagram, and text at 2 am when the plot bunnies hit. This book really wouldn't exist without you.

To K.D Fraser, N.Slater, Shalaena, and the rest of the WriterTok group: I wouldn't have finished this book with out you. Thank you so much for enduring all of my chaos and walking me through all my questions despite them having been answered before. The help and encouragement you've all given me has helped me personally and professionally and I would be nothing without the community we've built.

To Booktok: I rediscovered my love of reading through someone who I no longer speak to, but they introduced me to booktok so I can't regret the things that lead me here. It brought me a wonderful community of authors and influencers and small creators that the world needs more of. To Luna Laurier and Courtney Thorne who let me be a member of their ARC teams. I hope I can inspire the same amount of joy that you bring me.

To Scarlett St. Clair: We saw you at JosephBeth's in Lexington December of 2022 and hearing you talk about your writing struggles and the thoughts going into your head was so freeing for me as a debut novelist. It was really nice to know that popular authors such as yourself go through the same struggles I do when it comes to my writing. I was the emotional support goblin for my book bestie who asked you a question (Without stuttering go her!) and you giggled at our friendship. She kept looking over at me every 3 seconds because a lot of what you talked about she had already told me was fine. This book is no longer on fire and everything is fine.

To my own spicy community, the Alphas and the Brat Pack: I genuinely believe the signs lead me to you. I was lost and I stumbled across y'all right when I really needed you. Without realizing it you helped me learn that there was nothing wrong with me and everything wrong with the world. You helped me find confidence in myself that I had only seen glimmers of beforehand.

To my past therapists who don't know this book exists: Thank you for teaching me that trauma shapes everyone differently. Just because I'm happy and eagerly greet each new person and each new day after everything I've been through doesn't make my trauma less. It just means I'm handling it differently. All versions are acceptable.

To Bret: One of the best things I got to keep after a breakup, second only to my son. You're a great friend and deserve the world. Thank you for giving me the peace of mind that it wasn't me. Also, thank you for giving me a safe space to ask ALL THE QUESTIONS about men.

Finally, to those I've learned to set boundaries with and are no longer a part of my journey. You may have lost me along the way to completion of this novel, but it's okay. I found myself in the process.

About the Author

Siri has been writing short stories since she was 10 years old. At 13 she started publishing fanfiction on various sites and recently decided to make a huge leap of faith into self-publishing. When she's not writing the sugar to her author friends' spice she's upholding her title of her work's Emotional Support Goblin, causing chaos with her bestie, and terrorizing her 13-year-old son and their home office supervisor: an absolute unit of a black and white tuxedo cat named Figaro.

www.ingramcontent.com/pod-product-compliance
Lightning Source LLC
LaVergne TN
LVHW011949060526
838201LV00061B/4259